A SECOND KISS

"Come this way," Barton said, guiding her down another path.

It was dark, and Linnet, aware that for the first time the man at her side had used her given name and that it had not sounded at all strange on his lips, felt the cool night air envelope her. "Ah," she sighed. "This is much better."

"I agree," he said, his voice hushed.

They passed by a couple who lingered in the darkness of an alcove. Lin glanced at them, only to see that they were kissing passionately. Her breathing increased as she remembered the one hasty kiss between her and Barton. Would he try to repeat it? Would she let him?

"Lin, I . . ."

Linnet drifted closer to him as they stopped. She could hardly see his face, but as she tilted hers up, she could feel him getting closer, his warm breath touching her lips like a caress. "Nic," she whispered.

"Yes?"

But she had nothing more to say. She surrendered to the inevitable, and his lips closed on hers as she sighed.

From "Love Lessons" by Donna Simpson

<u>BOOK YOUR PLACE ON OUR WEBSITE</u> <u>AND MAKE THE</u> <u>READING CONNECTION!</u>

We've created a customized website just for our very special readers, where you can get the inside scoop on everything that's going on with Zebra, Pinnacle and Kensington books.

When you come online, you'll have the exciting opportunity to:

- View covers of upcoming books
- Read sample chapters
- Learn about our future publishing schedule (listed by publication month *and author*)
- Find out when your favorite authors will be visiting a city near you
- Search for and order backlist books from our online catalog
- Check out author bios and background information
- Send e-mail to your favorite authors
- Meet the Kensington staff online
- Join us in weekly chats with authors, readers and other guests
- Get writing guidelines
- AND MUCH MORE!

Visit our website at
http://www.kensingtonbooks.com

MY
DASHING
GROOM

Shannon Donnelly
Donna Simpson
Hayley Ann Solomon

ZEBRA BOOKS
Kensington Publishing Corp.
http://www.kensingtonbooks.com

CONTENTS

BORDER BRIDE

Shannon Donnelly

One

She had been mad to agree to this. Stark, staring mad. So of course it must be love.

But now, staring down at the ladder, with its top rung still some four feet below her bedroom window, Claire found it difficult to remember just how much she did love Harry.

What was she doing to think of running away with a man she had known a scarce month?

It had all seemed so sensible with Harry's arms about her. It had seemed the perfect answer when his lips teased the skin just under her jaw and his husky voice whispered to her that he would carry her across the Scottish border where no license was needed to marry. And where a parent had no say over the future of a woman who was nearly of age anyway.

But with the moon full and a ladder against Roxburgh House, Claire found her heart thudding and her stomach knotted. And it all seemed madness.

She glanced behind her again, her gaze darting around the bedroom that had sheltered her life. Her watercolors of the exotic lands that she had imagined hung upon the wall—shadows she could not distinguish. Her shelves of books—geography, travel guides, and histories—seemed for once so empty of comfort. Tucked between the heavy volumes were hidden the novels that her father scorned and that her mother had smuggled to her. But those stories told of how uncomfortable adventures were. And her bed stood opposite the window, looking solitary and virginal in the moon's light.

Silence cloaked the house, other than for the creak of aged wood, a sound so empty that Clarie's throat tightened and unshed tears stung her eyes.

She would leave it all if she stepped out onto that thatcher's ladder. That and her family.

Her hands tightened on the bundle she held. "Pack light," Harry had said. "I'll buy you gowns in Lisbon."

And so she had taken only the miniature of her parents, her grandmother's pearl brooch, a second gown—in a serviceable dark green—one extra pair of stockings, a comb, and her locket with a clipping of her sister's hair.

It all seemed so little to take to a new life.

Could she even do this?

A rattle of pebble against glass pulled her focus back to the open window. The summer breeze billowed the drapery around her, bringing the damp smell of soaked ground. Thank heavens it had at least stopped raining.

Taking her lower lip between her teeth, she leaned forward and peered outside again.

The dark figure at the base of the ladder, burly and masculine, offered some comfort. Moonlight flashed off the silver braid on his uniform. She could picture even now how dashing Harry had looked when she had first met him at the Huntingdon Assembly a month ago. He was dashing and handsome; what lady would not have fallen in love with his reckless smile and the wicked glint that danced in his gray eyes?

She took a deep breath and let it out again. This was what she wanted—a life of adventure, a life of passion, a life with Harry. She repeated that litany again in her mind. But it could not quite silence the voice that whispered, "Oh, you are making the most awful mistake this time."

Wrinkling her nose against that voice, she put back her shoulders. She had made her choice. And if her impulsive nature got her into trouble yet again, well, it could not be any worse than the other option that faced her.

In truth, it had been a simple enough decision. Go with Harry, or forever bury herself in dull, soul-killing security. She was not going to do that. She was not going to marry Lord Haltwistle. Not. Not. Not!

Five days ago her father had come home, delighted with himself for securing her future.

"Four thousand a year, and a title as well. And not a cent spent to launch you! Damn, if I've not done better than when I shuffled Jenny off to that squire of hers."

Sitting in the drawing room, Claire had stared wide-eyed at her father, at his burly figure and his drink-reddened face. His eyes glittered, but she knew—as did all the household—how to judge if he had gone from jovial to belligerent to self-pitying to dangerous. And he looked just a few glasses over congenial.

With her embroidery folded in her lap and her stomach churning, she watched her father splash burgundy into a glass. Then she summoned her courage, wet her lips, and said, her voice almost steady, "But . . . but, Father, he's fifty!"

Her father turned on her, eyes flashing, and Claire dropped her stare. She glimpsed, but did not need, the warning glance sent to her by her mother.

She kept still as her mother said, her voice quiet and filled with its usual long-suffering, "Mr. Roxburgh, our dear Claire is not yet twenty. Perhaps this could be put back un—"

"Twenty! And what did we marry Jenny off at? Eighteen it was. If this one gets any older, not even Haltwistle

will want her. And you, my girl, mark that you are polite
to him tomorrow when he comes to call. I told him you
like children, and you'll have three ready-made for your
care, so do not start simpering to me. It's a good match!"

Claire stood, long-suppressed rebellion erupting.
"Good? For whom? I do not—"

Glass slammed down upon polished wood, startling
Claire into silence. Then the yelling had started. She
could have borne her father's anger. Lord knew, she felt
its heat often enough. But it was her mother's tears that
had finally ended her defiance, so that she gave in,
meekly agreeing to see his lordship.

Her chest tightened even now at the memory of how
awful it had all become. She had fled tears and recrimi-
nations, running to the orchard, her own tears hot on her
cheeks and a sharp ache in her chest.

They would make her do it, she knew. She would give
in to her father's demands, and he would marry her off
to a gentleman more than twice her age.

It had seemed providence to have Harry find her sob-
bing on the grass. Of course, they had been meeting in
the orchard in secret since their first encounter at the
assembly, but for him to have found her there, on that
day, seemed a sign. And when he had suggested that they
run away to Gretna Green—only a few days' ride to the
north—well, it seemed so reasonable a course.

Claire stared down at the ladder again, at the dark
masculine form that waited for her. She took a breath
and closed her eyes to say a prayer. Then she tossed her
light bundle out the window.

A muffled curse rose, and she winced at her own bad
aim, but then she swung her leg over the sill before she
could change her mind. Holding in her mind the memory
of Harry's arm about her shoulder and his words teasing
her ear, she set her mouth and her determination.

Soon she would be in his arms, and it would feel right again.

But, oh, she wished she could silence that doubting voice at the back of her mind.

Her slippered foot found the first rung on the ladder, though she had to stretch her toes to find the rough wood. Clinging to the windowsill, she settled her feet more firmly; then she hung there for a moment, her pulse racing and her throat dry.

She had not worn gloves, nor a bonnet, with the idea that she needed a firm grip on her descent and an unobstructed view. But her cloak tangled about her legs, blown by the wind. Cold fingers shook as she braced them against the wall and felt downward with her foot for the next rung.

One more reached.

Then one more.

She strained to hear a shout from her father or a cry of alarm from her mother or a servant. But her father had drunk himself to sleep in his library, as he too often did, and her mother never came out of her own room at night. And the servants kept to their rooms, for they knew what was best for them.

Another step, and then Claire gripped the top of the ladder with her hands. A breath shuddered from her. She wet her lips, feeling more confident now.

Twisting, she tried to glance down and gauge how much farther until she stood on solid ground. As she did, her kid slipper skidded off a wooden rung. She let out a cry and muffled it at once—but too late.

Numb fingers clutched at the ladder, but it tipped with her weight. She let go, instinct taking over as she fell.

And then, somehow, arms caught her, solid and strong and all too awkward. Her skirts ended up around her knees so that her garters showed. Her cloak tangled around her. But she was caught fast, with one arm around

her waist and another around her legs. Breathless, she
clung dizzily to him.

Then his scent—male, touched with the lightest of
spice—shot alarm through her. She noted at once the
difference in the massive shoulders, the daunting height,
the startling size of him.

Stiffening, she braced the heel of her right against the
silver braid of his regimentals. "You're not Harry!"

Two

Alan Carlton's mouth twisted as he stared at the girl in his arms. Well, now he knew why Harry had concocted this mad idea of eloping with some gentleman's daughter when he should have been thinking that they were soon due to rejoin their regiment.

Lit by moonlight, she seemed a slender fairy child, all golden curls, pale round face, and glimmering dark eyes. Her curves lay sweet and easy against him, and he could see very well that Harry had been thinking with the wrong part of his anatomy.

That was not going to make any of this easier.

So he frowned at her, put her on her feet, and took up the bundle she had dropped onto him.

Her head just topped his shoulder, but she stood with her face turned up to him, her expression not quite visible in the full moon's light. Her words came out fierce and low. "Who are you? Where is Harry?"

He kept his own voice hushed as he answered, "Captain Alan Frederick Carlton at your command, Miss Roxburgh. Harry sent me to fetch you, with his deepest apologies. I am to tell you he is winning you a ring, and the cost of your wedding."

He waited to see how she would respond to this information. With luck, she'd take it badly and would climb back up that ladder and they'd have done with this folly.

In the moonlight, he saw a frown pull together her

delicate, arched brows. For an instant, he hated to see
her troubled, and he could have kicked Harry for creating
this predicament. But that had never done any good before. Harry would be Harry. And it was up to Alan to
try to make this right.

"Well, then, you had best take me to him," she said,
her chin up.

She had courage. He had to give her that. And then
he tried to think of arguments he might give her to convince her to change her mind about this. He had re-
hearsed a dozen of them on the ride here, but with her
staring up at him, expectant and all too pretty in the
moonlight, he found he had nothing to say. All his sensible phrases dried in his mouth, and he knew he was
going to have to find another way to do this.

Turning on his heel, he started for the horses. He left
her to follow, half hoping she would not. And when he
did not hear footsteps behind him, he turned back.

She had hesitated on the grass, tilting her head to stare
up to her bedroom window—at least Harry had gotten
right which room was hers. He hoped she was debating
the wisdom of this madcap idea. Lord knew, Harry
wasn't one to ever think twice about the wisdom in anything.

Please think again, and yet again on this, he willed
her. Harry didn't need a wife. Not when it meant an end
to their days as bachelor-brother officers. Which is why
he had offered to come fetch Harry his bride. It was
proof enough to him that Harry did not really love her,
not if was willing to allow the dice to take precedent.
And he had thought to come here and talk her out of
this.

Damn, why could he not find the words to tell her to
stay here and not marry Harry?

Should he tell her about Harry's worst faults? That
money went from Harry's pockets as fast as it filled

them. That Harry was quick smiles, impulsive, overly generous, and a good fellow to have at your side in the thick of it? None of it seemed likely to sway her. And Harry had sworn that a wife was just what he needed to steady him.

Steady him! Alan had almost laughed at that.

Perhaps Harry was right, however. He had seen miracles in his life, such as the one that had gotten both Harry and himself home on medical leave and out of that great victory and hellish mess called Talavera. Perhaps this fairy bride was such a gift to Harry.

And then his mouth pulled down again.

Harry needed a bride about as much as he did.

And it was his duty as a friend to convince Harry that was so. Only how did he do that?

At last she turned away from her home and began to follow.

He led her to where he had tethered the horses, on the other side of the hawthorn hedge that enclosed the house and its gardens. Mud sucked at his boots, and he wondered if Miss Roxburgh had worn sensible, sturdy shoes, or something as delicate as she.

But it was not his place to ask. She was not his bride.

Oh, damn Harry.

When they reached the horses, it took but a moment to tie her bundle to the D rings at front of the saddle— he'd brought spare leather thongs with him. Then he lifted her up onto Trojan—his own second mount—and fitted her foot into the side saddle's stirrup. Of course, Harry had not thought of a saddle for her, and Carlton had been tempted to mount her astride. At the last minute, his own gallantry had been his undoing, and he had changed his mind and bought a side saddle from the innkeeper.

Folly. It was all folly.

He waited only long enough to see that she handled

the reins with ease; then he swung up on his own Finn, an Irish-bred chestnut gelding big enough to carry his weight. Turning Finn for the road and the tavern where Harry waited and gamed, he urged the gelding to a brisk trot, leaving Trojan and Miss Roxburgh to tag along.

Time for her to get a taste of what it would be like to follow the drum as an officer's wife.

By the time they had reached the George and Crown, Claire's mood had gone from puzzlement to an aching sense of resentment and ill-use.

How could he do this to her? How could Harry have left their elopement to a stranger? Oh, the gentleman—what was his name? Oh, yes, Carlton. Captain Carlton. Well, the captain had behaved well enough, but his looming bulk beside her left her nervous. And he said not a word to her once they were mounted.

Even when they were well beyond the range at which anyone from the house might hear their voices, he kept his horse to a steady trot, and he did not even so much as look behind him to see if she kept pace.

It was beyond all that was polite!

Harry would have smiled and asked how she fared. He would have kissed her hand and reassured her. He would have said things to make her forget her caution and doubts.

Only Harry had not even come for her.

Oh, how could he?

Halting before the half-timbered inn, the captain swung off his mount and gave his horse's reins to her. "Wait here," he ordered.

She opened her mouth to protest, but he strode into the inn before she could utter a word. Well, of all the incivilities! Not even to be asked to come in for a cup of tea, or to be offered to dismount and take her rest. It was true enough, however, that they had traveled not more than five miles from Roxburgh, and she had no need of tea or rest. But it would have been nice to have been offered them.

Pressing her lips tight, she tried to fight down her pettish ill humor. Harry was winning them money. That ought to count for something. In his stead, he had sent someone who seemed quite trustworthy. That certainly bespoke his concern.

So why did she have the urge to burst into hot tears? Why did this seem an even worse mistake?

And then Harry came out of the inn, his grin flashing white in the moonlight.

"Harry!" she cried, unhooking her leg from the side saddle's pommel and slipping down so that her footwear squelched in the mud.

In three strides he had her in his arms and swept her up and spun her around, then kissed her cheek. "What, did you think yourself forgotten, my pet? Not a bit of it! I've fifty guineas in my pocket for your dower, and a ring as pretty as your eyes, though not nearly as green, and a story to keep you amused on the road."

The pungent aroma of ale washed over her as he spoke, and she pulled back, unpleasant associations with her father's drinking stirring.

Harry just grinned at her. "Oh, don't be shy in front of Alan, my dear. He's practically family. Aren't you?"

"Practically," Captain Carlton said, his tone dry. "And if we are to be practical, we should mount and ride. The moon sets in two hours."

Harry grinned again, squeezed her waist, then let her go.

As he led her back to her mount, she could not help but ask—the hurt still nagged inside her—"I know you were winning us money, Harry, but is that really more important to you than I?"

"More important? My delight, my angel, my soul— you are the most important woman in the world to me.

And I shall make it up to you. I vow I shall. Only now Alan is scowling at us, so we must both behave, for his scowls have been known to make the Frenchies tremble in their boots—and me as well."

A rude snort came from the direction of the hulking shadow that was Captain Carlton, but Claire decided to be charitable and to think that it must have been his horse.

Harry threw her up into her saddle, then left to claim his own mount from the stables. And when he rejoined them, they turned their horses to the north, with Harry charming and chattering, and Claire started to feel that at last her future and her life had begun.

Yes, this was what she wanted.

And she told herself exactly that every five minutes, in case her wayward self forgot it.

The sensation of falling woke Claire with a start. She jerked upright, blinking, then realized she had nearly toppled into sleep on her mount. Stifling a yawn, she squinted at the light that glowed in the darkness before her.

The moon had set an hour ago, and Captain Carlton had said they must find a place to sleep. He had argued for bedding down in the nearest field, but Harry would not allow that.

"Not with coins in my pocket and Claire to keep comfortable!" Harry had insisted, sounding outraged.

Claire had been pleased that he had thought of her. But after an hour more on the road, she began to think that soft hay sounded rather better than the hard, creaking leather of her saddle.

Finally, they reached Alconbury. Harry and Captain Carlton had dismounted to see about rooms at the Red Lion, but it seemed to be taking forever.

The innkeeper—portly and looking both cross and be-draggled in his nightshirt and white nightcap—stood on the steps before a small inn at the edge of the darkened village. By what little she could see in the light from the lantern that the innkeeper held, this simple structure could house no more than a few rooms. But the man seemed to have sharp standards, for he scowled at them and gave Claire scornful looks that told of his low regard for single women who traveled with military men and no other female escort.

Perhaps a field or barn might have been better, Claire decided, shifting uncomfortably in the saddle.

Smiling and talking, Harry seemed to be getting no-where, and he was starting to lose his temper. Claire could see that by his tight smile and abrupt gestures.

But then the captain said something, his voice pitched too low for Claire to hear, and the innkeeper's expression changed to uncertainty and then widened into a smile.

"Well, why did you not say so in the first place?" the landlord said, his voice carrying to her.

Claire frowned. What magic had the captain used to work this miracle?

With a rather exasperated expression on his face, Harry dug into his pouch of coins as the captain turned and strode to her side.

"Come, we've rooms and breakfast secured," he said.

Unhooking her leg from the side saddle's pommel, Claire slipped to the ground.

And nearly collapsed.

The captain's large hands caught her by the waist. She reached out to grasp him, grateful now for his size.

With her hands on his arms and her face warm, she glanced up at him. "Thank you. My legs seem to have decided that it is past time for sleep."

For an instant he stared down at her, silhouetted with

the lantern light behind him and his dark form looming before her.

He muttered something inaudible, his voice tense; then he turned. "Harry, your bride needs your aid."

Straightening, she frowned at him. "No. I can manage. But tell me—"

"Tired, my pet?" Harry asked, coming to her and interrupting with an easy grin.

She smiled. "A little. But what did—?"

"Well, come and rest. Alan insists we need an early start tomorrow, in case your father follows."

The warmth in Claire's face drained away, and her heart skipped. She had not even considered that possibility. Surely he would not. And then she thought how her father hated to be crossed.

"Follows?" she repeated weakly.

Harry's grin widened, and he brushed a careless finger across her cheek. "Oh, no doubt he'll be too busy ranting at you to do more than strike your name from the family Bible. But when I come home a hero and a general, you'll have a warm enough welcome, I'll wager."

Captain Carlton's rumbling voice broke in. "General, is it? Perhaps you could also promote your bride to a bed before she collapses. She's not accustomed to a night ride."

"She will be soon enough. Won't you, my pet?" Harry said, then offered his arm to Claire. "Now come along, like the good trooper you are."

With a smile to the captain, Claire disengaged herself from him and allowed Harry to lead her into the inn.

The innkeeper, with his nightcap shed and his nightshirt stuffed into a pair of dark breeches, had woken a stable boy to care for the horses. That done, he bowed them to a set of rooms at the top of the stairs—one for the captains to share and one for Claire. Then, with a wink at Claire, he left them his candle and maneuvered his portly bulk down the creaking stairs again.

"What did the captain tell him to make him so accommodating, Harry? I vow, at first he looked ready to wish us all to perdition as unsavory guests."

Harry gave a careless shrug. "Never mind that. It's to bed with you." His face softened with a smile, and Claire forgot about the landlord.

The candlelight caught flares of red in Harry's golden hair, and the shadows sharpened the straight line of his nose. His mouth—all sensual curves—lifted in a smile, and his gray eyes danced for a moment with an enticing delight. He started to lean closer, and Claire knew that he meant to kiss her.

Eyes drifting shut, she lifted her face. It would all feel right again in Harry's arms.

And then a deep rumble made her start, and Harry pulled away.

Three

He ought to have let Harry kiss his bride good night, but the sight of her—eyes half closed, hair golden in the candlelight, lips parted—had torn it for him. His temper flared, and so he had cleared his throat to interrupt, making her jump and Harry scowl.

A touch of guilt added to Carlton's surly mood. But he was not going to stand by and watch Harry dig himself even deeper into this madness.

Then Miss Roxburgh turned to him, her face softening into a smile. "Oh, it's you, Captain. I was just saying good night to Harry." She glanced back at Harry, hesitated, then gave him a quick smile and slipped into her room.

Harry rounded on him. "Could your timing be any worse?"

Carlton's mouth edged up. "You're the one who asked me to help with this nonsense. I told you then that you would regret this night's work. Why do you not send her home before it is too late?"

Harry's mouth pulled down. "And that is what you call help?" A grin flashed suddenly. "I just want to be there when you fall in love! Now go to bed. You always turn as glum as a bear when you've not enough rest."

That was not what was making Carlton moody. However, he saw at once that the more against this he said, the more obstinate Harry would become. He was simply going to have to allow Miss Roxburgh and Harry time enough to see how badly they were suited. And he hoped to heaven that happened before they reached Scotland.

The sky had barely warmed to gray, with a heavy overcast hiding the dawn and threatening rain, when Claire found her way downstairs again. Her riding dress was rumpled, but she had found cold water in her room to wash, and she had at least thought to bring with her a comb for her hair.

She had slept far better than she had expected. Yesterday had taken its toll on her, with anxiety, a three-hour ride in the dead of night, and far more hours before that spent pacing her room. In the morning's dim light, her natural optimism resurfaced. She was on an adventure at last.

And she was simply ravenous.

The clatter of pots at the back of the inn informed her that she was not the first to rise. It was the tantalizing aroma of bread toasting, however, that drew her to a paneled parlor at the front.

Peering into an open doorway, she saw Captain Carlton seated in a wooden chair near a crackling fire, a toasting fork in hand.

She knocked softly, and when he turned and rose, she came into the room. "Oh, please do keep toasting. Is there enough for two?"

He eyed her for a moment, his craggy features rather daunting, and Claire understood now about Harry's cautions that the captain's frowns could make anyone waver.

But then a slight smile softened his features. "There is a fresh loaf on the sideboard if you would care to cut it."

"Oh, I would. I am famished," she admitted. She moved to the maple sideboard, took up the bread knife, and cut into the loaf, which was still warm from the oven. Then she glanced back at the captain.

He had resumed his seat by the fire, his attention on not burning the toast in the flames. In the dawn's pale light—and the warmth of the firelight—he seemed far less intimidating than he had last night.

Or perhaps that was because he was sitting down and not looming over her like some enormous shadow.

The blue of his hussar uniform fit snug across his wide shoulders, and the silver braid across the front seemed designed to make his broad chest even more imposing. In dress and manner, he seemed such a contrast to Harry. His buckskin breeches looked comfortably worn—not tight and gleaming like Harry's. And while light glinted off the tassels of his Hessians, his boots lacked the mirror polish of Harry's.

And where Harry was devastatingly handsome, Captain Carlton looked a rugged man, with a strong nose and a determined, square jaw. He wore his dark-brown hair cropped short, unlike Harry's stylish golden red curls.

However, he was attractive in a way, she had to admit, if one had a preference for large, imposing gentlemen.

He glanced up, and her cheeks warmed. He had lovely eyes. They were a deep brown, framed by long lashes and with rather interesting crinkles about the edges.

"Toast?" he asked, pulling the bread from the fire.

"What? Oh, thank you, but you should eat that slice, and I shall wait for the next."

"I know far better than to keep a lady waiting—particularly a hungry lady." He slid the toast off the long-handled fork and onto a pewter plate, then took up the slice that she held out to him. "There is hot tea as well," he added.

With her stomach rumbling, she sat at the table, buttered her bread, slathered on jam from the pot, and bit into a mouthful of strawberry, warm toast, and butter. A small sound of contentment slipped out.

"I see I shall have to order a second loaf," the captain said, amusement in his rumbling voice.

With a full mouth, rather embarrassed by her greed, Claire glanced over to him and found that those interesting crinkles around his eyes were from how he smiled. It was not so much that his mouth lifted, though it did a little, but even more so, his eyes narrowed and warmed.

She would have told him not to bother with ordering more bread, only she had no room for words. So she ate, and the captain toasted.

Four slices later, Claire let out a happy sigh. Pushing away her plate, she pulled closer her teacup. How odd it was that it should be so easy to sit there with a man she did not know at all, and to have him toasting her bread.

As he finished browning a fifth slice, she told him, "No, you must eat that, for I fear I've eaten half the loaf already. But I shall butter it for you—and then you may tell me, if you will, how you met Harry."

He handed over the toast into her care and then gave a shrug. "I've always known Harry. We were born on the same day, in neighboring houses."

"Really? But you look . . . That is, I thought you older than Harry."

His eyes crinkled again.

"Oh, that was not very well put, was it?" she said.

"Not at all. I am accustomed to it. Everyone thinks I am older, but it is only by a matter of minutes, I assure you."

"Do you mind looking older than Harry?"

"You may ask me that when I carry another five-and-twenty years on my head. Now if there is any jam left—"

"I did not eat it all. At least, not mostly all."

"Well, give me what is left, then."

She did so, and then buttered the next slice for him as he toasted one more for himself. A dozen questions hovered in her mind. She wanted to ask him what he had said to the landlord last night to change his mind about the respectability of a lady traveling with two military men. She wanted to ask him about Harry—and why it was that the captain was eloping with Harry and herself.

Not that I mind, she told herself. But, in truth, she rather did mind. This was not the romantic dash to the border she had envisioned.

Yet, she had to admit that it was rather pleasant to sit here and talk to him about Harry, although she did not feel daring enough to ask the most obvious question—why are you here with us?

Carlton answered her questions and tried very hard to cling to his disapproval of Miss Roxburgh. As soon as he had heard from Harry about this elopement, he had wanted to think her some flighty female—the worst sort of woman for a military man to marry. A woman filled with romantic nonsense and no brains at all.

Instead, her questions showed a lively, curious mind. And the questions she did not ask showed that she had some sensible caution in her, as well as restraint.

But that still did not make her the right sort of woman for Harry.

They were military men. They had careers ahead of them, if they kept each other alive and their minds on the art of battle. There would be time to marry later, when peace came again and opportunities for advancement on battlefields lessened and a wife could be taken along to some military outpost somewhere.

But with Miss Roxburgh smiling at him and asking questions, it seemed rather difficult to remember that she really ought to be in her own house, with her own family.

No wonder Harry had fallen so willing a victim to her charms.

Damn! Why could she not have stayed at home and waited for Harry? Harry had mentioned something about her father's attempting to marry her off, but the girl could simply say no to that.

And so he tried to think how she must honestly be flighty somewhere under that shy smile. And how she would hold Harry back, for he'd be thinking of her, not of his men in the field. And he told himself that it was still not too late to send her home—though the truth was that her reputation was in tatters now that she had spent a night on the road with them.

Still, that didn't have to be Harry's problem—or his— if she broke it off and headed for home on her own.

So, he talked about Harry and himself, with an emphasis on all of Harry's worst faults. And as he warmed to the subject, he made it as clear as he could without directly saying so, that any woman who married Harry would have to be more than tolerant, more than understanding, and have to be part trooper herself.

It looked a scene of domestic bliss that Harry walked into, with Claire smiling at something that had been said, and Alan brushing the crumbs from his uniform.

Jealousy shot through him.

His hand tightened on the doorknob, his jaw clenched, and a hot hammering drummed in his chest and head.

Then Claire turned to him, her smile widening. "Harry! We were just talking about you."

Instantly, he relaxed. What a fool he had almost acted. Of course they would be talking about him. Was not Alan the best of fellows? And was not his sweet Claire as besotted with him as he was with her?

It seemed quite obvious that since they held him in

common between them, they would use that to become better acquainted. Relief eased into him, as did a touch of shame. He ought to have paid more attention to his bride. Even Alan there was glowering at him—and to think he had almost believed that Alan had thought Claire would come between their friendship.

With a grin, he greeted them both, and then set about to entertain them. Alan, of course, kept to his usual blockish expression—though Harry knew that was the farthest from the truth about the fellow. But he refused to do more than offer a word here or there when appealed to for enhancing their military glory. Claire, however, sat wide-eyed, exclaiming at the proper moments, although he could swear that at times her expression seemed a touch troubled.

Honestly, though, he could not ask for a better bride. Or a better audience.

Then Alan spoiled it all by rising and saying, "We should see about the horses, Harry."

"Oh, after a decent breakfast, we shall."

Claire frowned, then forced a smile and said, "Whatever you like, Harry."

She had listened carefully to Captain Carlton's stories about Harry and what he would need in a wife, and she had determined at once to live up to that list, daunting as it was. Harry needed a patient, understanding wife, someone who did not make demands on his time, and someone whom he would consider a good friend. A fellow soldier, almost.

And she could be that.

Or at least she hoped she could.

Her offer had the captain scowling at her and Harry staring at her in surprise. "Whatever I like? But, my pet, it is my aim to please you. And you are tired of waiting, aren't you?"

She was, but she smiled. "Oh, not at all. Not if you are not."

Frowning, Harry looked as if he was ready to argue over how she actually felt about matters.

The rattling of a carriage pulling up outside the inn drew Claire's full attention, and she remembered what Captain Carlton had said about her father following them.

Turning toward Harry, she asked, "Oh, no, what do we do if that's my father?"

Four

Carlton went to the window, almost hoping to see an irate gentleman step out—that would certainly put an end to this elopement. Instead, two elderly ladies stepped from a traveling coach. He turned back to the others. "I presume your father does not wear a gown?"

Claire let out a breath, then turned to Harry. "Please, I do not mean to be a bother about this, but if you do not mind, can we not start out at once? Did you not say it will be at least another day on the road?"

"That and probably a bit more," Harry said, quite cheerfully. "So we shall set out at once, my pet."

Claire managed a smile, but she began to wonder if Harry had any idea how long it actually took to ride from Huntingdonshire to Scotland.

Within a quarter hour they were on the road again. Harry urged a brisk pace, and Claire happily agreed to a gallop, but Carlton merely said, "Too fast a pace and we'll blow our mounts and have to hire fresh horses."

Harry laughed at that and told his friend he was a worrier, but he agreed to a slower pace so that they could save themselves the expense of having to change mounts.

Three hours later they had crossed over the Welland River and into Lincolnshire; at Witham Common near Grantham, Claire was more than happy to dismount for a rest. Aching in every muscle, she kept her expression cheerful and swore to herself that she would not complain. The captain had said that Harry needed a wife who did not complain.

However, she could not keep from asking, "How much farther will it be to Gretna?"

"I daresay it must be less than a hundred miles," Harry answered with a smile. "Now, what say you to some tea while Alan and I have a pint?"

She agreed to this, but his uncertainty of the actual distance made her wish that she had a map and a sense of where she was actually going.

The day had warmed, and as they had ridden north the clouds had blown apart, revealing deep blue sky. They took their refreshments in the back yard of the Black Bull, under an oak tree.

It was quite pleasant, and Harry amused them with stories of trying to fish off the docks in Lisbon. When his tankard emptied, he went off to see about refilling it. "Just one more for the road, my pet. Another for you, Alan?"

The captain declined, and Claire's smile slipped away as she watched Harry walk into the inn.

"He does like his drink, you know," the captain said.

Claire flashed a strained smile. "I did not know. But it is a warm day. I could see why he would be thirsty."

Carlton let her answer lie. He had tried his best to paint an unflattering image of Harry, but this girl seemed determined to see only the good. Oh, Lord, perhaps it really was love between the two. That thought did not make him happy.

Then he realized that Miss Roxburgh had asked him a question. "Beg pardon?"

"I asked how long you think it will take us to reach Scotland. Will it be another day, or two?"

He gave a shrug and put down his own tankard on the sun-dappled table. "With Harry, who knows. I've seen him ride a hundred miles in a day, and seen it take a week for him to travel to only the next county. It all depends on how many distractions he encounters."

"Distractions?" she asked.

As if to prove his point, Harry came out of the back of the inn, a wiggling black-and-white pup in his arms. Grinning, he strode to Claire. "Look what I found!"

He put the pup in Claire's lap, where it did its best to climb the front of her dress and lick her face. She laughed at the pup and smiled up at Harry. "Oh, he is adorable."

"I'm glad you think so, for he is yours."

Claire's face fell. "But, Harry, I cannot carry him on horseback. And he is so young—how will we feed him?"

He smiled. "Oh, you'll think of something. You ladies are amazing what with that maternal streak of yours."

Claire gritted her teeth, kept smiling, and told herself that Harry really was only trying to be sweet. Then she glanced down at the pup—its eyes dark and shining and its ears not even standing yet—and her mood softened.

They spent a short time more playing with the pup and arguing over names, and then Claire glanced up at the sky, the sun now well into the west, and asked if perhaps they should not be going on again.

Harry agreed quite readily, but when he left to settle their bill, she glanced over to the captain. That doubting look that was starting to irritate her was on his face again, and it left her uncomfortable enough that she said, her chin coming up, "It is the most adorable pup!"

"As I said—distractions," the captain said, then rose and left for the stables.

Claire buried her face in the pup's soft fur and let its tiny pink tongue wash her ear. "Oh, never mind. I do not think he really likes us."

However, when the captain came out of the stables with their horses, he also handed to Claire what looked like a sling made of black cloth.

"I've seen the peasant women in Portugal use these to carry babies, so it might suit your furry friend."

She stood up, and Carlton patiently arranged it over her head and shoulder and helped her tuck the sleepy pup in the folds so that it lay nestled close to her.

A very lucky dog, he thought, as she bent to coo at the animal. *And so is Harry, damn him. Or he would be if this girl would only wait at home for him.*

The pup slowed their travel. Claire found it uncomfortable to trot, for the pup bounced against her side or had to be held close. She could manage a canter, but Captain Carlton said in that dry, doubting tone of his that the now hardened mud would lame their mounts. The fields had been planted, so the only times they could cut cross-country was in wooded stretches.

Mostly they walked their horses, stopping when the pup cried, so that it could answer nature's call and lap water from the streams they crossed.

Skirting Grantham, they followed the main road north-west, crossing over into Nottinghamshire and passing through Newark.

Harry told her they would pass near to Sherwood Forest and asked if she would care to stop and explore. They would be passing Cumberland Park, the seat of the Duke of Newcastle, as well as the Duke of Portland's estate at Welback Abbey. Claire smiled and shook her head, and prayed that Harry would think it dull to tour the great houses. She let out her breath when he smiled and went on to change the subject, asking what she wanted to name her pup.

The late summer twilight still lingered when they drew rein before the White Hart in Budby. Harry had been chattering on, telling stories, but it was Captain Carlton who suggested a stop for dinner and an early bed, and Claire could only be deeply grateful that Harry agreed.

She was proud that she had not complained once, but

she could not help that she had started to slump in her saddle. The newly christened Troubadour also had begun to live up to his name again, and had started to sing low whimpers, indicating that he needed a walk.

The inn was crowded—not a private parlor to be had and only the smallest of rooms up in the attic left to let. Harry soon discovered the reason.

"A mill! Can you believe our luck. Tomorrow at noon."

Claire blinked at him and wondered why he would ignore the palaces of dukes but want to see a flour mill.

Captain Carlton must have noted her puzzled expression, for he leaned closer to explain, "He means a sporting event—boxing."

She stared at Harry, a little horrified. "I should have thought you got enough of fighting in battle."

"This isn't fighting. Boxing is a rare science. There's strategy, technique, and stamina. Besides, they're giving twenty to one against the challenger, so I must back him, which means I must stay to see the outcome."

He glanced at Claire, a frown tightening his forehead as if he had just recalled something. "I say, you don't really mind, do you, my pet, if we get a late start tomorrow?"

Claire glanced at Captain Carlton's craggy features, which were set in that skeptical look again. Then she looked back to Harry's beseeching eyes. The captain had said that Harry needed an understanding wife.

She forced a bright smile. "I do not mind in the least."

Grinning, Harry swept her up in a fierce hug. "I knew you were a capital find! Now, let us see about some food for that ravening beast of yours."

For the rest of the evening Harry could not have been more attentive. He procured a deck of cards and insisted on teaching Claire the finer points of whist, though she already played quite well, she thought. She had to eat in her room—since it was unseemly for a lady to eat in the taproom—but Harry insisted on keeping her company. He took Troubadour for a walk—and shortened the dog's name to Trout.

And by the time Claire was starting to wish for her bed, she was also starting to feel quite happy. Both for Captain Carlton's guidance on dealing with Harry, and for being so accommodating of Harry's desires.

She could wish, however, that Captain Carlton was not always hovering nearby every time Harry seemed to want to kiss her, so that he did no more than drop a peck on her cheek. And it would be nice if the captain stopped scowling at her, as if he somehow disapproved.

Was she not proving how well suited she was to fitting into Harry's life?

Oh, bother the man!

By morning, the captain was the least of her concerns.

Troubadour—now Trout—had kept her awake most of the night. He fretted; he fussed. She tried to keep him in bed with her, but he would not settle. She slipped down the stairs and outside to see if he needed to relieve himself, but then he ran off and she spent so long catching him that she caught a chill as well.

When the maid knocked on her door to wake her, she felt as if she had only just fallen asleep. Heavy-eyed, she dressed and went downstairs with her now sleepy pup.

The captain wished her a good morning as she came into the barren taproom, which smelled of ale and smoke.

She barely managed a smile, then slumped into a chair.

Rising, he came over to her and took the pup from her hands. "Done in by the ride yesterday?"

Straightening, she poured herself tea from the pot on the table. "Not a bit." Then she glanced at the captain and slumped in her chair again. "He is rather exhausting."

"Harry? Or your dog?"

"Actually, I meant Trout. What an awful name for a dog that is. I shall have to think up something else for him."

"Yes, well, have you considered instead finding him a good home here? I understand the landlord has a son who might find a young pup just the right sort of companion."

She shook her head. "I could never give away Harry's gift."

A smile crinkled the corners of his eyes. "The joy of Harry is that he lives almost entirely in the present moment—he is not likely to notice the pup is gone for a day or so. Of course, the misery of Harry is that he lives almost entirely in the present moment. Whatever is before him has his attention, and it is devilishly difficult to get him to focus on future plans."

She frowned at this bit of news, then reached out to scratch Trout/Troubadour's head. The pup seemed quite happy in the captain's large hands. He had nice hands, and those long fingers now rubbed the pup's black ears with slow, mesmerizing strokes.

How nice it would be to have someone stroke her with such love and care.

She let out a sigh.

"Please. Will you leave him to me?" he asked.

The appalling urge to burst into tears swept through Claire. Lack of sleep mixed with sore muscles so that all she could do was nod.

"Good. Go back to bed, and I'll have the maid wake you later with a bath if you wish."

"Oh, would you? That would be so kind."

He gave her a smile—a real smile, one that curved his lips and transformed his face into something alarmingly handsome. "I would have to be made of stone not to show you some kindness this morning. Go back to bed, Miss Roxburgh, and dream of your wedding."

With a smile, she thanked him and went back to her bed.

But oddly, as she lay her head on her pillow, it was the image of the captain lazily stroking the pup's soft black ears that stayed with her as she fell asleep.

Claire woke to the sound of a drunken man yelling and the clatter of carriage wheels. She bolted upright, then flung back her covers and hurried to the window to throw back the drapery. Sunlight streamed into the room, and she squinted against its glare. Then she focused on the gentlemen in the yard.

London gentlemen, to judge by their tight, fashionable coats and their tall, rakish hats. One of them staggered, grinning like a fool, and then the trio stumbled from their carriage and into the inn.

Claire let out a breath and rested her forehead against the windowpane.

Not her father.

Oh, she would not feel safe until she had Harry's ring on her finger and his protection as her husband. Only then would she truly be beyond her father's legal right to control her.

She started to dress, then recalled Captain Carlton's offer to arrange a bath for her. Tempting as it was, she would rather be on the road north again if Harry's boxing mill had ended. So she dressed and made her way downstairs.

Bosky, harsh male laughter boomed out from the taproom, and Claire paused on the stairs. She had no wish to go in there in search of the captain. So she turned instead and made for the kitchen.

She found Trout/Troubadour playing with a boy of six, indulging in mock battle with his rather grubby hands. A plump woman in her twenties bobbed a curtsy and then came over to ruffle the boy's hair. "Oh, my Tom is right pleased, miss, with his pup. Tom, thank the fine lady now for bein' so kind."

Rising, Tom gave a shy, awkward bow, the puppy in his hands.

Claire's heart turned over. She had no idea how she was going to explain that she—or rather that the captain—had given away Harry's present. But she could not separate this boy from the pup he so obviously adored.

She smiled at him, then asked the innkeeper's wife where she might find Captain Carlton, and if he was in the taproom, could he please be sent outside to the yard to speak with her.

Outside, the inn's sagging roof betrayed its great age. The buildings formed a square around a dusty yard, with three sides being taken up by rooms and the fourth for the stables.

Lacking anything better to do, Claire strolled over to the stable doors where she paused to pet a cat that sat just outside the darkened entrance.

Then she heard a heavy step, and she straightened to see the captain striding toward her.

When he reached her side, she put back her shoulders and told herself that she must remember to be firm but pleasant about this. It simply would not do to have him taking liberties with her life.

"You should not have given away Harry's gift to me."

He came closer, and she had to tilt her head back to stare up at him. She felt ridiculous lecturing a man so large as he, as if he were a boy of Tom's age.

He must have thought so, too, for the lines around his eyes crinkled. "You said you would leave all to me."

"I said nothing. I thought you offered to look after my pup, and now—"

"He has a far more comfortable home than he would in Portugal where he might end up shot or in someone's stew pot or trampled under a too-hasty retreat."

She frowned at him. "You think I would have cared so little for him as to have allowed any of that to occur?"

For a moment, silence stretched between them.

That was exactly what he had thought, she decided. Her frown deepened. He did not like her. She had sensed that from the very first night. And by all that he had said, she knew that he did not think her an able wife for Harry.

Finally, he said, "Miss Roxburgh, may I speak plainly with you?"

She started to answer him, but the sound of a carriage driven at breakneck speed made her turn instead.

The captain's large hand closed on her arm, and he pulled her into the shadows of the stable just as the carriage plunged to a halt in the yard.

She barely noticed the captain's hand on her, for she was far too busy staring in numb panic at her father's coach.

Five

There could be no mistake. Last autumn the coach had lost a wheel and had collapsed on the right rear axle. This carriage still bore the marks of that damage—the scrapes along the rear panels—for her father had not wanted to pay for anything beyond restoring the wheel.

Heart pounding, Claire stared at the coach as the door opened and her father stepped out and strode into the inn.

"Oh, dear God."

Carlton glanced down at Miss Roxburgh. He had pulled her aside, thinking only that whoever was thundering into the yard at such a pace was a danger to her and anyone else standing there. At her whispered words, he realized this must be her father. Oddly, there was no sense of relief that at last he had a way to get Harry out of this tangle.

The sensible thing, of course, was to advise her at once to go to her father and ask his forgiveness and forget the whole idea of a hasty marriage. She ought never to have run away with Harry, and Harry ought not to have been courting her without her parents' blessing.

He told himself all those reasonable things. But the rigid tension in her shoulders, those wide, frightened eyes, the tremor in her voice scattered his reasons like a line of infantry breaking under cannon fire. All he was left with was the quite unreasonable urge to put his arm about her.

Blast it, but that was Harry's job.

And then she turned a too pale face up to him. "Please. You cannot let him find me. If he . . . Oh, he has the worst temper, and he . . . He'll take me back to Lord Haltwistle."

"Who is Lord Haltwistle?"

"Did Harry not tell you?"

Carlton frowned. Now he remembered—something about her father forcing her to marry an older gentleman. It sounded absurd that in this age a lady could be forced to do anything, but her fear was not the least bit absurd. It shimmered around her, and it left him uneasy as well.

She wet her lips and asked, her voice almost steady, "You are going to give me away, too, aren't you? Just as you did Harry's pup."

His face burned as if she had struck him. He could only stare down at her as she grasped his sleeve.

"Please, you asked to speak plain—well, here is plain speaking. I know that you do not care for the idea of my marrying Harry, but—"

"It is just—"

"Oh, you made your reasons clear. You think I shall be as underfoot on a military campaign as that pup. You warn me of Harry's character, as if I did not know he is all quick moods and more impulsive than myself. But I love that Harry is as ready to smile as he is to frown. And I would not have agreed to come with him if I did not think to change myself and my circumstances."

"What of your parents' worries over you?"

Her stare fell for a moment, and her hand dropped away from his arm. Then she looked up at him again. "If my father is not willing to consider my feelings, I am not going to consider his. I do not like to wound him—or my mother. But when I put my foot on that ladder, I made up my mind that I was not going to live with regrets for someone else's choices for me."

His mouth twisted. "And why do you not tell this to your father instead of running off in this imprudent fashion?"

"I cannot tell him anything! He tells me. And if I go back with him, he will shut me up in the house and tell the servants—and even my mother—not to talk to me, or even notice me, until I bend or break. I know him as well as he knows me, and he knows that I cannot bear to be shut out. So, yes, I run. Because I have no other choice. And Harry, if he were here, would help me!"

"I am not Harry."

"No, but I thought you his friend. Only you will not give me a chance, will you? Oh, go and do what you must! I suppose that is all any of us can do."

With a shake of her head, Claire turned from him. She did not trust herself to say anything more without her voice betraying her emotions.

Oh, Harry, why are you not here for me? she thought, desperation tight in her chest.

But he was not here. A flare of hot impatience rose in her, only to be dampened by fear. What if the captain was right? Perhaps she ought to be given back to her father. He would be furious. And perhaps Lord Haltwistle would no longer be interested in her now that she had ruined herself by spending two nights on the road with two gentlemen. Only now that she was out of it, she did not want to go back to that house of silences and hot tempers.

She ached for her own life.

Scowling, Carlton hunched a shoulder. He did not like that she had turned away from him. Even more, he disliked the thought of her being shut up in a house and ignored.

How in blazes could any man do that to his own daughter?

She must be exaggerating, making up melodramatic nonsense to justify the notion of a romantic elopement.

With a curt, muttered curse, he turned on his heel. Then he paused and glanced back. "Wait here," he ordered.

She looked up at him, betrayal showing in her eyes, and he wondered if she would wait, or if she would saddle her own horse and ride off to find Harry.

Well, if she did, she would be Harry's problem, which is what she ought to be.

Turning, he strode for the inn.

A man's shouting carried to him from the taproom, and Carlton checked himself on the threshold of the inn.

To the right lay the door to the taproom, half ajar. The gentleman from the coach—Mr. Roxburgh, it must be—stood with his back to the door, his hat off to reveal ruffled, graying hair, and his back rigid with anger. The landlord faced him, looking sullen and as if he wished he were anywhere else as Mr. Roxburgh listed his inadequacies for not knowing the whereabouts of the two military men who traveled with a lady.

"I'll have the law on you for aiding their theft!" Roxburgh shouted. "I'll sue the lot of you for damages! She's tarnished goods, now, and what am I to do with that?"

Carlton's jaw tensed, and his fists bunched. Blazes, but he could not hand Miss Roxburgh over to a man who acted as if she were a piece of property. Tarnished goods, indeed! If this was what she got at home, no wonder she had leaped for Harry's arms, for a kind word and a soft smile.

He hesitated a moment, rationality warring with instinct. His innate sense of gallantry tipped the balance. He had not just his friendship with Harry to think of—he had Miss Roxburgh as well. Lord, he was a fool!

But Miss Roxburgh's father sounded an even bigger fool as well as a cruel bully.

Taking the stairs three at a time, Carlton made for their rooms. He knew how to move quickly—how many times had they had to break camp at a moment's notice for a day's march? He threw together his things, and Harry's, and then stopped in Miss Roxburgh's room for her light and already tidy bundle.

Mr. Roxburgh had worn his voice raspy by the time Carlton came back downstairs.

Meeting the innkeeper's wife, who now listened wide-eyed outside the taproom, Carlton slipped her a guinea extra, saying, "For an hour's grace—can you give us that?"

She frowned, shot a worried glance inside the taproom. The pup that Carlton had given her son came scampering out of the kitchen. She bent and scooped it up, soothed its ears, then straightened and seemed to make up her mind.

"We'll send him on to Worksop, sir. It'll be what he expects. But that's all we can do, mind."

Carlton nodded. They would cut west to Holbeck and skirt through Derbyshire before heading north again. It would be a longer route, but a quieter one. He scratched the pup, gave the innkeeper's wife his thanks, and then headed for the stables.

He found Miss Roxburgh waiting, but he noted that she had not had their horses saddled. Was that because she had not known what to expect, or because she had trusted him?

Worry still tightened her forehead, but when her glance fell to the bundles the tension eased from her slim form.

Giving her their gear, he began to saddle the horses. "I did not know if you would still be here."

His voice sounded grave, but Claire noted the crinkling around his eyes. It would be all right. The captain would look after her. She gave back an answering smile. "A military wife ought to be able to take orders, should she not?"

His mouth curved, and delight gathered in Claire that she could draw a real smile from him. She had been right to obey her instincts, to ignore the voices in her that warned not to trust a man she barely knew. No, she knew this man. In her heart and soul she knew enough to trust him and to rely on that feeling she had had that he would be a staunch friend.

Was he not that for Harry?

He led her horse to her and handed her the reins, his hand touching hers.

She looked up at him. "How do I ever thank you enough?"

His eyes darkened and he stared down at her for a long moment, but then he merely said, his voice brusque, "Come along. We must find Harry."

They waited until the innkeeper's wife distracted her father's coachmen with tankards of ale. Then they led their horses out of the stables, with the captain keeping his mount between her and her father's servants. She winced at the loud clopping of steel-shod hooves on cobblestone, but no one shouted for them to halt, and when she risked a glance under her horse's dark neck, all she saw was the side of her father's coach. No one peered around it to glimpse them.

Once outside the inn's square yard, the captain tossed her lightly into the saddle, his wide hands easily spanning her waist, then he mounted himself and they set off at a gallop.

Harry had said the boxing match was to take place at Clipstone, which lay within Sherwood Forest, and which meant that they would have to turn back on their route and ride south.

The forest rather disappointed Claire. She had had visions of it being dense and dark—the greenwood of Robin Hood legend. Instead, it looked like any other woodland: tidy, any fallen branches scavenged by villagers for firewood, its most ancient tress culled for lumber, and its wildness long-ago tamed.

A few carriages—late goers to the match—gave them direction enough to find the clearing at the edge of the woods, not far from the village. But once there, Claire gazed at the dozens of carriages assembled—the high private gentlemen's drags that created their own grandstands, the open gigs and smart curricles—and at the sea of top hats and coats. Her heart dropped.

"How will we ever find him?"

The captain swung off his mount. "Finding Harry is as nothing. One simply looks for the most laughter and the most trouble, and there is Harry in the midst." He glanced up at her. "This is no place for a lady, however. Can you wait for us at the village green?"

She opened her mouth to protest having to wait yet again, but then she noticed the measuring look in the captain's eyes. Pressing her lips tight, she decided he was testing her to see if she meant what she had said about learning to take orders.

Reaching down, she took his horse's reins. "Yes, sir!"

Without a glance back, she rode away, leading his horse with her. But as she rode she wondered just how it was that the captain's good opinion of her had begun to matter so much.

Claire sat on a bench underneath a willow tree, heartily bored. She had watched clouds move across the sky and noted the sun's steady crawl west, and she had no idea how long she had waited. She had decided, however, that she had best become accustomed to this, for she had the feeling that as a military wife she would do quite a lot of waiting.

She tried making a list of things to be grateful for—such as the fact that every man and boy in Clipstone seemed to have gone to Harry's mill. No one bothered her. The women of the village gave her curious looks, but otherwise they left her alone.

Also, her father had not come after her—riding south had indeed been the wiser course.

And Captain Carlton had not given her away.

She had to smile at that.

He was such an odd gentleman—so opposite of Harry, and yet they must have some things in common to be such close friends. Perhaps he was drawn—as was she—to Harry's easy, outgoing nature. She had the sense that Captain Carlton was not such an easy gentleman.

The steady pounding of hooves on the ground took her out of her thoughts.

Standing, she turned to the thundering and saw Harry riding toward her, his horse in a flat gallop. She steadied her horse, and Captain Carlton's, as Harry's mount plunged to a halt before her. Harry swung off his horse, landed light on his feet, and strode to her.

"Are you all right? I came as soon as Alan told me what happened. By heavens, I did not think your father would come after us—he must be angry as blazes!"

Taking her hands, he held them tight, then smiled. "But you are all right, and I shall not let him take you from me!"

Claire frowned. It had been Captain Carlton who had looked after her, and she glanced around now, wondering where he was, and then she realized what must have happened.

"Oh, Harry, you have left Captain Carlton behind to walk here, have you not?"

Six

Harry's smile faltered. "Of course I did. I came the instant he told me what happened."

"Well, that was not very kind of you after all he has done for me!"

"Nonsense. Alan knows better than to expect me to be kind."

"Does he? Well, I do not. I do expect you to be kind—and to be there—and you were not any of those things today!"

To her dismay, angry tears stung her eyes. She had not meant to reprimand him, and here she was, scolding like a shrew, her intentions to be brave and cheerful in tatters and her real feelings spilling out.

She pulled her hands away and turned from Harry.

"My sweets . . . my pet . . . Alan was there. He looked after you, just as I knew he would. There is no reason for you to be so upset. Has it not all worked itself out?"

She glanced at him, her chin down and her lower lip still trembling. What he said made sense, but still the wound inside her refused to close. He had not been there for her. And she could not deny that she wanted to think him dependable, a gentleman she could trust with her heart.

Tentatively, she put a hand on his chest to finger the

rough silver braid. "Tell me it will not happen again, Harry. That you will be there to look after me."

His face eased into a grin, and he slipped his arm around her waist. "Of course it won't happen again. These things always work out, don't you know. Now, stop your fretting."

"But what of Captain Carlton?"

"What of him?"

Claire straightened and pulled away. "Should we not at least go find him? I feel awful that he must walk here on his own. You know, he might be quite tired of always having to look after others with never anyone to look after him."

Harry seemed amused at this, but he agreed pleasantly with her suggestion. After boosting her into her saddle, he swung up on his own mount. She urged him to ride ahead and take the captain's horse to him, but Harry refused, saying with a grimace that he was not leaving her, and Alan would not mind.

The sight, however, of that lone figure trudging along a dusty road, head down, wrung a sharp pang from Claire's heart.

But when they met up with Captain Carlton, it seemed that Harry had been right. The captain seemed not the least put out by having been left on his own, and Claire could only wish that she had his fortitude.

They covered more distance that day than they had in the other two put together, but Claire noted that they now kept off the main roads.

After crossing through Derbyshire and into the East Riding of Yorkshire, they skirted the town of Sheffield. The land had steadily changed from the tidy farms and fens of Huntingdonshire to pasture and woodland, and now the countryside opened into rugged dales best suited to grazing sheep. The roads became a tangle of intersecting lanes, bordered by tall hedges, with only the occasional signposts to mark directions.

Captain Carlton noted that they were bound to lose their direction if they did not soon find a way out of those country lanes and hedged pastures. So at Huddersfield, they took the turning toward Leeds. That city they also skirted, striking out north afterward, on a dusty road with a signpost to Harrowgate.

Claire's longing for a map deepened. Her aching muscles told her they had ridden a good many miles, and she knew they still had the North Riding of Yorkshire to cross, as well as the counties of Westmorland and Cumberland. A hired carriage—and frequent changes of horses—would have been far faster and infinitely more comfortable.

When she suggested this to Harry, he smiled, cheerfully agreed, and then added, "I daresay I should have thought of that when my pockets were well lined."

She frowned. "But I thought they were."

With an easy grin, he shrugged. "Oh, they were. And I nearly doubled what I had—and that, my pet, would have been more than enough for the grandest of coaches for you. Only Rimmer would start losing. And then Alan said you needed me, so I left without waiting for the end of it. Serves me well for backing a Lancashire man with all my purse."

"All? Do you mean to say that you bet the money that was to get us north on that boxing match?"

His grin faded and a hunted look came into his eyes. "Yes, well, what if I did? The odds were too good not to have a high stake in it, and Rimmer might have pulled out a victory, you know, only I did not stay for it. Anyway, I thought you wanted me to show you that you were more important than any bets."

Scowling, Claire opened her mouth to tell him that what she wanted was a little sense, but then she caught

Captain Carlton's expectant stare. The captain had lifted an eyebrow, and he watched her, as if waiting for a demanding tirade.

She glanced back at Harry, who now looked sullen and unhappy, and she took a deep breath. "Thank you, Harry, for making me more important than such a wager."

Brightening, he straightened. "Of course you are. And I shall get you an even better ring than that other one—it was only a rather shoddy emerald, anyway. You would not have liked it."

The hurt flashed through her that he had lost her ring as well—the one he had hinted at being her wedding ring. Firmly, she pushed away the twist of pain. She would not allow it to matter. She loved Harry, and she was as good as married to him now that she had spent all this time in his company, and she was going to make him a good wife.

He is far better than Lord Haltwistle, she told herself. And if he was not quite what she had thought him, well, she would look on his positive traits—his good nature and his easy temperament.

She kept repeating that to herself while Harry did his best to amuse her with his enthusiastic stories of the excellent bottom shown by Rimmer in taking a tremendous number of bare-knuckled blows.

Not long after the sun set they took refuge in the ancient ruins of an abbey not far from the tiny village of Studley Roger. Claire did her best to remain cheerful even though they could not afford the price of a room. Her body ached for a soft feather bed and her stomach growled for a hot meal, but she might have to face far worse on campaign with Harry in Portugal, so she would simply consider this training for her new life.

Harry seemed pleased with her good spirits, for he gave her a squeeze and a smile, saying, "Don't fret. My luck always comes about." Then he mounted his horse and set off to "forage for our dinner," as he put it, promising to return in a trice.

Claire turned from watching him ride away to find Captain Carlton studying her. She forced an even brighter smile and kept her back straight. "Where do you think is the best place to sleep?"

The cellarium still had its vaulted stone ceilings, but Claire found the silence in the darkened, hollow chamber rather unsettling, as if the monks still walked here, mourning Henry VIII's dissolution of their abbey. She hated to admit such imaginings to Captain Carlton, so she suggested that sleeping under the stars on soft grass would be better than hard dirt.

The captain gave her a skeptical look, as if he knew full well her uneasy thoughts, but he led her to the ruined chapel, with its towering stone windows now empty of glass but still arched in the shape of praying hands.

Only the rectangular shape of the church remained, a shell of its ancient glory. However, Claire liked the feeling of peace and the comfort of the summer breeze and the soft grass underfoot.

The captain chose a spot in a sheltered corner, and he soon had blankets spread, horses hobbled, and a fire going. True, the blankets smelled of horse, and Claire's stomach rumbled, but when Harry returned after more than a good deal longer than any "trice," he brought with him eggs still warm from a hen's feathers and a pork pie that set Claire's mouth to watering.

"Don't ask what windowsill the pie came from," Harry said with a grin. Then he set to work with a pan and the eggs, swearing, "I shall make you the best omelet you have ever eaten."

It was. And though Claire tried not to be greedy, she ate every bite of her share of the food. Harry apologized that she would have to make do with water instead of wine tonight, but he promised to win her money enough for such comforts that she became a little nervous about just how he would fulfill these vows.

"Please, Harry, do not make wagers on my behalf—besides what else do you have to stake?"

"Why, my horse, of course."

Visions of having to walk the rest of the way to Scotland flooded Claire, leaving her hands chilled and the pie heavy in her stomach. "Please, Harry, promise me you will not risk our horses."

"But, it's no risk, if the bet is a sure thing."

"Harry, please!"

"Oh, very well. If you insist."

She smiled at him and hoped he would be as good as his word.

With the fire dying and little else to do, Claire excused herself and left to roll up in her blanket on the ground. Rolling over, she faced the silent gray stones of the abbey.

For some time, she lay there, listening to the low rumble of Captain Carlton's voice and to Harry's easy laughter. The ruffle of cards being shuffled added to their companionable sounds, and Claire's throat tightened.

Loneliness cut through her, sharp as a December wind. She longed to sit up and join them, but she would only be in the way between them, really. They had so much in common, so many shared experiences.

Miserable, she tried to burrow deeper into her blanket, pillowing her head on her arm. And she knew with a shameful certainty that it was jealousy of Captain Carlton's easy friendship with Harry that was making her so unhappy.

Carlton came awake with the instant, full awareness that five years of army life and battle had trained into him. He lay still a moment, eyes open, allowing his vision to grow accustomed to the darkness.

The moon had set, but the sky glittered like magic, the thick swath of winking stars strewn with careless abandon across the blackness. Not far from him, a steady snoring told of Harry's presence and that he slept as he always did, deeply and oblivious of the world.

Then Carlton heard Miss Roxburgh stir and pull in a shivering breath, and he knew what sense had woken him.

Seven

"Are you cold?" he asked, his voice pitched soft so as not to startle her. It was odd that her quiet stirrings had woken him, but perhaps it was not so unusual considering that he had never before had a lady to look after.

Unlike Harry, he had never gone in for the petticoat line. Ladies generally left him feeling graceless and awkward. He had no skill or interest in flattering them, and working to charm smiles from them seemed a ridiculous amount of effort. But Miss Roxburgh required neither charm nor flattery—she had those from Harry. And since she was as good as married to Harry, she would have no expectations from him.

Which is why, he told himself, he felt so comfortable in her presence. It must be why.

Of course, it did not hurt that she was so easy on the eyes. Nor that she seemed quite ready to offer smiles.

But she was as good as married to Harry, he reminded himself again.

The fire had long ago died, but dull embers gave off a faint heat and enough light to see her pale face and her slender curves as she sat up to face him. "I thought I was the only one awake. Does Harry always make such a noise?"

He smiled. "Often enough. I generally shake him until he at least turns over."

"That does not wake him?"

"Not Harry. He would sleep through a cannon barrage, if allowed."

Dragging her blanket up around her, she glanced at Harry and then back to Carlton. "I wish I had such a gift. I cannot sleep for every pebble underneath me, every damp spot in the grass, and every rustle I hear."

"Yes, but think of all he is missing. The starlight. The stillness. The scent of summer in the air. And there's a rare gift in sleepless nights, for it's a time to turn a problem over and see it from a new perspective."

In the starlight, her eyes gleamed and her voice held a smile. "What lovely thoughts. I shall have to remember that. Well, since it will not wake Harry, do you think we might have a fire again?"

Carlton sat up and stripped off his jacket. Rising, he moved to her side and tucked her into his coat, pulling the front closed around her. "We've no more wood, but that should keep you till dawn."

"Thank you, but . . . well, will you not become chilled?"

He settled next to her. "Chilled, Miss Roxburgh, is a day's march through icy rivers and snow. It is a winter's night in the saddle with your toes aching and your fingers tingling. It is a wet so drenching that you cannot even light a fire. That is chilled. This, Miss Roxburgh, is heaven."

"You must start to call me Claire. Please? After all, how can we keep up formalities when we are sleeping under the stars?"

"Hardly sleeping, but I should like that. And if you'll call me Alan perhaps we can cry friends at last."

A white hand slipped out from under her blanket and his jacket and extended to him. "But of course we are friends . . . Alan."

He took her hand in his, its softness fitting easily into

his larger grip, and then he tightened his hold. "You are cold."

"Only a little."

She started to pull her hand away, but he would not release it, and said instead, "No. Come along. Give me both of them."

For a moment she hesitated, but then she put forward her other hand. He bracketed her hands with his and rubbed gently.

Claire swallowed hard. Her pulse thudded heavy in her throat, and pleasure tingled along her skin. Parting her lips, she tried to think of something light and friendly to say, but she could only think how very much better it was to have his warm hands engulf hers.

She let her eyes drift closed. And then a loud snort jerked her upright. Harry muttered something in his sleep and rolled over.

With her face hot, and guilt heavy on her chest, she pulled her hands away and told herself not to be silly. She and Captain—she and *Alan* had done nothing wrong.

Only perhaps it would be better not to allow Alan to rub her hands. Or at the very least, not to allow it to feel so very good.

"Thank you. That was very nice," she said, and winced at how prim and starchy she sounded.

It is just the night, and having his coat wrapped around me—oh, but he does smell so very nice.

"You do not want more? You are not still chilled?"

She forced out the lie, telling herself all the while that it was only a very small one. "Not at all. But please do not allow me to keep you from going back to sleep."

He stretched out his legs and leaned back against the stone foundations of the church. "Once I wake, I'm awake. Shall I tell you stories, instead, as Harry does?"

She kept quiet for a moment, and then she asked, "Are they about boxing?"

He gave a low chuckle. "No boxing, I vow. Though the ones I have about military life would interest you as little, I'm afraid."

"Oh, no. I actually think that is rather exciting. How did you come to be in the army, Cap—Alan?"

"It's Harry's fault, of course. I think he was born army mad. And when he joined, well—"

"You had to go, too, to look after him?"

"Something like that."

"And who looks after you?"

"Me? Oh, a giant of a fellow such as myself needs more looking out for than looking after. However, my mother does her best to dote on me, and I've two sisters who knit me the most wretched stockings and gentlemen's unmentionables."

Claire gave a gurgle of laughter. "Now you are saying shocking things to me—and to think your sisters so indelicate as to even knit you the unmentionables that go between your clothes and your skin."

Sobering, Claire's face flamed hot, and she blessed the darkness for hiding her. She ought not to have mentioned his skin, for an image had flashed into her mind of just how well he must look in his skin. All that male muscle, and broad chest, and . . .

No, she really had to stop thinking such things.

It was the darkness, she decided. It wove into its magic this sense of intimacy, which made it so easy to say whatever popped into one's thoughts.

"Tell me about your sisters," she said, leading the straying conversation to safer shores.

He did. And the warmth in his voice told her that he loved them dearly. They were both married, with children—two boys for one and a girl for the other and one on the way. He had, as well, an older brother.

Envy wormed into Claire as he talked. How wonderful to have such a large, easy family, and to be able to speak so fondly of them. She told herself to be happy for him instead.

Just as she thought that, he added, "However, my father does not care to have me in the army. We quarrel about it each time I go home."

Claire hugged her knees tight. "You must hate that."

His grin flashed in the night. "Hate is a rather strong word. My visits certainly have some unpleasant moments, but when he rants, I listen and nod and agree with him, then do as I please."

"Oh, how I wish I could do that."

"Why can you not? It only takes resolve. Your father must have your best interests in mind, and if you were to tell him—"

"Tell him? I cannot tell him anything. He has always been bitterly unhappy that neither I nor my sister is a boy, and he thinks of us as burdens to dispose of as best as possible. I am supposed to marry, have children, and do nothing more."

"And you want more?"

Sitting up, she turned toward him. "Oh, much more. I want to go places—places I have read about. I want to meet people—different people. Why, when Harry told me about Portugal, and about India, it sounded so amazing. So wonderful!"

"It is not all wonderful," he said, caution heavy in his voice.

"It could be. I mean, yes, adventures can be rather trying—only look at having to sleep in a ruined abbey. But someday I shall tell my children how I rode off to Gretna Green with their father, and they will be so amazed—and so shall I to think that I was once so young and daring and so much in love. We all need adventures—we need them to remind us that we are alive."

Infectious passion lay vibrant in her voice, and Carlton understood entirely now why Harry had fallen in love with her. It was not just her lovely curves, nor the smiles she offered so readily. No, the brightness that burned in her was far more compelling than any surface charms.

Damn, if Harry had not gone and done it again.

What luck that fellow possessed to have a lady such as this run off with him, ready to marry him and follow him.

For the first time in his life, he could wish Harry to perdition.

Ah, but Harry deserved a good wife. Despite his flaws, no one could fault him for his generous nature, and no man could ask for a more steadfast friend. Were the circumstances reversed, Harry would have looked after his choice of bride.

So he owed the same to Harry.

But it was going to be blazingly difficult to remember that.

With a smile, he reached out and gave Harry's bride a pat on her hand. A friendly pat. And he made quite sure it remained only that.

"You will have a wonderful life with Harry."

"Yes. Yes, I shall, because I love him," she said. Silence lay taut between them for a moment, a crackling silence that seemed to have its own life and expectations. But Carlton knew better than to step into that silence. Possibilities lay in that silence. Far too many of them.

After a moment longer—such a very long, aching moment—she said, "I think I shall try to sleep just a little more."

She turned and lay down again.

And Carlton was left with only his thoughts for company, wondering if he was just a bit of an idiot to be thinking now of helping Harry into a hasty marriage. Or was he even more foolish not to think only of helping himself?

* * *

Claire opened her eyes and lay still, joints stiff and muscles protesting with cramps. Bleary-eyed, she sat up.

The gentlemen were not present, but she could hear the rumble of their voices not too far distant, and she could only be grateful. If they had been there, she would have snapped at the first one to speak to her.

What she would give for a cup of hot tea, a mirror, and a proper bath.

Rising, she stretched. Then she gathered her comb and stomped toward the splash of a river, determined to put herself in a better frame of mind and body.

Cold water on her face helped. So did combing her hair and plaiting it into a tidy braid that she then pinned up. She could do nothing with the wrinkles on her dress, but at least she no longer felt as ragged as a tinker's orphan.

Cupping her hands, she drank some of the cold, fast-running water, but that did nothing to ease the rumbling in her stomach. With wistful thoughts of last night's pie, she returned to the ruined chapel.

Harry greeted her, cheerful, more handsome than ever with sunlight glinting from his hair and winking off the silver on his blue uniform. He bent to kiss her, but she turned to offer only her cheek, shy under Captain Carlton's watchful stare.

"So Alan tells me you two were up half the night talking while I slept."

Eight

Claire's gaze dropped to the flattened grass and the charred circle where their fire had burned. Then, with a lump in her throat, she lifted her stare again. "Yes, and I'm sorry, Harry."

"Sorry? For what?" He grinned and slipped an arm about her waist for a quick squeeze. "You have no need for beauty sleep, for you're as radiant as the dawn."

She looked at him, searching his face. "You don't mind. I mean, that Alan and I . . . that the captain and I . . ."

"That you what? Cried friends? Why, I could not imagine a better thing than to have the two of you be the best of friends."

He grinned again, and Claire tried to offer up a smile. She ought to be happy that he was not the least angry or suspicious of them. Yes, she really ought. Only part of her wished that he had been just a little jealous. And that he wished that it had been himself and her sharing confidences under the stars.

At least he kissed her and hugged her, and that ought to be good enough to show that he cared for her. Oh, she must stop this dreadful wanting him to be different than he was.

So she turned her thoughts to breakfast, asking if they possibly had enough coins to buy something to eat.

Harry gave her a wink. "Don't worry about that, my pet. Something always comes about."

She bit down on the cross answer that leaped to her tongue—that if she wanted to worry, she would do so, and it was no right of his to try to coax her out of it.

Thankfully, Captain Carlton stepped forward. "Harry, I think your bride needs something more substantial than a promise just now."

Harry glanced at him, then at Claire, his expression startled. "My pet, are you really that hungry?"

Not trusting her voice to remain calm, Claire could only nod.

"Well, why ever did you not say so? Alan and I shall contrive something at once. Just you wait here a bit."

"Wait a bit," Claire muttered, as the gentlemen turned to their horses. And then she let out a long breath.

She walked the ruins as she waited, leading her saddled horse with her, pausing to let the animal graze and wishing she found grass as appealing.

At last, hoofbeats announced the gentlemen's return, and she watched them ride up to her.

Harry dismounted with a flourish. "Sorry to take so long, my pet, but Alan would barter our time for these." He handed her a handkerchief, and she unwrapped two meat pies that smelled divine.

Manners made her stop before she took a bite. "But what of you?"

Harry grinned. "Don't worry about us old campaigners. We had something already."

Carlton's eyebrow lifted at that casual comment. What they had had was a half hour of aiding an old woman bringing in her pigs. Not the most pleasant of work. And the reward of two meat pies. However, Harry was right. They were both accustomed to doing without meals, sleep, and whatever else a campaign might require of them.

Claire had no such training. With some luck, it would not be required of her to endure such hardships. However, they were going to have to do something about their now nonexistent funds.

Seated on the ruins, Claire ate her breakfast, tidy and delicate, though Carlton had the suspicion that she was hungry enough to have consumed the pies in one bite each.

With her fed, her mood seemed to improve, and they mounted and turned their horses toward the road.

The land grew wild enough that Carlton recommended they keep more to the main road. Harry urged that they stop in Richmond, telling Claire she would adore the castle that towered over the river Swale. And then he went on to spin stories of how legend held that King Arthur and his knights slept in a cave under the ancient keep, and how a secret tunnel led to a hidden treasure.

"Well, we could certainly use the treasure, for I really would rather sleep in a bed tonight," Claire answered.

Harry laughed at that, and then began to talk of Richmond's theater. Carlton turned his mind to the more practical matter of how to get Claire a bed that night.

In the end, they did stop for a few hours in Richmond. Harry insisted on showing Claire the town, but as there was nothing on the playbill for the theater, he had to be content with simply walking Claire about the streets.

Carlton excused himself from their company, and when he joined up with them again at the Bull and the Bear, he was able to order a reasonable meal and ale for both himself and Harry.

Claire gave him a sideways glance as he paid their bill, but she did not question him until they were on the road again. Then she allowed her horse to drop back, so that she rode next to him.

"You are a man of mystery, Captain."

"I thought we were to be Alan and Claire to each other?"

"Ah, but friends know about each other, do they not? And what I know of you is that you talk innkeepers into giving us rooms—though a lady traveling with two gentlemen hardly appears respectable—and now you make money appear from nothing."

"Actually, it appeared from under the sign of three balls."

"Three . . . Well, I am not so ignorant as to not know of pawnshops. What did you give over?"

He glanced at her, the creases around his eyes deepening. "And how is it that you know of pawnshops?"

"Oh, Mother uses them. She swears it is the only way to make the household allowance last the full quarter. Every second month into the quarter, her diamond brooch goes into a discreet establishment in Huntingdon. Then every quarter day it comes back again. Mother, of course, thinks that neither I nor Jenny ever knew what she was doing, or what three golden balls signified. Now, are you to answer my question?"

"It was nothing much that I gave over."

"What nothing?"

"You are not going to let this go, are you?"

"No. I am actually remarkably stubborn. My father calls it willfulness, but I prefer to think of it as determination."

"It was a watch."

She nodded. "We shall stop on the way back down to London to retrieve it for you."

He glanced at her, surprised. "Retrieve it? With what? Harry's charm and your good looks?"

Smiling, she lifted a shoulder. "Well, you said yourself that Harry's luck always changes. When it does, I shall make certain a little something is set aside."

With that, she gave her horse its head and trotted on

to catch up with Harry, and Carlton decided that she just might be the making of Harry after all.

They crossed into Westmorland that day, passing through Starnmoor Forest. The wild lands left Carlton cautious of straying too far from the roads—he did not want one of the horses to put a foot in a rabbit hole. But Claire exclaimed over the beauty of the rugged landscape.

In Appleby, Carlton hired rooms at the King's Head, and he gave in to Harry's urging that they see a bit of the ancient town.

Surrounded on three sides by the river Eden, the town boasted Roman heritage, though Claire was disappointed to find not a trace of ruins. Still, she found it pleasant to walk the streets, her hand tucked into the crook of Harry's arm, and Captain Carlton on her other side.

Dinner passed pleasantly. Since there was no private parlor, they ate early in the taproom. When other gentlemen arrived to drink their pints, Claire excused herself and retired to her room.

She hoped that Harry would come up to bid her good night—he had promised to come up early to see her. So she waited. Finally, with her candle guttering, she gave up and took off her dress and undid her hair. Still, he did not come.

At last, she lay in her bed, her room now dark. Listening to the deep, male laughter from the taproom, a hollowness rose inside her. How much nicer it would have been to have stayed with Harry. Only she was a lady, and ladies were not welcome in a taproom. At least, it would be nice when she could look forward to Harry coming up to her room, after they married.

Only what if Harry came to her smelling far too much of strong drink?

Oh, this was all getting to be so much more complicated than she had ever thought it would be.

* * *

The sound of rain woke her.

Rising, Claire padded barefoot to the window to peer outside. Gray clouds huddled close to the land, with the rain falling from them in thick droplets. She glanced down at the muddy road that wound past the inn.

How much nicer a coach would have been.

Still, it was a good education for her. She would not, after all, have a coach in the Peninsula when Harry returned to his duties.

With that in mind, she turned from the window to start her day.

The maid had brushed and sponged her dress, so that it now looked presentable. Claire washed and tidied herself, then went downstairs.

Harry seemed in spirits, and when she commented on his cheerful mood despite the gloom outside, he informed her that he had borrowed ten shillings last night and had won five times that amount.

"Dice," he said with a grin. "I should know better than to ever forsake the bones for cards."

For a moment Claire frowned at him, unhappy that he seemed unable to keep from taking the most foolish risks with their scant funds.

His own smile faded. "You aren't happy with me, are you?"

"Oh, no, Harry, it is just that . . . Well, what if you had lost and we had to sleep in the rain tonight?"

He stared at her blankly for a moment, then said, his voice puzzled, "But I didn't lose, now did I? Oh, I see. You're hungry for breakfast, aren't you? Some hot tea and a good plate of food will soon set you right."

Claire pressed her lips tight to keep back the harsh words that she wanted to say. How did she argue with his logic, such as it was? Well, if he could not be prudent, she would have to do what she could for her own peace of mind.

When he had her seated at a table in the empty taproom, with tea before her and a meal of cold beef, buttered eggs, mackerel pie, boiled mutton, and hot Yorkshire cakes, Claire summoned her courage.

"Harry?"

"Yes, my pet?"

"Harry, since you won so very much, would you give half of it over to me?"

"Half? Whatever for?"

"Oh, I just . . . Well, I might wish to buy something. Husbands generally make their wives an allowance, and you are about to bestow upon me your worldly goods, so why not begin now?"

Harry grinned. "I am about to do that sooner than you think, my pet, for we're only a little more than forty miles from the Scottish border."

Nine

For a moment, Claire could not move. The air seemed suddenly chilled.

Forty miles.

She gave a small shiver. They could cover that distance in five hours—less if they galloped. But the rain would thicken the roads, making it unwise to ride fast for fear of a horse pulling a tendon. Only why should she now wish for any delay?

She wanted to marry Harry, didn't she?

Still smiling at her, he took her hand. "It'll be all right and tight with us once we're married. You'll see."

He gave her hand a pat, but she rather thought his smile seemed a little stiff, as if he, too, was not very happy at that thought. Oh, she must stop this doubting. She loved Harry.

But did she love him quite as well as he deserved? Was that why her treacherous mind kept looking between Harry and Captain Carlton and comparing the two?

This was so unfair—to Harry, to Captain Carlton, to herself even. She ought to be comparing herself to the captain's example of trustworthy behavior and loyalty. How could she admire him and not demand those same traits in herself?

She had run off with Harry. And they would be quite happy once they wed.

Smiling brightly, she covered his hand with hers. "Yes, Harry. It shall be all right and tight when we marry."

And then she became aware of being watched.

Turning, she saw Captain Carlton in the doorway, his craggy features immobile and his eyes impossibly dark.

A band tightened around her chest, but she told herself firmly that what she felt did not matter. Feelings were fleeting things that passed. But she could not stop the thought that things might have gone very different if she had met Captain Carlton—Alan—before she had met Harry.

Of course, the captain would not have asked her to elope. He lacked Harry's impulsive, romantic nature. But she had come to care a good deal for the captain's dependability, his calm manner. He was a rock she could lean upon.

Harry would never be that.

Only she had made her choice. She had given her word to Harry. She must live with that. And she must find some way to ignore this attraction toward another. Toward Alan. No, not Alan. She must think of him always as the captain. As her dear Harry's friend.

Pulling her hand away from Harry, she asked the captain if he had broken his fast, then poured tea for Harry and chattered on about the bad weather so that the silence would not swallow them all.

By ten, the rain had lightened to a drizzle, and Harry said they ought to push on. However, he did not rise from his chair. Carlton glanced at the clock in the taproom, then put down his cup with its now cold tea.

"I'll see about the horses," he said, then rose, reluctant to do so, yet knowing that they really ought to ride on.

The muddy roads would delay a carriage, which would drag at coach wheels. But a persistent man—a vengeful man—would find a way here. And he had certainly seen enough anger from Claire's father to know he would follow her for no better reason than pure spite.

However, he disliked the thought of taking Claire out into the wet. He firmly ignored the other feelings that had stirred in him at the sight of Claire and Harry, heads together and hands intertwined. They were as good as married, after all.

Harry was a lucky fellow—damn him.

Striding from the taproom and out into the drizzle, Carlton went to order the horses saddled. And he told himself to stop thinking about Harry's bride.

By the time he led the horses from the stables, the wind had risen, tumbling the clouds into billows of white and offering glimpses of blue sky that gleamed like fair promises. As Carlton mounted, Harry tossed Claire into the saddle and then swung up on his own horse.

They made good time, soon crossing over the Lowther Bridge and into Cumberland. Harry insisted upon a stop at Penrith, swearing he was parched, and then, with a promise to be but a moment, he disappeared for over an hour. He returned with a bantam rooster tucked under his arm and the tale of the most excellent fight he had seen between the bantam and a Malay.

Dismayed, Claire frowned at the rooster. "But, Harry, whatever do you mean to do with that?"

"Why fight him, of course."

She glared at him, appalled.

Stepping forward, Carlton took Harry aside. The two gentlemen spoke for a few minutes, Harry gesturing passionately with his one free arm and Carlton's voice pitched so low that she could not hear it.

Harry glanced back at Claire once, scowling, and she wondered if he was blaming her for dampening his fun. For an instant, shame stung her. But then she realized that carrying a fighting rooster about on horseback could not possibly be anyone's idea of fun. So she lifted her chin and gave him back his stare.

Finally, Harry threw up one hand, then thrust the rooster at Carlton.

Stomping back to Claire, Harry folded his arms. "Well, Alan is to sell back the most prime rooster I've ever seen! Are you happy now?"

Resentment simmered inside Claire. "I did not ask you to sell him—or buy him. But I do not know what you were thinking to want to ride from here to Scotland and then back to London with a rooster struggling in your arms! Honestly, Harry, you could be just a little practical once in a while!"

Sullen, he stared at her a moment longer, and then the edge of a reluctant smile lifted his mouth. "I suppose it would have been a nuisance having the thing crow at dawn."

"Yes, it would."

"And it might well have ended in the cooking pot in Portugal—provisions sometimes are devilishly scarce."

"If they are, then I certainly should have ordered him cooked, and you would have been really cross with me then."

His smile widened. "Yes, I should. Alan said I was not thinking very much of you—or your comfort."

She blinked at him. "He said that?"

"Just took a strip of my skin off, he did, for my not being a better husband to you. Oh, Claire, I am sorry. I honestly do mean to do well by you. Say you'll forgive me."

Her face warmed and her stare fell to the grass under her boots. "Oh, Harry, I never meant to change you."

"But I must change. Alan swears I must if I am to make you happy, Claire."

She frowned at this, troubled by the truth in this. What if he did change—into someone she did not really love?

Into someone bitterly unhappy and resentful because of having to make those changes?

Before she could form her worries into words, Captain Carlton returned. He pressed a few shillings into Harry's hand, and then he and Harry were off to fetch the horses, leaving Claire with her growing uneasiness.

Oh, I am making this far too muddled by thinking too much, she scolded herself.

Still, even as Harry helped her into the saddle, smiling and joking again, the dread settled into her that perhaps she and Harry really were not two people who ever ought to be married.

After Penrith, the sky cleared, except for a few clouds that strayed like idle sheep, and the day warmed into summer again. The grass along the roadside dried enough that they found good stretches for cantering, alternately slowing the pace to a trot or a walk to rest their mounts.

Within a few miles of Carlisle, Carlton drew his mount to a halt and stood in his stirrups, his head turned, as if listening.

Harry glanced back at the winding road and started to say something, but Carlton held up a hand. He stood like that for a moment. Both he and Harry had tied their shakos to the D rings at the front of their saddles, and now the breeze ruffled Carlton's short, dark hair.

When he turned back, his eyes—the color of strong tea in the sunlight—met Claire's. "There's a coach coming—fast."

Her heart skipped a beat. Wetting her lips, she glanced down the empty road, but with the ground soft she could hear nothing. The captain must have extraordinary senses.

Harry gave a laugh, and Claire glanced at him. "You two! You should see your faces. What, do you expect every carriage to carry your father?"

Urging his horse forward, Carlton drew up next to his friend. "Better a cautious expectation than a bad meeting. Come along, Harry. Let's show Claire how we make ourselves scarce from French scouts."

Grumbling at such bother, Harry turned his horse to follow after Carlton.

The road lay open to either side, for the land had risen into stony mountains and grassy hills. Carlton set his horse to a canter, riding toward a small wooded area, and in less than a minute they entered the shaded grove and Claire had to bend low, ducking branches.

Harry and the captain drew their mounts to a halt, and Claire twisted in her saddle just as a mud-spattered black coach, horses struggling with the deep footing, thundered past, harness jingling.

Harry frowned, then glanced at Carlton. "It could have been anyone."

"Yes, so many have excellent reasons to make a mad gallop for the border. We'd best bypass Carlisle. He'll have to change horses there, if not sooner."

Carlton glanced at Claire, who still watched the bend where the coach had disappeared, her expression pensive. The urge rose to reach out a hand to her, but he checked his movement.

"Harry, look to your bride. I'll scout ahead," he said, and then dug the spurs into his horse.

As Alan galloped off, Harry steadied his own mount to keep it from following; then he glanced at his bride. What exactly was he to look to her for? She was a touch pale. But, thank heavens, she was not complaining about anything. He gave her an easy grin.

"Nothing like a bit of danger to spice our ride, eh?"

She turned toward him, her eyes troubled. "Danger?"

"Well, I mean, stands to reason your father would be none too happy with me, if we were to meet just now.

Not that he would shoot me, but, well, you know how tempers can fly."

"Oh, Harry, maybe we should let him catch up to me. Maybe we made a mistake about all this."

Ten

"Mistake?" He stared at her a moment, then grinned. "Rather late to be thinking that, my pet."

"We are not yet married."

"Stuff and nonsense. We are as good as, for you have spent three nights on the road with me, and do not let me hear another word about it. I would not have run off with you if I thought it was anything but a fine idea. So you may stop fretting—you are fretting, aren't you? Yes, well, you should not frown so much or you'll line your face forever like that.

"Now, come along and give me a smile. . . . Come on. Yes, that's it, just a small smile. There, now you look like the beauty who first caught my eye. And don't you feel better? Of course you do. Good girl. Now, let's ride on."

Harry spurred his horse forward, cantering after Carlton with utter certainty that Claire would follow.

Must be wedding nerves making her so jittery. Heaven knew, he felt them, too. Had been ever since he had realized just how close they were to that proverbial anvil they could marry over in Scotland.

And, truth be told, he had not cared one bit for that little tiff over that fighting cockerel. Bloody shame to have to pass up such a game one as that bantam. Still, it would have been a nuisance. So it was a good thing that Alan had talked him out of it. Yes, it was a good thing.

He glanced back, saw that Claire had not kept pace but that she was slowly trotting after them.

Lord, now she had him doing it! Mistake! Ha! He was not making a mistake. No, by heavens! He loved her. And she was wrong to accuse him, as well, of not being practical.

Indignation tightened in his chest. Why, he was always the most practical of fellows. Had he not thought up this excellent elopement! Why, yes, he had.

And it was all going to be just fine once they were wed and could start their happy ever after.

It would be.

His mood lifted, and he began to whistle.

But he broke off midnote, for a nagging thought had occurred to him. Was it not superstition that it was bad luck to whistle on your wedding day?

"Well, there it is—Greta Green."

They had crossed the Sark River and into Scotland only half a mile ago, and now their horses stood at Headlesscross, the track that led off the main road and into the village. A few cottages with thatched roofs stood beside the track. In the open green, a cow grazed and smoke curled up from one of the larger, square stone buildings closer to the village center.

Claire swallowed the dryness in her throat, then turned to Harry and put on a bright smile. "Here at last."

"Yes. Yes, indeed. Well, best get to it."

He urged his horse forward at a brisk trot and Claire followed, with Captain Carlton trailing behind.

They had not seen any other riders—or carriages—on the road, and Claire could only be grateful. Some part of her worried, however, that perhaps it would have been better for her father to find her and take her home. She could only hope that the fact he had not was a sign that this marriage was meant to be.

The village ended at what seemed to be a blacksmith shop, and Harry halted his horse and swung off his mount. Tossing the reins to Carlton with a wink to Claire, Harry strode inside the building.

Claire sat fiddling with her reins, but in a moment Harry came back.

"Seems we want a Mr. Elliot—it's only a so-called blacksmith who does the marrying up here, for he has to strike a different sort of shackle while the fire is hot."

Claire frowned, but she allowed Harry's comment to pass.

A few moments later they halted in front of a plain, two-story house with three chimneys.

"Here, you, boy," Carlton called out to a barefooted youngster as they dismounted. He gave the boy a penny to look after their mounts. Then they went to knock on the door.

A dark-haired man in his middle years opened the door, his jaw square with a dour expression. He looked them over, then said, his brogue thick, "Must be a wedding you're here for. Come in, come in, now. I know that eager look, only which of you might the lass be marrying?"

Harry frowned. "Me, sir. And I would appreciate it if we could do this in all haste."

"Aye, sir. Haste is what we do. You've just to say you came of your own free will and I've a certificate to fill in, sir." The dour Mr. Elliot stepped back, leaving the door open.

With a shrug, Harry sauntered in. Claire glanced at Captain Carlton, then also stepped inside, while the captain followed, closing the door behind him.

A small hall, with narrow stairs that led to the upper

floor, opened into a larger room with whitewashed walls. The large desk and stacks of papers seemed to indicate this was the office—not quite the place Claire had pictured for her wedding.

A rocker sat before an unlit fireplace. Bare of decoration, other than a tattered rug, the room was clean, though it smelled of brandy and tobacco.

Mr. Elliot stood before the desk, fussing with papers—the wedding certificates, no doubt. Claire's mouth had dried until it felt as cold and dusty as the ashes in the fireplace.

Glancing up, Mr. Elliot eyed them again. "And who's to be your other witness? It's two you be needing."

Harry dragged a hand through his hair. "Two? Oh, bother! Well, I suppose I can hire that blacksmith fellow. Here, you wait with Alan, Claire. I'll be but a moment."

She opened her mouth to protest, but he strode out the door before she could utter anything. Pressing her lips tight, she rubbed the back of one hand with the other. Carlton moved closer to her, and she glanced up at him. All she could think of, however, were the other occasions on this elopement that Harry had promised to be but a moment and never had been.

She let out a breath, then realized how shaky it was. "I suppose all brides feel awkward."

"I suppose." He frowned, then took her hand. "Claire, I want you to know something."

She glanced up at his face again, taking in the rugged contours, the edges and creases, the sun-worn lines. "Yes . . . Yes, Alan?"

"If . . . Well, if you ever need anything, I . . . I would not be much of a friend to Harry if I were not a friend to you."

She glanced down at his hand, and then looked up at

him again, longing and confusion welling inside her until she did not know what to say or do.

The clatter from outside saved her from answering. Carlton let go of her hand and moved to the window to glance out. He came back, his face grim.

"Elliot, you must have some experience of this. What do brides generally do to avoid an irate parent?"

"Father?" Claire muttered, her hand going to her throat. She had thought a few moments ago that it would be better if he came to claim her. Now, faced with the reality of confronting him and having to return home with him, cold terror trickled down her spine. She could not do it. Frustration welled in her that she seemed to have only wrong options before her.

Eyes narrowed, Mr. Elliot glanced at her and then back to the captain. "First bedroom upstairs and to the left suits most. Costs five shillings more, mind."

"Here's ten. Keep the gentleman who is about to burst in upon you as long as you can."

Carlton grabbed Claire's hand.

"But whatever are you doing?" she protested as he pulled her after him, almost dragging her up the narrow stairs. "Father must know we are here, and when Harry returns—"

"Your father will already have departed, or he will if this goes right."

Stopping on the second-floor landing, he took her shoulders. "Claire, do you trust me?"

His fingers pressed into her flesh, hard and vital. She stared up at him. In that moment, she knew that what she felt for him was far more than trust.

She nodded.

His eyes crinkled, and Claire's heart turned over.

"I hoped you might," he said, and took her hand again. He pulled her into the first room on the left, and no sooner had he shut the door behind them than a commotion of loud voices erupted downstairs.

"Oh, he sounds in an utter temper," Claire said, wincing at the curses that carried to her even at this distance.

Carlton listened at the door for a moment; then he glanced at Claire. Would she agree to this? He hoped so, for he could see no other choice. And he would be a damn bad friend, indeed, if he allowed that despot downstairs to drag Harry's bride away.

Starting to unbutton his jacket, he turned to Claire. "Take off your dress."

Her eyes widened. "You cannot mean . . ."

"I do mean. You did say you trusted me, Claire." He finished unbuttoning his jacket and dragged it off, then sat down on the bed to pull off his boots. He would certainly see now if she honestly did trust him or not.

In a moment more, he had off his boots and slipped his cravat from his neck; then he pulled his shirt over his head.

Turning, he found Claire in only her shift and corset, staring at the bed, hugging herself.

He gave her an easy smile. "It's like diving into cold water—best done in a rush."

She glanced at him, smiled, and then dove into the feather softness of the bed with him.

Her skin smelled of sunshine, and he had to remind himself that he was doing this for Harry.

Putting an arm around her shoulders, he pulled her closer. "It's just for show."

She nodded, her eyes enormous now, sparkling like the green of Devon in spring, and although he knew he ought not do this, he might never have the chance again. So he put his finger under her chin, tilted her face up to his, and kissed her.

Claire's world spun into the oblivion of sensation.

Alan's arm tightened around her, his mouth opened against her, and she gave in to him, holding nothing back.

The pounding on the stairs, the crash of the door slamming open, echoed distant in her mind.

Her father's sputtering finally pulled her back to the world. "How . . . How dare . . . How . . . !"

Alan lifted his lips from hers, but she could only stare up at him, head spinning, thoughts befuddled.

Then she glanced at the doorway. "Oh, hello, Father."

He glared at her, his face reddening. "Hello? Is that all you have to say?"

She pulled the sheet up to her chin, then said, "I am sorry you came all this way for nothing. But I told you that I did not want to marry Haltwistle. Now, you look tired, so you had best go and take a room in Carlisle before traveling home."

Mouth open, he stared at her. Then he snapped his mouth into a thin line and turned to Carlton. He glared at the man a moment. "Do not think, sir, you will ever be welcome in my house!"

The captain's arm tightened around Claire, and she put a hand up to his chest. The touch of his bare skin against her palm warmed her and made him glance at her for a moment. She felt the tension ease from his shoulders before he turned back to her father.

"That, sir, is your business. Your daughter is now mine, and I would be happy if you left her to me."

Roxburgh gave a rude snort, but his shoulders slumped. He gave once last glare at his daughter. "Do not think to come to me when you are a penniless war widow!"

Angry now, Claire started to sit up, but the captain's arm's around her kept her still.

"She will never be that, sir. My family has a large enough estate in Devon that Claire will always have a welcome there. But I do hope, sir, we may bring your grandchildren to sometimes visit."

With another rude snort, Roxburgh turned and strode out, slamming the door behind him.

Claire swallowed hard, and then the flush started along her skin. She was lying half naked in a bed with her husband-to-be's best friend.

She straightened at once. "I . . . I do not know what else to say to you other than thank you. And I . . . I . . ."

She let the words trail off, uncertain herself of what else she wanted to say. She knew what she wanted to do. She wanted to throw herself back into his arms. She wanted to tell him that it was he whom she loved. But how could she do that when he had just been so wonderful to her? He had saved her—for Harry. How could she place him in the impossible situation of having to betray his friend?

She was now more trapped than ever—and more certain than ever that she had chosen the wrong husband.

Her love for Harry was the love a friend would have for another—it was a pleasant, delightful, light feeling. But what had stirred inside her when Captain Carlton had kissed her had knocked that love over like a wave crashing against a sand castle.

Dropping her stare, she covered his hand with hers, and she vowed that she would not tell him what she felt. But at last she knew with a delirious, utter certainty that if she had it all to do again, she would do the same. If she had not run off with Harry, she would have never met Alan.

Now, she would do whatever lay in her powers to keep him in her life.

Looking up at him, she smiled. "I seem to say thank you a good deal."

His hand came up to brush her cheek. "Claire, I have no right to say this, but I—"

The door crashed open again. Claire jumped, and next to her she felt the captain tense as Harry stood in the doorway, staring at them.

On the bed, Claire's hand tightened on the captain's.

For a heartbeat, no one said anything; then Harry muttered, "Well, I'll be!"

He came forward a step, and Claire braced for his accusations, and she tried to order the explanation she owed him for this scene.

But then Harry grinned. "Dash all, Alan, if you are not the best friend ever!"

Coming around the side of the bed, he took hold of the captain's hand and began to shake it.

Carlton's shoulders relaxed. "Then you know the truth of it? You spoke to Elliot?"

"Elliot? Oh, he told me you were up here. But I ought to have known a hundred miles ago what was in the wind—you, dog, you. Ought to call you out for stealing my bride, I ought, but how can I when I'm nothing but relieved not to be marrying her myself."

"Relieved?" Claire said, both surprised and at the same time a touch dismayed.

He turned to Claire. "Not, of course, that you are anything but the most delightful of ladies, my pet. It's just that all your talk about mistakes started me thinking that perhaps I'm not quite ready to marry, you know."

Carlton glanced at Claire. "You told Harry you thought it a mistake to marry him?" She nodded, and his frown deepened. "And why did you not think to tell me this?"

She began to knot the bed linens in her hands. "Well, you are my friend—but you are Harry's, too. And I, well, I have to marry someone, and I did not want to burden you . . . and . . ."

Harry leaned closer to Carlton. "I think this is where I take my exit. I'll have this anvil priest and that honest blacksmith fellow over to whatever passes for an inn hereabouts while you sort this out." He winked. "Take your time."

Then he came around the bed. "Claire, my dear, you are getting the better man, but I daresay you realized that some time ago. I do, however, reserve the right to be godfather to your children and spoil them utterly."

"Thank you, Harry. And I do love you, you know. But I also think I might want to murder you if we did marry."

"Can't have that, my pet. I do not like to be murdered."

Taking her hand he kissed it, gave her a wink, and left the room whistling.

Claire turned to the captain. "You must think I am awful—promising to marry one gentleman, and in a space of a few days deciding that I am in love with another."

"Is that why you did not want to tell me about this? You thought I would think badly of you?"

She nodded.

The lines around his eyes crinkled as he took her in his arms. "My love, I always knew you weren't the right bride for Harry. But you may have fair warning that I do not intend for you to ever change your mind again about your affections."

"Oh? And how will you accomplish that?"

Carlton smiled. A weight had lifted from his chest when Harry had walked in on them and smiled. He would have been content to be Claire's friend, but oh, it would be far sweeter to be far more than that to her.

Tightening his hold on her, he tilted her face up to his. "It's very simple, my dear. I am going to love you forever."

He was smiling still as he bent to kiss her, and he

rather thought that it would be quite all right to keep Harry waiting for once.

And then he forgot all else except the sweet pleasure to be found with his border bride.

LOVE LESSONS

Donna Simpson

One

"You cannot marry your whore, Cedric. It is just not done."

Cedric, the eighth Earl of Cairngrove, did not look at the speaker. Instead, he frowned at the papers—marriage settlements newly prepared by his solicitor and sent around for his approval—splayed out in front of him. He made a careful notation in the margin of one paper and turned it over on his massive oak desk, one of several enormous pieces in the stately library of the Cairngrove London residence. "Wrong, Nic," he said, gazing over his glasses with an expression that mingled affection and irritation. "I can, and I certainly will." He paused, and his expression hardened, the soft, jowly lines of his face becoming granite. "However, if you refer to Jessica as my whore one more time, I will call you out."

Unfazed by the threat, the younger man said, "You shall be the laughingstock of London." He paced away from the desk toward the window, but then whirled and returned, planting his hands on the burled oak surface and leaning over to emphasize the urgency of his words. "Nay, of all of England. You must see that you will make of the family name a mockery!"

Dominic Barton—Nic to his intimates—the younger of the two men, was also the more striking. The hands that he laid on the desk as he leaned across it were not soft, but they were immaculately kept, with a ruby insignia ring on his right ring finger. His arms were solid and clad in the finest of superfine wool, part of an exquisitely well-cut coat. Where the earl was descending comfortably into middle age, advancing into his forties with a spreading of the stomach and thinning of hair, Barton, at thirty, was just coming into his most attractive years, lean and athletic, with broad shoulders, narrow hips, dark hair, and intense eyes almost coal black.

But where good humor and lively intelligence sparkled in the earl's eyes and danced on his lips, the younger man's features told a tale of self-indulgence, debauchery, almost, and . . . Well, there was no other word for it. Strangely enough, there was a *priggish* cast to his expression that hinted that though he was quite content to indulge his own carnal appetites, there was a definite line between what he thought fit for himself and what he thought was owed his family name and history. For all of his man-about-town airs, Mr. Dominic Barton was a bit of a puritan, and never more so than where his family was concerned.

"Nic," Cairngrove said, taking off his glasses and polishing them on the cloth that lay next to his inkwell, "I do not care if people laugh. Not one whit. Let them. Let them have a jolly great roar at my expense." He frowned at an inky smear on his glasses and wiped it off.

Nic slapped his palm on the desktop. "But a Cairngrove has never wed a whore!"

Cedric stood swiftly, and his ringed hand, bearing the insignia of his old and respected title, flashed out. But the young man was quicker and caught the earl's hand before the slap was delivered.

"Really, old brick," Nic drawled. "I thought you more tolerant than that. And swifter." He dropped the older man's hand.

"I meant what I said," Cairngrove growled. "I will

have no one speak ill of Jessica in my hearing. She is to be my wife, and the man who dishonors her in my hearing will pay for it with the slash of my sword. I mean that, Nic. I will spill even my own brother's blood."

Barton gave him a long look and said, "Cedric, old man, you know I would never accept a challenge from you. It would be just too drearily Cain and Abel." He faced his older brother across the desk. Dark eyes flashing in the sunlight that pierced the deep gloom of the high-ceilinged library, he continued. "Remember this, though, Brother, you may be able to control what people say to your face, but you cannot command what they say behind your back. And behind your children's back. What price will *they* pay for your decision?" He turned on his heel and marched out of the room, the heavy *thunk* of his boot heels evidence of his disapproval of the recent turn of events in his older brother's life.

Cairngrove slumped back down in his green leather chair and passed one hand over his eyes. He hated this chasm between him and his only sibling, but it did not change his determination. How could he bring Nic to understand what it felt like to be deeply in love for the first time in all of his forty-three years?

And damn it, he had earned his happiness! When their father died unexpectedly at a relatively young age, Cedric had done his duty, marrying, at the tender age of twenty-one, an eminently suitable heiress, Lady Wilhelmina Stuart. Together they had produced five children, three of whom had survived to adulthood. William, Viscount Darden, the Cairngrove heir, was now twenty and in Vienna as a diplomatic assistant. Allan, eighteen and William's younger brother, was also in Vienna with the horse guards. Their sister, Melanie, Allan's twin, was married and touring the Continent with her new husband.

With his children settled in life, what had he to do now but please himself?

And marrying Jessica would please him. He knew it was unconventional. And good Lord, he knew no Cairngrove had ever done it. But he was going to make his mistress his wife, and be damned to the world.

If Nic could just once experience love—just once—then he would understand that there was almost nothing in the world one would not sacrifice for it.

Linnet Pelham, an elegant young lady of twenty-three, gazed at the gauzy material in her hand and said, "Jess, I hope this turns out all right. I had such high hopes of it when I started, but I should have known I am not the dab hand at stitchery that this fussy work requires. I should have left it to the milliner."

Jessica Landry, a fretful expression on her narrow face, turned onto her side and said, "It doesn't matter, Lin. Don't finish it if you don't want."

"Jess, I did not mean that! I meant . . ." She trailed off and gazed over at the other woman, who lay in bed, pale and wan after another bout of nausea. If only Jessica would allow her to call in a doctor! But she wouldn't hear of it, becoming violently agitated whenever it was mentioned. "Jess, you do *love* Cairngrove, do you not?"

Tears filled the young woman's blue eyes before she squeezed them shut. "I do."

"Then you do want to marry him."

"Yes . . . No . . . I don't know!" She thrashed around on the bed, turning onto her back again, then onto her other side. Finally she rolled back over, hugged a pillow to her thin bosom, and stared at Linnet again. "Why can't he just leave things as they are; why did he have to make such a fuss?"

Exasperated, Linnet threw aside the awkward attempt at a veil she was sewing and said, "He wants you to be his countess. You should be ecstatic! God, Jess, he loves you! Is that so hard to understand? He loves you and he wants to be with you always."

Great, fat tears rolled down the other woman's cheeks. "Don't be angry, Lin, I just . . ."

"Oh, honey, I'm not angry!" Linnet knelt down by the side of the bed and put her arms around the weeping woman.

"I am his m-mistress," Jessica sobbed, almost doubled over as she curled into a ball under the covers. "I never expected him to m-marry me!"

"But now he wants to."

"People will m-mock him! G-Gillray will make drawings, and others will poke fun, and . . ."

"Jess, stop it!" Jessica was quickly making herself hysterical, and Linnet felt it was time to inject some common sense into this emotional bathos. "Listen to me! If anyone can weather the storm that will erupt, it is Cairngrove. He is a strong and intelligent man and he *loves* you! There is a clear path here; either you love him and will marry him, or you do not love him and will break it off."

A little calmer, Jessica said, "It is not that easy!" She sniffed and used the handkerchief Linnet gave to her to blow her nose. "I am only thinking of him. And . . . Oh, God, Lin, what about his children? They will hate me!"

Linnet stood awkwardly and rubbed the feeling back into her legs. "Don't be an ass! They will not hate you." Forced into honesty by her own realization that Jessica could have the right of it, she finished with, "Or if they do, it will be their own problem, not yours. Cairngrove will support you."

"But I will not stand between him and his family!"

Sighing in exasperation, Linnet said, "Then if you think that his spoiled daughter and sons' hurt feelings are of more importance than Cairngrove's happiness, go ahead and break it off."

"I didn't mean that!"

"Then *don't* break it off!"

"You just don't understand, Lin, and you never will. I'm exhausted; I am going to sleep for a while." Jessica turned to face the other way.

Linnet gazed at her steadily for a moment, then said, softly, "Sleep, Jess. I will be close by if you need me."

Perhaps she had been too impatient, Linnet thought. She had no idea what Jessica was going through, what doubts, fears, inadequacies. And Jess had not been well for some time.

Linnet, after all, had only been there for a couple of weeks, at loose ends after being told abruptly, at the end of Easter term, that her services as English mistress at Fox Hall School for Young Ladies were no longer required. Her sin, she thought, though it had never been stated outright, was in telling a girl of fourteen what would be required of her in the marriage her parents were contracting for her fifteenth birthday. The child was astoundingly callow, and being somewhat acquainted with the girl's mother, Linnet knew that the poor girl would go to the marriage bed woefully ignorant. Linnet could not delay the marriage, but she *would* have the child aware of what would be expected of her.

How could she have known that Ellen, the girl in question, would then rebel at being expected to do such intimate things with the "poxy old fart" as she referred to her intended bridegroom? The wedding never took place, the mother of the bride blamed Linnet, and Linnet was "released" from her employment. In secret she gave a quick "hurrah" for Ellen's new-found independence and her stubborn resistance to marrying her fifty-three-year-old prospective bridegroom. But still, though she had no regrets about her actions—Ellen's future was worth the sacrifice—she did regret her lack of a wage, the impossibility of getting another teaching job with no reference from Fox Hall, and the necessity of descending upon Jessica unannounced and unexpected.

And yet it appeared she was not a moment too soon. Masterful at breaking up a wedding, could Linnet now save a marriage she fully believed would lead to great happiness for both parties? She recovered, from the bedchamber floor where she had tossed it in her fit of pique, her lamentable attempt at creating a marriage veil fit for the future Countess of Cairngrove, and slipped from the room as Jessica's breathing became deep and even. Down the hall in the room designated for the seamstress creating a lovely ivory dress for Jessica's wedding, she handed over the veil to the woman inside, saying, "Mrs. Semple, if you can make something of that, I shall be eternally grateful."

The woman took one look at it and said, "Looks, miss, like an ideal strainer for Cook's whey."

Laughing, Linnet closed the door on the sight of yards and yards of frothy silk and Brussels lace, and headed down the dark hall toward the stairs. Her reflection flashed by in a mirror in the hall and she paused, glanced at it, and then glanced away. Every time she looked in the mirror these days she found herself wondering, could she, *dare* she, take the same path Jessica took a few years before—should she go on stage? Should she try to find a new way to make a living, since there was no likelihood of her finding employment as a schoolmistress again?

But Jessica had had a natural talent, a dramatic flare that broke the audience's heart and held them spellbound, unable even to summon the brass to pelt her with rotten oranges or sing loud drinking songs, as audiences were wont to do. If Linnet ascended to the stage all she would do is act as target practice.

So what would she do with her future? With Jess making such an astounding match it was possible that Linnet, on the earl's coattails, could wheedle her way into society, insinuate herself into some man's good graces and elicit a marriage proposal. Cairngrove was an absolute lamb, and if Jess asked him to, he would, without a second thought, foist a shabby-genteel spinster schoolmistress onto the *ton* and pass her off as marriageable. But since she had already dismissed her dramatic abilities, she did not see herself any better able to act demure and conceal her natural streak of acerbic wit and untimely sense of the ridiculous. No, and neither did she see her way clear to becoming one of the earl's pensioners, though she knew Cairngrove well enough by now to know he would give her a wage as a companion to Jessica. But she cringed from that thought. She was not and never would be a sponge. No, she would just have to find her own way to make a living.

She descended the first flight of stairs to the landing and turned the angle to go down the rest when she heard a commotion at the door. Her lips firmed into a straight gash of displeasure across her face. Another troublemaker. Boxley Square, the site of Jessica's town home, was in a moderately well-to-do section of the city, but still they had their share of hawkers and peddlers.

Linnet straightened her back, took a deep breath, and descended the last set of steps. There had been a spate of importunate visitors to the door of late. The news of the Earl of Cairngrove's marriage was not supposed to have leaked out yet, but there had been numerous visits from silk merchants and such, all with absolutely the best prices in London on cloth from India, china from the Orient, and jewels from the French royal family's treasures. Linnet found a kind of satisfaction in turning them away with her natural brusqueness.

"I will handle this, Meg," she said to the maid who had answered the door. She pushed the exasperated Meg out of the way. "What can I do for you?"

"Are you the, uh, *lady* of the house?" His tone inso-
lent, the man at the door had marked off the word "lady"
in such a way as to surely intend to give offense.

Narrow chin down, Linnet felt an almost savage joy
in the fury she would now unleash, and yet . . . and yet,
this man in front of her looked like no peddler, nor even
the Fleet Street type she had ever chanced to meet. Too
handsome, too self-assured, too well dressed. Too high
up in the social hierarchy. Within seconds she had as-
sessed him. His unassailable position in society was
spelled out in immaculate linens, perfect tailoring,
gleaming Hessians, and a diamond stickpin.

Who was he? She was not one to swoon over masculine perfection, but from the top of his glowing Brutus
cut to the tip of those Hessians, he was something out
of the ordinary, his dark eyes piercing and intense, his
aura commanding.

From the "no" her mouth was about to form, in answer to his question, she stretched her mouth into a
"yes." Regardless of who he was or what his position
in society, he was clearly not a visitor to the residence
or he would already know she was not Jessica Landry.
And he was no friend of the earl's, she was sure; he was
quite a bit younger than Cairngrove. Linnet would not
have Jess disturbed. There was only one way to handle
this.

"I am she," she said, lifting her chin in an unconscious
display of hauteur she had adopted during her years as
a teacher at Fox Hall.

Nic, his booted foot in the doorway, was startled.
Though he had been out of the country for some time,
even on the Continent he had heard of Jessica Landry
as a great beauty, but she must be . . . He did rapid cal-
culations in his mind. She must be all of eight-and-
twenty or so by now. This woman was beautiful, tall,
slim, and regal, but with a porcelain loveliness that fit

more with eighteen than twenty-eight. She was exquisite and graceful and glowed with health and vigor.

And yet Cedric said she had been ill lately. She did not look ill. She looked . . . blooming. Delicious. Her slender frame, clad in a sober gown of navy sarcenet, was not boyish but rather feminine in a willowy, lithe fashion. He was instantly attracted to her beauty, and a spurt of jealousy trembled through his limbs that his older brother should possess nightly such loveliness. If he had seen her on the stage, as Cedric had, he would have taken her under his protection, too.

But still, one did not wed one's whore. He hardened his heart. That was all she was, a whore. He pushed his way past her into her home and glanced around, knowing even as he did so that he was being insufferably rude, but past caring. The jade must be used to this kind of treatment as an actress and then a kept woman. So this was what his brother's money had bought, he thought, glancing around him at the paneled walls and elegant paintings. He could find no fault with the decor, which displayed a restrained and elegantly modern taste. She must be a valued mistress indeed, he thought, for the home was stately, respectable, no whiff of the brothel or even lower-class tastes here.

He turned back to the woman and noted the tight-lipped frown on her lovely face and the anger that flashed in her brilliant eyes. He would soon change that expression to a more pleasing look, or his name was not Nic Barton.

"Who are you, sir? And why do you force your way into this . . . into my home?"

"I have come, Miss Landry," Nic said, boldly assessing her slim figure, raising his quizzing glass, and raking her up and down, "to make you a bargain."

Two

Again she frowned. He saw quick calculation in her eyes, and then she stepped back, allowing him in. She escorted him past a collection of potted palms into a parlor off the main hall. Nic swiftly decided on a change of plans. His original intention on meeting his older brother's mistress was to impress upon her the impossibility of her upcoming nuptials and how he would do everything in his power to bring the pressure of the *ton* to bear on her. In short, he meant to make sure no household in any *ton* circle would admit her. It would have been difficult to actually do—after all, Cairngrove held much more power and social cachet than he did—but he had counted on her ignorance of *ton* ways, added to his own natural self-assurance to carry him through.

He had thought long and hard before going to her door, and he felt reasonably secure in making certain assumptions before even meeting Cedric's mistress. One such assumption was that entrée into the great houses of the *ton* was one of her objectives in marrying Cedric. If he could assure her that she would be doomed to disappointment on that head, perhaps she would retreat from her demand for marriage. But if she insisted on going ahead with the wedding, he would rally the natural repugnance of the *ton* for scandalous goings-on—at least those thrust into their faces and not decently kept under covers—to aid him in his ostracism of Miss Landry and her unprecedented gall.

But . . .

But he had clearly miscalculated a couple of things. Now, looking back, he was not certain what he expected from Miss Landry, but assuredly he had not counted on her absolute loveliness and the purity of her appearance. She stood at the door of the parlor asking the maid to bring tea, and he scanned her face and form. No, he had not expected this, this quickening of interest, this heat that swept over him when he watched her move. It changed things. Subtly, but definitely.

As a soldier he was accustomed to planning strategies as new information came in, and he must apply those skills to the present battle, he felt, the war to save his brother's reputation and family name. A mistress. For a girl of such loveliness and natural grace—and seeming gentility—to stray so far from the path of modesty must mean a need for money and . . . what else? A certain moral lassitude, perhaps? Or was that just hopefulness speaking? Perhaps there was ambition there, too, ambition that he must thwart.

He watched the sensual, unstudied sway of her hips and the little movements that told him more about her inner needs than any amount of talk ever would. His interest quickened. She was filled with repressed sexuality, he would bet. What would it take to release that? And had Cairngrove ever found the key?

No, he really did not think he had. The man was besotted, yes, but was that as much for what he could sense but not attain as for what they actually had between them? Nic rejected, in that moment, that his brother truly was in love. It was just the infatuation of an older man for a younger woman, the first lover he had probably taken after the death of his wife. And ultimately, marrying her would be a tragic mistake. So clearly Nic was doing the right thing, saving his brother from a horrible mistake that he would regret for the rest of his days.

And if this girl was unwell, as Cairngrove claimed, then Nic must be on his deathbed, for he had never seen so healthy a young woman. That must be another stratagem Miss Landry was using to quicken the earl's sense of haste in marrying. She was putting on no languid, sickly airs with him, he noticed.

"Now, sir, what do you want?" she said, facing him and coldly eyeing him with distaste.

Her voice was well modulated, well trained, but not what he would have expected from a retired actress. Her tones were too clipped, her enunciation too perfect. "What do I want?"

"Yes, that is what I asked. Are you a little deaf, perhaps? Shall I raise my voice?"

He grinned. Little termagant. He liked her already. But then he gave himself an inner shake. The face of an angel and personality of a scold did not make her anything more than the whore she was. It was important—nay, vital—that he find a way to separate this young woman from his brother. Cairngrove would regret his hasty and impetuous action; he knew it clear down to his bones. If it had just been a matter of regret, though, Nic would not be taking such pains over the whole affair. Let Cairngrove make an idiot of himself.

But what of William and Allan and poor Melanie? How would they ever hold their heads up among the *ton* again if their stepmama was a retired actress, a *whore?* It was unthinkable. For their sake, and ultimately for Cedric's, he must do this thing.

But how?

"Raise it if you like, but I am not going deaf. Surprising, really, when you consider what the proximity of cannonade can do."

"You were in the military?"

"I was a captain," he said, amused at the quickening interest in her voice.

"Where did you see action?"

"I was involved in the Peninsular campaigns and then was sent over to Canada until we attained peace. From there I moved on to Belgium, and then Vienna. I returned only months ago."

She seemed to remember their purpose in speaking and shook her head, frowning. "You said something about making a bargain. I would have you know that I am interested in neither silks nor jewels."

"You would be the first woman of my acquaintance who was not, then," he said with a wry grin.

She stiffened. "I am sure your . . . *acquaintance* with women of that sort is wide and deep, sir, however that does not concern me. State your business or get out *now.*"

"I am not a peddler," he said.

A maid arrived with a tea tray, but the young woman ignored it and waved the girl away. Then she sat down in a rigid chair and stared at him silently, elegant eyebrows raised.

Very well, then. "Miss Landry, allow me to introduce myself. I am Dominic Barton, Cairngrove's younger brother."

Linnet felt her mouth gape open and slapped it shut, her teeth jarring together. Good Lord! Cairngrove's brother? "You are his *brother?* I am so sorry, sir, for . . ." She shrugged and shook her head. Why should she apologize, really? She had been unspeakably rude, but then he hadn't identified himself so what more could he have expected? Even worse, he thought her to be Jessica Landry, his brother's intended bride. She opened her mouth to clear up the confusion but Mr. Barton was already talking.

"Yes, I am the earl's brother. I am sure you wonder why I have come here, unannounced and without old

Cedric. I came, as I said, to offer you a bargain, a deal, as it were."

Linnet frowned. What kind of May game was he playing? Since he mentioned it, yes, it was odd that he had come for the very first time without the earl to his future sister-in-law's home. "What kind of a deal could you possibly have to offer me, sir?" Her natural skepticism was apparent in her tone, but she made no effort to temper it.

"Are you not going to offer me tea?" he asked, a smile on his lean face, his dark eyes sparkling with repressed amusement.

Linnet, confused between her instinct toward politeness, especially since the man was Jessica's future in-law, and her suspicion that there was something not quite right in this visit, found herself unaccustomedly flustered. "Of course." She poured, and Mr. Barton sat in the chair by hers and accepted a cup of tea. He dropped a lump of sugar into it and stirred.

He drank some, then sat back. "I have been away a great deal in the last years. Even since the peace with America I have been attached to my unit in Belgium. We were pressed into service when Napoleon refused to stay put on his island."

"Your brother must be grateful that you have come back with no injury," Linnet said, still unsure what to say, how to tell him she was not, after all, Jessica Landry.

Barton nodded and then said, his voice hardening, "I come back to the news that he is intending to marry a woman no one in this town will even speak to once he weds her."

Ah, there it was. He intended to feel her out, find out her intentions. Then perhaps it was time to tell him the truth and let him meet the real Jessica. Linnet would prepare her for the visit first, because it would not be easy. This steely eyed man might not be best pleased that his brother was marrying his mistress, though it was not absolutely unprecedented, and eventually, Linnet was sure, people would get over the shock. There was nothing to object to in Jessica's person, for she was lovely, well spoken, and intelligent. And her birth was adequate, too, though certainly not exalted. It was only this tricky business of her being Cairngrove's mistress to be overcome. "I think I should tell you . . ."

"No, Miss Landry, let me tell you." He set aside his cup and leaned forward in his chair. "You know, no one in this town will even speak your name much less admit you to their homes."

Instinctively recoiling at his aggressive posture, she stuttered, "A-anyone who married a man like Cairngrove would certainly have other compensations. Perhaps sh— uh . . . perhaps I do not care for society?"

"But Cairngrove has a position in the government and many friends among the *ton;* you will only be bringing him humiliation if you persist in this mad scheme to marry."

Linnet felt her anger begin to roil in her belly. That this was what Jessica had been saying made it that much worse. "I think, Mr. Barton, that you had best . . ."

"No, hear me out, my dear," he said, his voice lowering to a silky bass. "I am not done, not by a long shot. I told you I have a most interesting proposition for you, my sweet."

A shiver raced through Linnet and settled in her stomach. If she had been the type of woman easily seduced by masculine charm, she might at that moment be listening only to the timbre of his voice and not his words. His eyes were dark, almost black, and they were peering at her intently. She swallowed. When he reached over and took her hand from her lap, she jumped, startled.

"I have as much your interest at heart as my brother's, believe me, Miss Landry. I would not see such a lovely young woman hurt by the insensitivity of the *ton*. They can be brutal, and they would crush a fair flower like you," he said, touching her cheek with the back of his free hand.

Linnet almost could not breathe. Surely someone should open a window, for it was suffocatingly hot in this airless parlor, even though it was just barely May. "I am not fragile in the least, Mr. Barton. In fact . . ."

"How much better for you," he went on, talking over her words while he cupped her chin gently and rubbed his thumb over her sensitive bottom lip, "if you found a way to slip quietly away to live in opulence and comfort elsewhere. I could make that possible for you. Cairngrove has likely only given you an allowance, but I . . . I would be willing to make a settlement on you. Money of your own, to do with what you please."

Linnet, taken by surprise, could not respond. Barton's other hand tightened around hers and his thumb caressed her palm. Unfamiliar sensations jolted through her body, jangling her nerves.

His voice was even lower and as silky as fine French talc. "All you would have to do is slip away so old Cedric cannot find you. Just slip away in the night."

Stunned, revolted by the offer, Linnet was ready to let him have it. How dare he think Jessica would desert his brother? How dare he think he could bribe his brother's companion of two years so easily? He was insufferable, and she would tell him so to his face and then tell him to leave.

She glanced into his eyes and was riveted. There was more there than just an offer of money. His eyes scanned her, and she felt a heated flush rise over her body as if his eyes were burning into her, setting her aflame.

Was he suggesting? . . .

A jumble of confused emotions thrummed through her

like a drum tattoo. Was it really his intention to suggest that she become *his* mistress instead of his brother's?

It couldn't be, or . . . or could it? This was his brother he was talking about, and he would willingly seduce his brother's mistress away from him?

She was repulsed, and yet the heated flash of his eyes intrigued her. With an instant bolt of intuition she understood that the flare of passion that glimmered in his coal eyes was for herself, not herself as Cairngrove's mistress. She did not think he had come intending to offer her his protection in that manner. It was the impulse of the moment, inspired by his desire for her.

He released her hand and sat back in his chair, eyeing her with ill-concealed interest. His glance was like a touch, as if she could feel each point where his eyes rested, on her throat, on her shoulders, on her . . . on her breasts. Linnet was arrested by the novel sensations racing through her. She had always considered herself cold, and yet the simplest glance of this man next to her had sent her pulse racing and raised tiny beads of perspiration to her brow. What did he do? How was he different?

Ever one to avoid obfuscation, she looked at him directly. "Are you asking me, sir, to desert your brother and go away with you?"

Three

She was pleased by the startled look in his eyes. Good. Her forthrightness had clearly disconcerted him. It was like a pitcher of cold water poured over his head. But he recovered quickly.

"I had considered it." He crossed his legs at the knee. "Old Cedric is a wonderful person, but it has always been known in our family that in my bones lies all of the passion. Cedric is a diplomat, trained in subtlety and mildness." He changed position yet again, leaning forward, his eyes holding hers. "I am a warrior, trained only in fierceness, boldness . . . I *take* what I want," he said, holding out his palm and snapping it closed, "while old Ceddie negotiates for it." His voice lowered, became caressing and silky, and yet still his words throbbed with ill-concealed desire. "I would not disappoint you, my dear. If you have been used to love-making that is tepid, I will show you what it is like to make love with a man who has fire in his veins. I would give you love lessons, my dear, teach you what it is like to be consumed by a hungry man, ravished until you cry out into the darkness as you surrender to the exquisite domination of passion."

The dark carnality of his words sent a shiver through Linnet and she bolted upright from her chair, unwilling to face the susceptibility of her body to his manipulation. Voice shaking both from anger and from alarm at the flash of unwelcome heat coursing through her, Linnet said, "And now you have insulted everyone concerned. Your brother is a dear, *dear* man. Where he loves, he loves wholeheartedly, and you are not worth the end of his pinky finger, sir. If I *were* his mistress—" She saw the startled look in his dark eyes and enjoyed thoroughly his discomfiture. "If I *were* Jessica, I would have had you thrown from the house before now for insulting me and the relationship that exists with your brother. As it is I am glad I intervened, so that Jessica, my dear, sweet . . . friend, did not have to hear this abominably *filthy* suggestion. Good-bye, Mr. Barton."

Barton was on the doorstep and the door was shut firmly behind him before he recovered from his stupefying rout. He stood, staring at the green-painted door with the brass knocker, and his mind whirled through the events of the past minutes. Not Miss Jessica Landry. The young woman he had been speaking to for half an hour was *not* his brother's mistress. If there was a tiny knot of pleasure in the pit of his stomach at that news he was not about to acknowledge it, though he did recognize that it changed everything.

His change in plans, from bullying to persuasion, had been the work of a second from the moment he laid eyes on that lovely, lithe goddess. It had gone against the grain to try to seduce his brother's mistress away from him—it was a type of thievery, after all—but it was not only for his own pleasure, but for his brother's good, and so he had been able to rationalize that in this one case the end justified the means. But clearly he was going to have to rethink things. Perhaps this was for the best, for if she *had* been Jessica Landry and had had him tossed from the door, he would have had no recourse. It would have been the end of his campaign.

But the battle was not lost. A wise captain knew when to retreat, muster his forces, and find a new line of at-

tack. The danger was that she—who was she, anyway?—
would tell Miss Landry of this encounter. But he did not
think she would. Cairngrove had talked enough of his
paramour for Barton to know she was frail and sickly.
No one who cared about her would tell her such upset-
ting news.

He took a deep breath, willing his body to calmness.
Who was that gorgeous young woman? And what was
her relationship to Miss Landry? He stared at the door,
then turned and descended the steps, whistling a jaunty
tune. He had not mistaken the flash of suppressed desire
in her lovely eyes; of that one thing he was certain.
Whether she knew it or not, she was susceptible to him

Though she surely had been offended by his suggestion, she was tempted, or his name was not Dominic
Barton.

Linnet, shaking with anger, paced in the hall for a few
minutes, reliving the triumph of showing him the door
while his mouth hung open and he stared like a landed
fish, gasping and gaping. How dare he? Who did he
think he was, to offer *carte blanche* to his brother's mistress? It was unthinkable. It was outrageous.

"Ravished . . . to the exquisite domination of passion."

Humming beneath her outrage, like the faint thread
of a song one could not get out of one's mind, was the
insidious tug of attraction, a shocking wave of fascina-
tion for a man so totally outside of her experience. She
laid her cheek against the cool painted surface of the
door frame and gazed into the parlor they had just va-
cated. It still seethed with the energy of Barton's presence, the intense masculinity of his graceful form and
riveting eyes. He was right about one thing; Linnet had
spent many an hour in the presence of the earl and never

had she felt that allure, that pull, the force of magnetism between man and woman. Was that because Cairngrove was already bespoke, already consumed with love for Jessica? Or was there something between Linnet and Barton that was outside of the normal gravitation of female to male?

With an exclamation of disgust she pushed herself away from the door frame, restlessly pacing the parlor in search of some useful thing to do. There was absolutely no point in even thinking about it. As had just been demonstrated by what had passed between them, the only way a man like Dominic Barton would look at Linnet Pelham was as a possible mistress.

Though, she reminded herself firmly as she sat with her sewing basket by the window, there was absolutely nothing wrong with her birth. Her father had been a gentleman and her mother almost a gentlewoman, though in *her* family there was the hint of the shop. But on the Pelham side there was a baronet and a knight, and more of the untitled gentry. It was enough to make them genteel.

She picked a piece of embroidery out of the pile and stabbed at it with a needle. She would see how quickly she could destroy this piece that she had been working on haphazardly over the years, she thought, eyeing the crimson silk thread warily. The design was already starting to list badly on one side. Soon, if she continued torturing it, it would look as if it had been pulled into a whirlpool and twisted impossibly.

Her family was genteel, yes, she thought, stabbing the cloth, but poor. *That* she was forced to admit. Her parents, matched well in love for each other if not in equality of birth, had been prolific. As the Bible admonished, they had gone forth and multiplied. And *multiplied*. Mrs. Pelham had matched even good Queen Charlotte, bearing fifteen children, though four of her own had died in infancy compared to the queen's two losses.

And their father's income had never been adequate for his number of children. If they had been sensible they would have retired to separate beds after the first four. But they had not, and as a result the only time Linnet's mother was not with child was when she was nursing the last one, an expedient she had been forced to by the lack of money to retain a wet nurse for the last several babies.

That poverty was one of the many reasons why, after being sacked from her position at Fox Hall, Linnet had not returned home. She had left initially to work at the school out of necessity. She had not been raised to think she would need to work, but her father's death several years before, shortly after the birth of her youngest sister, had left her family destitute. She was not the eldest, nor was she the first to realize she would need to find employment, but at seventeen she had gone out as a schoolteacher and had spent six if not enjoyable then at least satisfying years in that position.

But being left without a job had forced her onto Jessica, for there was no way she could return home to her fragile mother, who was still burdened by the raising of several of the youngest children. She hadn't even told her mother yet about her lack of employment. But she would soon. She must—when she broke the news to Mrs. Pelham that her eldest daughter, in disgrace these last few years first because of her profession and then because of her manner of support with *no* profession, was marrying the Earl of Cairngrove.

Jessica was, indeed, Linnet's eldest sister. The name "Landry" was a fiction designed to save the "Pelham" appellation from the stain of the stage. In fact, Mrs. Pelham, caught up in her own worries, did not even yet truly know of her daughter's descent into the world of the *demimonde*. If she had a more active, inquisitive mind, she could have puzzled it out, even though nothing had ever been said outright to her. But she had never asked, and Jessica had never said, beyond mentioning, in her very occasional letters home, the earl as a "mentor."

And so there were numerous shocks coming to the frail Mrs. Pelham, but please, God, Linnet thought, not all of them would be unpleasant. Cairngrove had made it quite clear to both of them that one of his first priorities in the marriage settlements would be security for Jessica's family. Until now, Jessica, bound by love to the earl as well as gratitude, had not allowed him do more than pay the rent on the Pelham family's cottage in their Surrey village. But marriage would certainly change the family's situation and prospects.

Her sewing tossed aside, Linnet gazed out the window at the activity in Boxley Square. A hansom pulled up next door and disgorged an elderly woman of heavily painted visage. A tiny sweeper dashed across the road and cleaned up the reminder of the horse's passing.

The outside world might criticize, but Linnet understood the pressures that had driven her dearest of sisters into such desperate choices. Six years before, with all of the children still at home, their mother ill and their father newly deceased, leaving them, through his improvident ways, destitute, they were soon at the point of despair. Within months they would be cast upon the charity of the parish. Jessica, as lovely of character and temperament as she was of face, took it upon herself to make use of a tenuous acquaintance with a young woman from their village who had become an actress. She moved to London and started her work in the theater. Every spare penny she made, she sent home.

Linnet made the leap soon after, as young as she was,

to a teaching position, and, like her sister, sent every penny home. But still, it was never enough. Their younger siblings became ill at different times; they needed medicine, good food, clothes, education, none of which came free. Jessica soon realized that the theater did not pay as well as she had hoped. A virtuous young woman when she was first approached by an ardent earl, Lord Cairngrove, who wished to become her protector, she said no. But soon, getting to know him and liking him, she agreed. Linnet had been shocked when Jessica first told her of her intentions, but it was Jess's life, and she was besotted with the earl, as much in love with his charm and intelligence as she was his purse. She had justified the move by telling Linnet that, from her observation, most people placed actresses in the same category as mistresses and prostitutes anyway. It had the potential to be a downward move, for once a woman made that irrevocable step, she could lose her position and be forced to find sustenance in the arms of a man. And then another . . .

But love had come to both of them, an unexpected fairy-tale ending to an all-too-common story.

From his generous allowance she was able to divert a considerable amount of money to her family, and between them, she and Linnet managed to keep their family out of the poorhouse. Now, after several years, most of the children were married or working and the worst of the pressure was off their mother, who now only had her four youngest at home.

But still . . .

Linnet sighed and jammed the embroidery back in the basket and paced to the window, staring out of it and longing to run outside to some treed area, some cool and quiet preserve. But this was London. If cool and quiet existed, no true Londoner would acknowledge it.

But still, at this crisis point in her life Linnet had

avoided home and her mother. She loved the woman, but the depression that was ever near, hovering like the bill collector just outside the door, would have enshrouded the woman again at the knowledge that Linnet had been sacked, let go, and was likely not to find such a good position again.

And so she had come to Jessica. And she was glad, now, that she had, for she had found her beloved sister ill and afraid, unable at this critical time to accept that she could surmount all opposition and join with the exalted Earl of Cairngrove in matrimony.

There should be joy and celebration—after all, this was an unbelievable stroke of good fortune, this marriage, the little cinder girl's triumph just like the old fairy story—but all there was in the Boxley Square residence was gloom and dread. Why on earth was Jessica thinking of backing out of marriage with a man whom she clearly adored, and who loved her back with equal or surpassing fervency? It was impossibly puzzling. Yes, she was ill and perhaps not thinking clearly. Maybe that was all there was to it. Perhaps once she was feeling better she would be willing to take on the challenge of being the next Countess of Cairngrove.

But now there was this new spider in the pudding: Mr. Dominic Barton, come to add tribulation to Jessica's trials. If he was an indication of the wretched iniquity of the denizens of the *ton,* perhaps Jessica had good reason to fear the move into that exalted circle. Linnet could not help her with most of her worries, but in this one case she thought she could. She would rout Barton once again and as many times as it took to keep him from troubling her sister any further.

Despite his Luciferian good looks, despite his overwhelming attraction—how good he smelled, how piercing his eyes, how magnificent his form—she knew herself to be equal to the challenge. There was nothing he could say to her, no allurement he could use, now that she knew his true colors, to change her opinion of him. Nothing in this world or the next could convince her that he was anything but a serpent in the garden.

Four

Cairngrove smiled, the first genuine smile Barton had seen on his face for some time.

"Nic, I am so glad. You have made me a very happy man, and I'm now assured that Jessica will soon feel better, too. I have been worried for her—she has been so unwell, lately, but I fear that part of her illness is worry about how she will fit in, how she will be accepted. What you have just said will go a long way toward making her feel welcome."

Lord, but his brother was an easy mark. That he could be gulled into thinking Barton wanted to make up their quarrel and wished to be made known to his new sister-to-be, was remarkable. How had the man survived in diplomatic circles? Barton wondered.

"That is my most fervent wish, old man. I understand that she has not been well, but would not a cozy visit in her sitting chamber be just the thing, perhaps? I would not want to make this into an ordeal, so the less fuss the better." Barton leaned across his brother's desk and fiddled with the inkwell. "Does she have, er, a companion, or . . . or something of that nature?"

Cairngrove nodded. "Yes, her . . . uh, friend, is staying with her for a while. Just while Jess is ill."

A "friend." Cedric stumbled over that appellation. Did that mean his unknown inamorata was another actress, Barton wondered, out of work, perhaps? Who *was* she? He didn't even have a name to think of her by, yet. But that would come. First things first. "It might be best," Barton said, slowly, "to circumvent this friend, for now. I wish this to be just between myself and my new 'sister.' " He almost gagged on the words, but concentrated on making his expression a mask of pleasantness.

"I have an idea how to achieve a private visit," Cairngrove said, sitting back in his deep chair and laying his hands across his stomach. "Just leave it up to me."

Linnet walked slowly down Reed Street on the last approach to Boxley Square, one of the new squares planned and constructed during the recent building fervor. It was neat and modern, and the town homes were all lovely, with clean modern lines and gracious exteriors.

But it was still London. The miasma that drifted down alleyways, across the polluted Thames, down filthy streets paved with horse dung and rotting vegetation offended her nose and her visual sense of aesthetics. Give her a country lane any day. She actually found herself missing the rigid conformity of Fox Hall, if only because of the country walks she had taken with her pupils while they talked of Pope and Spenser.

She stopped in front of 34 Boxley, Jessica's house, but did not wish to go in just yet. She crossed the brick-paved street and let herself into the small gated garden that all of the residences of Boxley faced. It was a tiny green space, but treasured by Linnet because of the stately elms that shaded the path and the burgeoning spring gardens that rioted over the pathways.

Cairngrove had sent a message that he was coming to visit Jessica. That meant he wanted to see her privately, in the language they had worked out since Linnet came to stay. In a home as large as the town house she could certainly have found a place away from Jessica's suite, but she felt better leaving the house to give them as much privacy as possible. It was the least she could do.

And Linnet would do anything for Cairngrove, who had been the soul of kindness to her since her abrupt arrival and treated her already with the affection of an older brother. He knew that she was Jessica's sister, but at his lover's request had not made it known to anyone else, including the serving staff. Jessica was adamant. She would not divulge Linnet's relationship until her own wedding was a *fait accompli*.

Knowing how she had struggled with the morality of her life choices, Linnet tried to make Jessica's way easier by going along with her quirks, and she did understand. If Linnet ever intended to teach school again, it would never do to have it known that she had been a resident in the home of a doxy. And yet how could they avoid that knowledge getting around once the marriage occurred and it was known that Linnet had been a resident in the house? She shook her head. It was all a tangle. She would have to pick it apart thread by thread when she had a quiet moment to reflect.

She chose a bench, happy to have the tiny green space to herself for a half hour, and gazed at the row of town homes through the fresh green of the new leaves. Her mind wandered and she wondered what it was that Cairngrove wanted to see Jessica about that was private. Or perhaps . . . perhaps he just wanted to exercise the right of a man with his mistress. Linnet shifted uncomfortably on the bench. The idea made her feel hot and strange. She had never asked Jessica about that part of her life with the earl. It was none of her business, but she had to admit to a certain curiosity.

Especially since her own unschooled response to the earl's dangerous brother. Mr. Barton had managed to play upon her feminine responses with just a suggestiveness in his voice and a look of his dark eyes. Was the attraction between Jessica and the earl similar? It did not do to think about it. Rather she should think about Barton and his abominable behavior.

Unprincipled wretch! Let him try to break up Jessica and Cairngrove! It would not work, for she was aware of his intentions now and would guard her sister against his treachery.

It was good that he was so loutish, for if she had found him as pleasant in personality as he was to look at, she might have become as fallen as her sister. Not that she considered Jessica immoral. Her older sister had been persuaded to become Cairngrove's lover only after she had found herself actually in love with the man, and surely true love could never be immoral? She was the first of the two who knew her heart. Cairngrove had only gradually come to understand, Linnet thought, that Jessica had touched his heart, not just his body. If only the dolt had known it as quickly as Jess had! Then he could have married her immediately instead of proposing that most typical of actress/earl relationships, mistress and protector. Now it was going to be ten times as difficult to insinuate Jessica into society.

But Linnet would not believe that it couldn't be done. People among the *ton,* it seemed to her in her limited view of the uppercrust, had short memories, especially with a man of as much power and social cachet as Lord Cairngrove.

And speaking of the earl, she could see through the fence the man himself come out the door, descend the steps, and walk off toward Reed Street with a jaunty swing of his cane. Linnet stood and started toward the gate, not willing to guess at what had given him such an overwhelming appearance of well-being.

It was none of her affair. She and the earl had worked out a comfortable relationship; Linnet had taken over from Jessica much of the work of wedding planning—the earl wanted a splashy St. George's of Hanover Square ceremony, intended to show the *ton* his new wife was to be respected—and so she and Cairngrove had been together a great deal. She had found him intelligent, gentle, likable, and absolutely without pretension, unlike his dastardly brother. But there were many areas that were still completely private between Jess and Cairngrove.

She closed the gate behind her, crossed the street, and entered, doffing her hat and gloves as she walked through the door. It was a rather informal household, so there was no butler to greet her. She made her own way up the stairs, put her package away in her room, and paced the length of the hall down to Jessica's sitting room. She stood by the door for a moment, wondering if Jess was asleep or up to a talk, and was startled to hear voices murmuring inside. Her maid, maybe? But no, one voice was lower in tone.

Linnet tapped on the door and pushed it open. She slipped in and found Jess with flushed cheeks and a happy smile.

"Lin! Oh, Lin, I'm so glad you're home! Come in. Come in and meet Cedric's brother, Mr. Dominic Barton. He begged Cedric for a chance to meet me, and we have been having the most delicious conversation!"

Linnet stopped and stared into a pair of coal-dark eyes lit from inside with a humorous glint. Oh my, hadn't she been routed!

The next half hour was excruciating. Barton, with a wicked glint in his eyes, baited Linnet shamelessly. "I know that I have seen you somewhere before, Miss . . . what was your name again?"

"Miss Linnet Pelham," Jessica supplied helpfully. "My dearest friend in the world. Where could you have seen her, Nic?"

Linnet almost groaned aloud. Nic? How had her sister become so intimate so quickly with the scoundrel?

"I don't know," he said. "The theater perhaps?"

"Perhaps," Linnet answered. Her sole joy became putting him at a distance. It had quickly become apparent to her that there would be no way to tell Jessica now about Barton's abominable mission without crushing her. Linnet had not seen Jess so animated since she had arrived. Still wan and covered in a woolen coverlet of pale blue that matched perfectly the exquisite embroidered upholstery of her reclining couch, Jessica had a touch of rosy pink on each high cheekbone. And she was smiling. Barton, the snake, was teasing her, calling her "sister," and asking about her short career on the stage.

It was clear to Linnet how much this sign of acceptance from Cairngrove's family meant to Jessica, and it was killing her inside to know that when Barton snatched away his pseudoapproval in whatever cruel game he was playing, it would crush Jess's spirit. In Barton's eyes Jessica Landry was no more than a poisonous carbuncle festering on the edge of the earl's life, and he had set himself to lance and excise the blain.

And yet how charming he could be when he set his mind to it! Even Linnet had to smile at some of his sallies, as insincere as she knew them to be. At the end of the half hour, Barton stood and stretched, displaying an indecently well-set-up form that held Linnet's attention.

"Lin, will you see Mr. Barton out, please? I would get up, sir, but I am so sleepy. I feel that this visit has done me a world of good."

Linnet stood silently.

"Jessie, Jessie! You promised to call me Nic. I shall think you do not like me if you go back to the awful formality of Mr. Barton!"

"I am sorry, Nic," she said, smiling up at him as he

took her hand and bent over it. "I won't forget again. And you are coming back tomorrow afternoon, are you not? You promised me a game of piquet."

"I would not miss it for the world, Sister."

Jessica sighed happily as her maid entered and helped her up off the couch, guiding her into the bedchamber beyond. "Good-bye, Nic."

"Rather, *adieu*," Barton said, blowing her a kiss.

Linnet, cheeks flaming, led Barton down the stairs to the front door. As the man turned to take her hand and kiss it, she jerked it away from him. His dark eyes startled, he peered at her in the gloom of the windowless hallway. "Mr. Barton, you may have fooled my . . . my friend, but you have not fooled me. If you hurt her, if you offer her any insult, I will"—she gritted her teeth together, holding back the bitterest of condemnations—"I will make sure you pay for the deed, sir. I promise you that."

Nic gazed at her for a moment. "How do you know, Miss Pelham, that I have not decided to acquiesce to the whole obscene arrangement gracefully? What can I do, after all? Old Ceddie is an adult, even if he is acting like a foolish old man in his dotage."

"You have not changed your mind. You are toying with her. But I will not have her hurt; I swear it."

Nic, his eyes gleaming, swiftly placed one hand behind her head and pulled her close, pressing his lips against hers and kissing her deeply, sucking in the tender flesh of her bottom lip. Shocked, she staggered back and held one hand up to her mouth.

"You, my dear, are unconscionably lovely. Bear that in mind. I find you irresistibly attractive, and even more so when you berate me in that adorable fashion. I will see you on the morrow." Whistling, he exited the premises with a rakish swagger in his step.

Five

Nic did not repeat that indecorous kiss again in the next few days as he became a constant visitor to the overheated suite of rooms in the house in Boxley Square. But he did not forget it. He watched Linnet Pelham as she tended to her friend, Jessica being still too weak to even do some of the simpler things for herself.

Miss Pelham was a mystery to him. While Jessica Landry was open and simple, grateful for small favors, full of smiles for him when he arrived bearing a posy or a box of comfits, Miss Pelham remained a shadowy figure, seldom speaking to him, avoiding his gaze. Of course, unlike Miss Landry, the other woman had every reason to mistrust him. Damn, but it was too bad he had tipped his hand that first day. It had made her prickly and difficult. No wheedling her into his arms, he thought, eyeing her lithe figure hungrily. Perhaps a straightforward offer of his protection, then. Money might speak louder than desire.

If there was ever an opportunity. He never seemed to see her alone. He had been absolutely truthful in that he found her enchanting when she played the scold, but he would have given up some of his attraction in exchange for a more welcoming attitude.

It had been five days of constant visits. He had spent his time assessing Miss Landry, trying to discover her weakness, trying to see what would work to separate her from his deluded brother, but he was no closer now than the first day, he thought. He had spent his fair share of time in the boudoirs, often the arms of actresses. On the whole they were a willing lot and far less spoiled than the ladies of the *demimonde,* who made being a courtesan their life's work.

But Jessica Landry did not even seem like the more intelligent and ladylike of the actresses he'd known. She reminded him most strongly of the wife of one of his friends. A companion at arms of his, Major Barret Storne, had married a young lady of excellent family but indifferent health. But Barret, one of the strongest and most vigorous of men, doted on his frail darling. Jessica Landry had the same delicate complexion and gentle voice. But where Storne's wife was a trifle vacuous, Miss Landry was sweet-natured and uncomplaining. Even though she was clearly ill, she was not in the slightest weak of mind.

He wondered what exactly was wrong with her. She seemed to get neither better nor worse. Once or twice during his visits she had called frantically for her maid, only to be led away to her bedchamber beyond the sitting room. Such episodes would always end his visit. But the next day she would be herself again, and no mention would be made of the episode of illness. He would catch Miss Pelham casting worried glances her way, but nothing was ever said, no allusion made to her physical condition. Delicacy forbade him asking.

She was so pale and thin that Cairngrove seemed a giant to her haunting loveliness. He had spent one afternoon with them, and for all Barton could detect between them there was only genuine feeling, gratitude, and love on her part for his unending good graces, and adoration on his part for his lover. And yet her pale blond good looks did not attract Barton. She was pretty and seemed a lovely young woman, but she did not captivate him.

It was the tart-tongued, vigorously healthy Miss Pelham who drew his eye.

He was startled, as he approached Boxley Square on a brilliant spring afternoon, to find that far from scheming how he was going to break up Miss Landry and his brother, he was looking forward to spending the afternoon in her rather stifling boudoir. They would drink tea or sherry, talk for a while, play cards. He would tell stories of the army—only the ones suitable for a lady's ears—and he would look at the silent Miss Pelham, admiring her glossy chestnut hair, glowing skin, and lithe, graceful form. What a comedown for one of the premiere rakes of London society, to be satisfied with gazing on the face and figure of his future mistress with no plan yet as to how to attach her!

But as he entered the Boxley Square residence, Miss Pelham, he was informed to his disappointment by the maid, was absent from the residence that afternoon, though expected back momentarily.

He entered the dressing room of his brother's ladybird and sat in the heaviest chair in the room, always reserved for his more powerful frame. He gazed at Miss Landry, who was reclining as usual on her chaise. The room was warm, but she was wrapped in a woolen shawl. The curtains were drawn against the brilliant spring sunshine. How had he gone so far astray from his original mission of breaking up the cozy pair that was his brother and this pretty Paphian? He had found little objectionable about her so far. She was not to his taste, true, but if it was not for her wholly unsuitable employment—as a mistress, for God's sake—he might begin to think she was an adequate, if not brilliant choice, as second wife for his brother. Try as he might, he had never warmed up to his sister-in-law, Wilhelmina. She was a virtuous and pleasant enough woman, but chilly and formal in her manners.

Jessica Landry, on the other hand, was warm and appealing, good-natured enough, and seemed—perhaps only *seemed*—sincerely attached to Cairngrove. Today she looked wan but willing to be cheered.

"Nic, how good of you to come like this. A man such as yourself must have a thousand other things to do than to visit an invalid, and yet you come day after day. It is truly good of you."

He kissed her hand and made himself comfortable in the chair, though her unjustified praise made him want to squirm. *Enough, Nic,* he said firmly to himself. *You never did shy from an unpleasant task before—on the battlefield or in the boudoir. Think of your nephews and niece, and the notoriety attached to their father wedding his whore.*

"Jessie, you look lovely, as always."

"No Spanish coin, Nic. I know how pale and thin I have become. But I shall be better soon. I know it."

Assuming she had had a good report from her physician, Nic frowned down at his hands and tried to decide how best to approach the matter at hand. "So," he started, "when you are married, what will be your first move into Cedric's political sphere?"

Jessica seemed startled at the abruptness of his speech. "I . . . I beg your pardon?"

"My brother is a noted speaker in the House. Politics are very important to him. Surely you will have considered how best to make your move into his political circle?" He hated what he had to do. He had come to like Jessica, he thought, examining his nails, unable to look her in the eye. If she was what she seemed, and after five days in her company he thought she just might be, then she was a very pleasant young woman. If it had only been her birth that was objectionable, he might have retreated from his task. If it was merely a matter of no dowry or unsuitable parentage . . . But she was Cedric's mistress. She must be made to see, preferably for her own good as well as for the earl's, that a marriage between them would not work. Why could they not just go on the way they had been?

"But I do not need to move into his political circle." Jessica sounded a little bewildered, as though she had gone into a millinery shop only to find herself at a horse auction.

"Ah, but you must," Nic said, leaning forward. He could do this. He *had* to do this. He peered into her pale-blue eyes. "Surely you must know that a man of my brother's standing will require that his wife act as hostess to his political friends . . . and enemies. She must stand beside him, walk that fine line on the thin edge of grace and dignity, and politically astute impartiality."

"But I don't . . ."

"Now, Jess, unfortunately it is true. I know it is unpleasant. And boring, for a lady. You will be expected to talk politics and yet offend no one. You must be charming and witty and yet never outshine Cedric's more stolid abilities. A tricky place to be in, but as Countess of Cairngrove you must do it."

"No, you misunderstand, Nic. I do not need to move *into* Cedric's political circle. I have already met His Grace, the Duke of Wellington. He and Cedric are old allies. And Lord Castlereagh, poor man." She smiled sadly. "I liked him *very* much, but I sense a sadness in him. He is so burdened and yet he will not rest." She frowned and shook her head, picking at the cover. "We talked for hours the night Cedric had him and his aide over for dinner, just an informal gathering that time. Before I became ill . . ." Her voice drifted off, and she glanced toward the window. Her voice a little stronger, she continued. "As I was saying, before I became ill we had many dinners . . . just with the . . . the gentlemen, of course. The ladies could not attend. It is one of the things Cedric hopes will change, though he does not expect me to begin immediately, since I am ill."

Barton sat back in his chair, speechless. His one prized piece of ammunition was the hope that Jessica, once she realized how far out of her milieu she would be as Cairngrove's countess, would be content to remain as mistress rather than making the push to become countess.

"I have been even acting as his secretary," she said, with a guilty and yet smiling flush. "I have been writing his letters for him since Davidson has been away visiting his dying father. Your brother is very active in the push to reform Parliament."

Linnet at that moment sailed into the room with a brilliant smile on her face. "What a glorious day it is! I could almost imagine I was back at Fox Hall."

She brought the scent of sunshine and roses into the room, and Nic stumbled to his feet and bowed. "Miss Pelham! How ravishing you look this afternoon!" He had been startled into honesty. She wore a sky blue spencer and a delightful hat on which bluebells nodded.

Her expression died back into the sober, joyless mask she donned in his presence. Barton, not for the first time, regretted the way their acquaintance had begun.

"Mr. Barton," she said, acknowledging his greeting.

"Why do you not call him Nic, Lin?" Jessica asked languidly. "We have no need of formality here."

"On the contrary, Jess, a little formality can be a good thing." Linnet removed her hat and spencer and handed them to Jessica's maid, then set about tidying her friend's side table. She refilled Jessica's water glass from an elegant pitcher and moved a stack of linen handkerchiefs to within her reach.

Nic sat back down and watched her. How could he break through the iciness he had engendered? He gave a mental shrug, thinking all he could do was be himself.

She did not trust him, and he could hardly blame her. He turned his attention back to Miss Landry, still trying to see a chink in her armor, a weak spot to be exploited. "I have never heard the story of how you met my brother, Jessica."

The young woman blushed, her wan face flooding with color that gave her an aura of radiance. Fascinated by the change, Nic saw her in that moment as Cedric must have, delicate, ethereal, and yet with an inner light that was luminescent through her ivory skin.

"I . . . I had taken a position with Mr. Lessington's theater on Haymarket and was playing Ophelia."

"You didn't tell me you played that part," Linnet said, sitting and gazing at Jessica with wide-eyed interest. She clasped her hands together. "What a brilliant bit of casting! Mr. Lessington must have been pleased with your performance."

"He very kindly said so. Said I brought just the right—what word did he use?—Wistfulness. He said he always thought Ophelia was wistful and that I brought that to her."

Barton nodded. He could see Jessica as that tragic girl. "And so Cedric saw you in Hamlet?"

She nodded, her eyes gazing off into some indefinite distance. "He sent me flowers . . . white roses! I had been working for Mr. Lessington for two years or so, and I had my share of admirers . . . not that I—" She broke off in confusion and glanced at Barton. "Cedric was my first . . . my only—" She broke off again, and shook her head, unable to say what she wanted.

Linnet, her expression hard, glared at Barton. Holding his gaze the entire time, she said, "What you are trying to say, Jess, is that you had had admirers but had taken none of them as lovers before."

"I . . . y-yes."

Barton's first instinct was to snort with disbelief, but

he did not think that politic. So that was how they were going to play it? She would be introduced to the *ton* as not *really* a fallen woman because she had only ever take the one lover! It would not fly. Women of the theater learned quickly how to supplement the wages given to them by theater management. He did not blame them. A woman had her own way to make in the world. But to try to present Jessica Landry as an unsullied flower of innocence!

He kept his own counsel in this instance, though. He wanted to ask Linnet what parts *she* had played, what theaters *she* had worked for, what lovers *she* had taken, but he dared not at that moment. Besides, this conversation had given him the introduction to the subject matter he wanted to pursue.

"So Ceddie gave you white roses, hmm?" He sat back, at his ease, and crossed one leg over the other.

"Yes," Jessica murmured. "I wore some of them in my hair that night. But it was not the roses; it was the note." She smiled in misty remembrance. "He . . . he wrote, 'Doubt thou the stars are fire; Doubt that the sun doth move; Doubt truth to be a liar; But never doubt I love.' "

"Hamlet's words to the doomed Ophelia. And so you had met him already?"

"No. He . . . he made himself known to me that night. He said he had been to every performance of Hamlet we had done. He was so very ardent!"

Nic stifled a laugh. Cedric, *ardent?* His brother was born for many things—politics, diplomacy, the earldom—but as an ardent lover he would have made a jackass, in Nic's opinion. He chuckled. "And so, 'Quoth she, before you tumbled me, You promis'd me to wed. So would I ha' done, by yonder sun, An thou hadst not come to my bed.' "

Linnet felt a swelling of anger. He was laughing at

her. He was mocking Jessica! She was about to leap to
her feet to defend her sister, but Jessica's voice stopped
her.

"No, Nic, he never promised marriage and I never
asked him for it." Her voice was sad, and she looked
away toward the window. "I surrendered my . . . m-my
innocence to a man I loved for a number of reasons,
most of which are none of your business. But I do love
him. I loved him then and I love him now."

Nic shifted uncomfortably. Linnet shot him a hostile
glance and he met her gaze soberly. "Jess, I'm sorry,"
he said. "I did not mean to make fun . . . I didn't intend
to hurt you. I apologize."

Jessica, a sweet and watery smile on her face, said,
"It's all right, Nic. I know how this looks. I know it
appears that I am taking advantage of him. And I know
what people are going to say. But this is between your
brother and I."

Nic was silenced. But finally he said, standing, "I
must go. I truly am sorry if my words hurt you. I . . .
It was Hamlet, and after Ceddie's quote in his note to
you, and . . ." He shook his head. "I have no excuse. I
am sorry." He leaned over, took Jessica's pale hand, and
laid a gentle kiss on it. "I will come back tomorrow, if
you are not too angry at me."

"I am not, Nic. You know you are welcome."

Six

Linnet waited until he was out of the room, but then could not contain her ire. "I don't know how you can bear that . . . that egotistical, wretched, sophist. That snob, that knave . . ."

"Lin, stop it!"

Linnet looked at her sister in amazement. Jess had a look of sharp anger on her face.

"What is it, Jess?"

"Did you really expect his family to welcome me with open arms?" She moved irritably on her pillow. "Did you?"

"Well, I . . ."

"How naive! It is completely natural for Nic to have reservations about me. I am Cedric's *mistress!* Naturally this marriage is not at all what his family could hope for for him. Cedric is the Earl of Cairngrove! Do you know what that means? I am not fit . . ." Her expression crumpled and her face twisted. "Oh, *oh,* Lin, I think I am going to be ill!"

Linnet spent the next half hour helping Jessica and then putting her to bed. She was uneasy and descended the stairs slowly, trailing her fingers on the railing. Jessica did not seem to be getting any better but would not see a doctor. Insisted it was not necessary. If she persisted in such idiotic behavior, Linnet would just go ahead and find one for her sister anyway.

"Miss," a footman called, "the gentleman is still here and expressed a wish to see you alone." The footman bowed and indicated the parlor off the hall.

"The gentleman? Do you mean Mr. Barton?" Linnet was appalled.

"Yes, miss."

Linnet took a deep breath and stiffened her spine. If he was still here then he would bear the brunt of her rage. No one was going to disparage her sister and get away with it. She strode into the parlor to find Barton gazing out the window, his handsome face set in a serious expression. He turned as she entered and gave her a rueful glance.

He opened up his arms in a welcoming gesture and said, "Well, have at me, Miss Pelham. I deserve it."

It disconcerted her, his ready acceptance of her anger. So, being Linnet and hating to be predictable, she smiled instead, and said, "Whatever do you mean, sir?"

He let his arms drop and turned back to the window. "I was looking out at the garden opposite just now. It is gated and locked. Is that right? To lock away our only little bits of nature in this most unnatural of cities? It is like jealously guarding anything worth viewing so that those we deem unworthy cannot enjoy it. As if enjoyment of it by others somehow taints it for us."

Linnet shook her head. "I have no idea what we are talking about and cannot be expected to make a sensible answer."

He turned back and gazed steadily at her. "And are you so very afraid of making a nonsensical answer?"

"I do not wish to look ridiculous, if that is what you are asking."

"I suppose what I am really saying is . . ."

"What are you still here for, Mr. Barton?"

"Ah, no time for nonsense. It was not really nonsense,

you know; I had a point. But I can see you are in no mood to dally far afield."

"Do you blame me?"

"No. Miss Pelham, I wish to apologize."

"A-apologize?"

"Yes. For my ill-chosen words upstairs just now, but more particularly for my behavior the first time we met."

He strolled from the window toward her, and Linnet indicated a chair rather than have him approach too closely. She had never been able to erase from her lips the impression of his hasty kiss, and it disturbed her more than she supposed it should have. What was a kiss, after all? It could have as well been placed on her hand.

Though she would be lying to herself if she said it was the same.

"Go on, Mr. Barton."

He eased himself into a chair. Linnet studied him, contrasting him with his older brother. There were some years between them, she surmised. Cairngrove, she knew, was in his forties, where the man before her was not much above thirty. They were both tall, but the earl was bulky and broad where Mr. Barton was slim, quick-moving, though not at all negligible in form. He was muscular, she felt sure, blushing at the thought.

Barton noted the blush and wondered what was going on in her quicksilver mind. If he were conceited he would assume she was thinking some randomly lusty thought about him. But he had never been a peacock. Whatever she was thinking would stay locked in her own mind.

"I had no right to be so overbearing and rude that first day. I feel sure I have given you a disgust of me, but I would like to make it up to you."

She leveled a steady gaze at him. "By accepting that Jessica will make your brother a perfectly unexceptionable bride?"

He was silent. He looked down at the carpet and then back up into her eyes. "I cannot do that. It would be dishonest, and I have pledged myself to be, at the very least, honest with you."

"Then we have nothing further to say. You are obdurate and I am stubborn. We will advance no more."

Barton gritted his teeth, biting back words that need not be said. But unaccustomed as he was to subduing his natural reactions, they spilled forth anyway. "You are the most harrying . . ." He stopped, and took a deep breath. "I promised myself not to argue with you."

"Do you generally keep your promises? Are ones to yourself less worthy or do you break faith with others more easily?"

This time he did not rise to the bait. Instead, he sat forward in his chair, clasped his hands together, and gazed at her earnestly. "Miss Pelham, I have no idea of your history."

"And have no business knowing," she said.

She was being deliberately rude, he thought, and examined her flushed face. Was that a way to keep him at arm's length or did she genuinely despise him? Or perhaps a little of both.

"And have no business knowing," he agreed. He found himself, strangely enough, wishing to explain his actions to her, make her understand his concerns. She had become in the last week something more than just an obstacle to be gotten around. "But the *ton* is a closed circle. It is why young men are chivied into selecting their bride from among its ranks, and why young ladies choose a husband outside of its ranks at their peril."

"Then it is time the walls were broken down."

"Perhaps. I may agree with you on that subject."

She was silent, waiting for the exception that would surely follow. She did not need to wait long.

"But this is my family! My brother is clearly besotted

with Miss Landry. And now, having gotten to know her, I can see why. She is lovely, intelligent, good-natured. In short, she is everything I could want for him."

"But?"

"But," he agreed, "there is his family to consider." He saw her quick expression of disdain. "Not myself; I am not counting myself. I don't give a damn whom he marries." Again her expressive face showed her feelings, her eyebrow raised, just the one elegant curve arching up. "No, truly, I do not. But he has children, Miss Pelham. And they have lives, careers, and in the case of my niece, families to consider. She has married into a family that is very high in the instep."

Linnet was silent for a moment, admitting to herself the justice of his concerns. It was simple to brush off the consequences of what many would consider a scandalous marriage when they did not concern yourself, but for him, his nephews' and niece's well-being was his consideration. If Jessica and the earl married it would be more than a nine days' wonder. They would face opposition, gossip, even slander, perhaps. Certainly controversy and whispering would follow them for a good while. "Is that not more Cairngrove's business than yours?"

"True, it is. But he is not thinking clearly. I think this illness of Jessica's has worried him, and he wishes to be close to her more, to take care of her. It is in his nature to take care of those he loves."

"Then perhaps you should be allowing him to direct his own life. He is set on this course; it is his own doing, and he is an intelligent adult, capable of making choices for himself."

Nic appeared to consider that. He frowned, but said nothing.

"I am not insensible to the difficulties attendant on Jessica and Cairngrove's chosen path," Linnet went on.

"I know Jess worries about it, too. But Cairngrove is insistent, and I think it behooves all of us to help him make the transition smoother for Jessica, and therefore himself. In the far view of things, I think it is the only way to help. And I do not think the difficulties insurmountable."

"Perhaps you are right after all," Barton murmured. He studied the carpet for a moment, then looked up. "I suppose that is all I have to say. Is Jessica all right? She was not looking well before I left."

"She is better now. In bed and sleeping peacefully."

"I am glad. Have you seen anything of London yet?" he asked, standing. "I have no idea if you have been in London long, or if you have seen the sights."

Startled by the change of subject matter, Linnet said, "Well, I have really not had a chance. . . . I have been in London only a few weeks, and I have been taken up in caring for Jess. So, no, I have seen little of London."

He gazed steadily at the lovely woman in front of him and wondered why he was about to suggest what he was about to suggest. "Would you consider letting me be your guide? There is much to see: the Tower, Hyde Park, Vauxhall." His senses stirred at the thought of the darkened walks of Vauxhall and the lovely, slender young woman in front of him. His hands on her waist, pulling her closer, her breath in his ear as he kissed her neck . . . "Please say you will consider it."

"I . . . I don't think . . ."

"Please. You would be doing me a favor. And if, as you say, Jessica and Cedric are to marry, then it behooves us to become better acquainted, does it not? You are her best friend; I can see how she relies upon you. But you are shutting yourself up here when Jessica spends a good part of each day sleeping, I think."

Of the myriad responses she considered, the one that

actually erupted from her mouth was none of them. "I . . . I think I would enjoy that."

With a boyish grin, he bowed and said, "I will consider that a promise and will come to collect you tomorrow at eleven. We shall ride in the park."

The next few days were a revelation for Linnet. Never had she given herself over wholly to merrymaking. From the age of seventeen she had worked, and before that she had endless duties at home, most of which involved caring for small children.

But Barton took her to see a rehearsal at the opera, to the lending library, and the Tower menagerie. She was charmed by Mozart, overwhelmed by the sumptuous display of books, and brokenhearted over the poor caged beasts at the Tower. He walked with her in Hyde Park— not at the fashionable time of day, true, but Linnet did not want to be stared at by his friends—and strolled arm in arm with her along the Serpentine.

He was an utterly charming companion, well mannered, intriguingly intelligent, and she found they could talk for hours and never reach the end of their disagreements, which were always debated in a lively manner, sometimes dwindling to absurdity, which set them both to laughing like old friends. He was clearly still attracted to her, but he behaved well, keeping his preference reined in and his hands busy. As a result, she found herself thinking more and more about their first meeting and his suggestion that he was likely to be a more potent and thrilling lover than his brother. Had he only been trying to lure her from his brother, or was there an undercurrent of honesty in his words?

Occasionally she found herself wondering about the enjoyment she took in his company. How could that be, when she had promised herself to despise him, when he had given her ample reason to? But she saw that there was more than one side to the complex Mr. Barton. He was multifaceted and intriguing and totally outside of her experience. Perhaps it had been a mistake to encourage this intimacy, but never far from her mind was the truth of his reasoning, and even more than he could know. They were to be family when Jess and Cairngrove married. They must find a way to get along, and it was proving surprisingly easy, as long as he did not disparage Jess.

Finally, they went to Vauxhall; it was everything she had heard in some ways, and yet she found the crowd, the bumping of other people, the noise, distasteful. The fairy lights glinted off his dark eyes as Barton turned to her.

"You seem perturbed, Lin. Is everything to your liking?"

"It is just a little crowded and overheated," she said, struggling past a particularly large man who inconsiderately blocked the path.

"Come this way," Barton said, guiding her down another path.

It was dark, and Linnet, aware that for the first time the man at her side had used her given name and that it had not sounded at all strange on his lips, felt the cool night air envelope her. "Ah," she sighed. "This is much better."

"I agree," he said, his voice hushed.

They passed by a couple who lingered in the darkness of an alcove. Lin glanced at them, only to see that they were kissing passionately. Her breathing increased as she remembered the one hasty kiss between her and Barton. Would he try to repeat it? Would she let him?

"Lin, I . . ."

Linnet drifted closer to him as they stopped. She could hardly see his face, but as she tilted hers up, she could feel him getting closer, his warm breath touching her lips like a caress. "Nic," she whispered.

"Yes?"

But she had nothing more to say. She surrendered to the inevitable and his lips closed on hers as she sighed, the sweet taste of the wine upon his lips heightening her sense of heady adventure.

Barton felt his body stir, dormant desires surging to the fore, delicious sensations throbbing through him. The past few days he had been absolutely, impeccably a gentleman, but now . . . Now he released himself from the cage. Ravenously he kissed her, sucking in the tender skin of her lips, tasting her mouth, while his hands traveled over her back, down to the gentle swell of her hips.

When she moved away from him, he felt bereft. "Where are you going?" he asked, his voice strange and choked against the muffled sound of voices and fireworks in the distance.

"I . . . We must go back to the main pathway," she said.

"Why?"

"Because it is not proper, being alone like this."

"Not proper?" He wanted to laugh out loud. How was it not proper? Was she waiting for his offer? He was on the verge of making it, close to asking if she would be his lover, come to him with his protection.

But something in her tone made him stop. She really did not consider it proper to be alone with him. He had already discovered that she was not an actress, but surely . . .

"Lin . . ." But she had already started back to the path. With a muffled curse he followed her. Back in the lighted area he could see in her eyes a bewilderment. It puzzled him. What game was she playing? What did she expect of him? He had felt her sway toward him in the dark and had been certain that he was moments away from heaven. But then she had seemed frightened, confused even.

Lin was silent all the way back to Boxley Square. She was truly perplexed and perturbed by the affect Nic Barton had on her, and she was not sure if she wanted to face the implications. But never a coward, she admitted it to herself; she wanted him. She very badly had wanted to go on kissing him, feeling his experienced hands touching her, his tongue darting, dancing, fencing with her own.

And she knew what that meant to him, to any man of his stamp. And so, this would be their last outing. As much as she had enjoyed his company, as dearly as she had begun to care for him—she did not want to believe that was true, but it was—she must not see him alone again. For she was not willing to go down the path of heartache her sister had walked. Jessica had done what she had partly out of economic necessity; it had saved their family from the poorhouse, quite literally. And yet Cairngrove had never treated Jessica like a mistress, as casually demanding as he could have been. Jessica had, in her years in the theater, seen many such relationships, she told Linnet, and so had been pleasantly surprised by the courtesy he extended her, the care and consideration. He had never once treated her with the callous disregard some men did their mistresses.

But there would not be two such men as Cairngrove And so, as much as Linnet admitted to herself she wanted something from Barton, something more than casual friendship, she knew it could never be. She was genteel but impoverished. He would never think of her in any manner but as fit material for a mistress. As distasteful as the truth could be, she was never one to shy away from an unpleasant fact.

So when he handed her down from the carriage, she said sadly, "I shall be, uh, busy for a while, Nic."

"Busy? What do you mean?"

"There is much planning to do for Jessica and Cedric's marriage. I shall be consumed with work, work I have been neglecting. I will see you when you visit Jess, but I d-don't think I shall have time for rides or walks. Good-bye, Nic."

Seven

Cairngrove thrust one large hand through his thinning hair and paced the parlor. "I don't understand this, Lin. She doesn't even seem interested in the wedding! It is not natural for a woman to leave all the planning up to her sister and her husband-to-be! It just is not!"

Lin watched him, a worried frown on her face. She knew he was right, but it did no good for him to get in a fret about it. "She just is not feeling well, sir. When she is feeling better . . ."

He wheeled and strode to face her. "And that is another thing. Why will she not allow me to call in a physician? If she is ill, why will she do nothing to get better?"

Linnet shrugged helplessly. "I can't answer that. She just says that she will feel better presently. We cannot force a doctor on her. Why do we not go back to planning the nuptials, sir? I thought that since you wish it to be at St. George's, we ought to consider that there will be many in the church who do not know you or Jess, and that . . ."

"The seamstress, of all people, accosted me . . . *me* . . . today, and told me that Jess is refusing to try on the gown. How can the woman fit it if Jess will not try it on?"

Exhausted, Linnet gave up and sat back in her chair.

Just then a footman bowed at the door, and said, "Mr. Dominic Barton."

Nic sauntered into the room with his usual insouciant grace. Linnet watched him, aware that her feelings for him had undergone a sea change since the day she had first met him. He had proven himself to be far from the crude, lecherous knave she had first seen. His concern about his brother's marriage was not simply mindless class snobbery, but was bound up in his deep commitment and care for his family. And he had shown himself capable of compassion. But who was he really? She still was not sure. After all, she could not get past the fact that his first instinct had been to seduce his brother's mistress away from him.

"Good day, all. Is Jessica up to a visit?"

Cairngrove took his brother's hand. "Nic. Good to see you. She is not feeling at all the thing. I am going back up one more time to check on her." He turned and strode purposefully from the room, leaving Nic and Linnet to stare at each other.

They had not been alone for several days, since Vauxhall. Linnet felt her mouth go dry. Nic strolled into the room, circling Linnet as if she were prey.

"So, we are alone."

"Don't be an idiot, Nic," she said, shuffling the papers she had on the small desk at which she sat. She collected them into a sheaf, tapped them to settle them together, and slid them under the blotter.

"Why have you been avoiding me, Lin?"

"I have not been avoiding you. I told you I would be busy. I have been, in case you want to know, planning a wedding, and as you quite clearly do not approve of said wedding, I cannot imagine you would want to hear the details."

"Tart-tongued little wench." As disapproving as the

words were, the tone held nothing but affectionate exasperation.

Linnet felt him stalk her, coming close behind her and touching her neck, curling a wisp of hair around his finger. She shivered and stood abruptly, crossed the room, and deliberately opened the door.

He chuckled. "Do I make you nervous?"

Cairngrove, at that moment, stormed across the hall and demanded his hat and stick. Linnet raced into the hall.

"What is it, sir? What is wrong?"

Cairngrove, his broad face suffused with a dull brick red stared at Linnet, his gaze unfocused. His eyes were wide and started from the sockets. "She . . . she says she won't marry me. Told me to leave and not come back until I will stop plaguing her about marriage."

"Did you quarrel?" Linnet gasped.

"No," Cairngrove said, bewildered. "No, not at all. I told her I love her. Told her I demanded that she see a doctor . . . that I was going to have my own personal physician see her."

"And?"

"And she . . . she broke down in tears, told me I was a brute and ordered me to leave. Said she didn't want to see me again." He strode over to Linnet and said, his voice choked, "Talk to her. I can't do this, can't let her go. And yet if you had heard her voice . . ." He thrust his thick fingers through his disheveled hair. "God, Lin, I love her. Thought she loved me. What is wrong?"

"Give her time, my lord," Linnet said, her voice thick with tears. His anguish was unbearable to see.

"Time? She's had two years! If she loved me, she'd want to marry me." His voice was bleak and his expression tormented. And yet, as always, his words were perfectly polite. "Good day, Lin." Barton had joined them in the hall, and Cairngrove said to his brother, "Good day, Nic." He turned and exited the house.

Jessica, her face buried in a pillow, said, her words muffled, "I will not be bullied into seeing a doctor. And I do not understand all this fuss about a wedding. Why is it so important? Why can we not just continue as we were?"

Linnet sat on the edge of the bed trying to understand what was stopping her sister from grasping the only happiness she had ever had and her best chance of *future* happiness. "He wants more than just this, Jess. He wants to marry you and is willing to surmount any obstacle to achieve that end. Is that so terrible?"

Jessica removed the pillow and gazed sadly at her younger sister. Her eyes were red and puffy from tears, proving she was suffering, too. "You just do not understand. Nobody does. No one ever will. Oh, Lin, let's just go away from here. I don't like London. I have some money saved, and Mama does not need so much anymore. Let's go and get a cottage by the seaside."

"Now you are talking errant nonsense," Linnet said.

Jessica burst into tears, and Lin was immediately sorry. She hadn't meant her words to be harsh. Hadn't thought they were, really. Jessica's sobs turned into wrenching dry heaves; she vomited nothing, but made herself wretchedly tired. Linnet held her for a while and rocked her, until the other woman was drifting into a troubled sleep. She tiptoed out of the room after making sure Jessica's maid sat with her while she slept.

Barton was at the bottom of the stairs, concern on his handsome face. "I have been pacing this hour, waiting for you to come back down. Is Jessica all right?"

Linnet gazed at him, noting the sharp lines of worry carved in two sharp vertical slashes between his dark eyebrows. She took a deep breath. "She seems no better nor any worse. But talk of the wedding upsets her. It is preying on her mind."

Barton was silent. He gazed steadily at the finial on the finishing curve of the stair railing. He traced the smooth wood with his square-tipped fingers. "They both seem so unhappy. Is this what marriage does?"

"Apparently only when one party is set on the marriage and the other is resisting."

"So this marriage truly was my brother's idea and not Jessica's?"

"Of course," Linnet said sharply. "I thought that was clear. It is what I told you all along, if you had deigned to listen to me." She asked for some tea from a hovering maid and went back to the parlor. She was beginning to be sick of the stuffy confines of the house, but if she went out to walk right now Barton would be there, and she could not risk, in her current worried state, that his compassion would encourage her to lean on him. She was vulnerable, and he had shown, on occasion, that he could be kind. It was too dangerous a situation for her heart.

Barton followed her. He was worrying at the problem like a dog with a new bone. "Why do you think she does not want to marry my brother?"

Linnet sat down in a chair by the window and passed one hand over her tired eyes. "I don't know. I think it is the pomp and ceremony of it, but I am not sure. She will not talk about it. Perhaps it is worry about the social consequences for Cairngrove. Now she is saying what she did not say before, that she will not marry him at all. But I know she loves him! I do not understand it."

"Can it be that illness is clouding her mind?"

"No, she is perfectly lucid. The illness is not that kind. It expresses itself in other ways, but her mind is not affected." Linnet frowned and pondered his question.

"Though she *has* been unusually weepy lately. Jessica has always appeared fragile, but she is remarkably tough and strong. She would not have survived the theater world if she was not, for it is no profession for weaklings. No, I cannot believe her mind is affected."

"What does the doctor say?"

"She will see no physician. Did you not hear your brother earlier? It is that more than anything that has become a contentious issue between them. He wants her to see a doctor and she refuses."

"She has not seen a doctor?" He sat down in a chair opposite Linnet and watched her eyes.

"Surely you knew that! Have you seen any vials of medicine? Any lingering Harley Street quack?"

Barton frowned at the floor, but then, as he mulled over the possibilities, his expression changed. Could it be? He looked up at Linnet, who sat staring out the window with a troubled look marring her lovely face. "What exactly are her symptoms?" he asked. "Was she sick just now, after her quarrel with Cedric?"

"Well, yes. She had another bout of the nausea."

"Nausea?"

Linnet sighed. "Yes. It is part of her illness. She has these waves of nausea, and she cannot bear to smell food, sometimes. Except for certain things that she seems to eat to the exclusion of all else. Lately it has been asparagus. She cannot get enough asparagus! Cook has had to comb every market for the delicacy."

"Waves of nausea. Strange cravings." A secretive smile lifted the corners of Barton's mouth, and he sat back in his chair, steepling his fingers. "Would you say that she is also given to changes of mood, sudden and rapid?"

Linnet nodded thoughtfully. "Yes, you have that right. She started weeping the other day just at a kind message sent to her by Mr. Lessington. He had heard of her pending marriage and merely wished her luck in her new life; he regretted that the stage would lose one of its most promising luminaries. I thought at the time that she missed her old life, on stage, you know, but she swears that is not true and I must believe her."

Barton nodded. "It has to be," he murmured to himself, certain at last. "There is no other probable explanation. My dear Miss Pelham, has it occurred to you that your friend may be with child?"

Eight

"A b-baby? A child? M-my . . . Jessica is going to have a baby?" The truth struck Linnet forcibly. How had she not seen it? But though she had known that some women experienced nausea and other illnesses during pregnancy, it had never occurred to her with Jessica. Perhaps that was because their mother, through all of her childbearing, was never sick a day. In fact, she was much more healthy when pregnant than when she was not in that state.

Barton chuckled. "I would bet on it."

A baby. A little niece or nephew to adore and spoil. Linnet's eyes teared up and she covered them with her hands. For the moment it was almost too much happiness, this news. Jessica was the dearest person in her life, and to know that she was with child . . .

And yet . . . Jessica was not well and certainly not happy. She dropped her hands to her lap and frowned. Thinking aloud, she said, "Why has she not told anyone? Good Lord, why has she not told Cairngrove?"

"Maybe the child is not his," Barton said in an offhand, jocular manner.

It was the thought of a moment and abandoned in that same instant, and yet one cannot take back words once they are spoken and linger in the air like crystalline fog. The words were practically visible, hovering between them, ugly, sulfurous, and yellow with a distasteful odor.

Linnet glared at him and her hands balled into fists. "How can you even say that?" she muttered, her voice grating and raw. "How can you say such an evil, wicked thing?"

"I . . . I didn't mean . . . ," he babbled. But even as he spoke it was clear that it was impossible to neutralize the poison he had introduced.

Linnet stood and in one swift motion pointed toward the door. "Get out. Get out now and do not come back. You have shown who you truly are and how little you understand of Jessica and her relationship with Cairngrove. You are exactly who I first thought you were, a rotten bounder, a cad, and a knave!"

"Lin, I truly didn't mean . . ."

"Yes, you did," Linnet spat. "Be man enough to admit your iniquity, at least. Get out or I will tell Cairngrove what you have said."

"But Lin . . ."

"Get out!"

There was no room for argument and Barton knew when a retreat was the only sensible move. He was deeply troubled by his own casual cruelty, too troubled to even put into words how remorseful he was.

Woodenly, Linnet moved back toward the stairs. From joy to despair, she had risen too high and then tumbled too far. It was too much to take in.

Barton's offhand comment had hurt badly, and she realized that was because she had begun to like the man. . . . No, more than that—she had come to care for him, had begun to think there was more to him than the boor she had met the first day. But now, to find out that he really was that lout all along!

She gazed up the staircase. Jessica. She would concentrate on her beloved sister, who was going through some kind of torment. She went up and sat by her side for a while, watching her sleep.

When she finally yawned and stretched, coming awake gradually, Linnet smiled down at her. "You are so beautiful, big sister. Cairngrove is a fortunate man."

"Oh, Lin," she said on another yawn, "it is just because you love me that you think like that. I look a sight, and I know it. I am too thin, sallow, and my hair is like straw. I am so sick all the time." She stopped, and her expression clouded as she fully awoke. "Cairngrove fell in love with the vibrant, attractive actress. He will not want me this way for long. And when he falls out of love with me, when he finds a younger, prettier girl, what will I do?" Tears thickened her voice.

Linnet moved over to sit on the bed with her. She pushed back the heavy golden blond hair from Jessica's brow. "He did not fall in love with you because you are pretty, but because you are a special woman. And he will love you even more after you tell him you are carrying his child."

Jessica burst into tears, and Linnet cradled her and rocked her.

"You know! How did you find out? Have you told Cedric?"

"Never mind how I know, and no, I have said nothing to the earl. That is your job."

"Oh, Lin, I can't tell him. I just can't!"

"Are you sure of it? Is it really the . . . the child that is making you so ill?"

Jessica nodded. "I . . . I am only two or three months along, but I am sure."

"And why have you not told Cairngrove? He is worrying himself sick about you!"

"You don't understand." Jessica struggled to sit up, and Linnet plumped the pillows behind her, settling her more comfortably.

"Then *help* me understand. Tell me what you are feeling, thinking. We always talked before, my dear."

Jessica frowned down at her thin hands, picking at a ragged nail. "He has three children, all grown and on their own. That is why he thought this was a good time to marry. He knows it will be tricky, marrying me and introducing me to the public. He thought it best now because they are all out of the country. He has told them, but they are not to come back for the wedding."

"And? I still do not understand. Jess, every day you delay means you will be that much more pregnant when you wed."

"I cannot marry Cedric," Jessica said, with a tragic look in her beautiful eyes. "He has always said how glad he is that he married young and that his children are all grown and gone. No more noise, no more bother. He can enjoy life."

Linnet sighed. "That means nothing! It does not mean he would not welcome a second family. He has to know that is possible, marrying a young woman! Good Lord, the man is not ignorant of biology, I would assume."

Her chin raised, her eyes misty, Jessica said, "I just cannot do it. Cairngrove wants this enormous wedding at St. George's with all the world watching. He wants the *ton* to accept me, take me to their bosom. And I can't do it! Even if I was not going to have a baby I would not want that, but now—Lin, I will be big with child, and he will . . . I just can't!"

"What about a smaller wedding? Just in the country, with a few friends? Once Cairngrove knows about the baby . . ."

"No!" Jessica grasped Linnet's hands and squeezed. "You must not tell him! I can't do it, Lin. I mean it! I just could never live up to . . . His first wife was the daughter of a marquis! I am the daughter of an improvident country gentleman, and I became Cedric's *mistress*. How would I ever? . . . No, I just can't. And you must promise me, swear on our father's grave, that you will tell no one, least of all Cedric!"

She looked genuinely terrified, and Linnet promised she would say nothing to the earl. She had to promise, or Jessica would have been frantic. Her sister's rambling did not make a great deal of sense to her, but then they thought so differently on so many subjects. Lin had come to understand over the years that there was a deeply dramatic streak to Jessica. Every joy growing up had been ecstasy, every disappointment a tragedy. And so there was an element of that dramatization of life in this current difficult passage, but it did not change her determination, which was real. She was serious about not telling Cairngrove. Linnet, knowing her as well as one human can ever know another, recognized that and knew she must abide by Jessica's wishes. It was her life, after all. Perhaps they *would* have to leave London together and find a small seaside village to inhabit.

The next few days were miserable, and to Linnet was left the awful work of denying the earl the door of his own residence. He did not live there, but he *was* the lessee and legally could have demanded to enter. But he did not. Instead he haunted the door, becoming increasingly frantic, his stolid demeanor dissolving into desolation. Linnet did not know what to tell him. What could she say to comfort him that was not a violation of her promise? All she could do was counsel patience, though she no longer thought there would be any reward at the end for his forbearance.

And she had her own sadness, though she would not admit it as such. She thought often of Dominic Barton and their strange wooing. She had glimpsed a tender side to him, and a passionate one. She had caught a flash, as though in a mirror, reflected and yet not the true image, of the man she had thought he could be in different circumstances: kind, good-hearted, sympathetic, and companionable.

She caught herself in a lamentably mournful mood and gave herself a bracing talking-to. There was never anything between them. There could not be between the sister of his brother's mistress, for heaven's sake, and a man of such judgmental temperament. Her heart whispered that he was guilty only of such sins as the rest of society, no better nor worse, but whispers could not reach her brain, active with the loud voices of worry and regret.

And yet, in the city of London she was not the only one involved in introspection. Nic Barton, raised in luxury, hardened by war, and not accustomed to any deep thinking on his own part but that necessary to defeat a perceived enemy, found himself submerged in unexpectedly earnest soul-searching. He went about his business, conversed with friends, attended the opera, gambled at his club, and yet there were subterranean depths to his mind busily conning over the new emotions and thoughts he had discovered in the past weeks.

He thought the revolution of his feelings had started with the discovery of how sweet and intelligent Jessica Landry truly was. He had met his brother's mistress expecting a certain type of woman—cunning, seductive, charming in a theatrical way. And yet she had been nothing he had expected. Despite occasional flashes of a personality that thrived on drama, she had been just a lovely young woman, a little wan and sickly, but pretty and sweet-natured.

And then there was Linnet Pelham, her friend. He had been attracted by many women, had found their exterior pleasing, had seen something in their eyes that drew him, but never had he met with such a combination of artless beauty and deep intelligence. She was utterly unaffected, and he had met few women he could say that about. She not only had learned her lessons well, she had thought deeply on what she learned. He would not have thought he would find that an attractive trait. After all, he had been taught that ladies, not overly intelligent, were meant for amusement and decoration and the satiation of bodily needs. It was not that he had never met a clever woman, just that he had never found one who also made his breath come faster and his body tighten with desire.

And now he was in the damnably difficult position of having to admit that his ideas, hitherto, had pretty much been completely wrong. Jessica Landry, his brother's whore, was also the perfect second wife for him. She was good-natured, intelligent, and beyond everything, deeply honorable, not willing to take advantage even of her pregnancy—Barton had not had that confirmed, but it explained much if it was so—to capture the ultimate prize, the hand of a peer of the realm. It would be a scandal if they married, but not, he thought, impossible to survive. Cairngrove's solid reputation and Jessica's natural grace and elegance would go a long way to that end.

And Linnet Pelham, whoever she was, whether aspiring actress or mistress-in-the-making, was the intelligent, vivid, wildly attractive woman he had never thought to find as a possible mate, a completing half. Would taking such a woman as a mistress, with all of the subterfuge attendant on such a relationship, satisfy his growing urge to be close to her, his hunger to be something more to her than a friend? And in her present state of mind, would she ever even speak to him again? Life was becoming strange and uncertain, and he did not know what to make of it, nor of the serious turn his thoughts were taking.

All he knew was that he was a disgrace and deserved every condemnation the lovely Linnet could possibly level at him, and more. He had been casually cruel, unthinkingly callous.

Instead of helping his brother clear the way for Jessica's entry into society, using his social cachet and contacts to smooth her path, he had been putting up barriers. He had been selfishly making moral judgments on the actions of people he had no right to judge without thinking of the emotions already engaged in the affair, the deep attachment that existed between Jessica Landry and his brother. It was unconscionable, and he had to find a way to apologize and make up for his woeful behavior.

And yet he was afraid that in Linnet's eyes, anyway, he had completely blackened his character, letting her see into the ugliness of his own cynical, jaded soul. What could he do now that would make everything better? He did not know, but it had better be something good, and it had better be soon. Because he was fast learning that life without Linnet's daily company and conversation was becoming dreary.

Nine

"Miss, I don't rightly know what to do, an' he's bein' so insistent, an' . . ."

Linnet, sitting with a book on her lap, though she could not say what she had been reading, frowned up at Meg and tried to understand what the girl was saying through the gabble. The girl wrung her hands and twisted them in the tidy white apron that was a part of her uniform. "Who is being insistent, Meg? What are you talking about?"

"It's that Mr. Barton, miss, th' earl's brother. He's at the front door. I know I ain't supposed to let him in, but he's not goin' to leave, he says, and will start shoutin' in the streets, and with Miss Landry so ill . . ." Her voice trailed off, and she cast beseeching eyes on Linnet, whom all the staff had come to recognize as the person in the household most likely to help them out of a difficult situation.

Linnet set aside her book and rose. So Dominic Barton had the temerity to come to the door. What did he want, to try to buy off Jessica again? She recognized the bitterness of her reaction, but since that spleen had been a useful tool to keep her from thinking of the earl's brother without a wretched thread of longing, she did not suppress the rancor of her thoughts.

Taking a deep breath, she surged into the hallway and

toward the front door. Barton stood in the open doorway, gazing down at his boots.

"What do you mean by coming here and bothering us? Have you not already been denied the door?" She was proud of the iron tone of her voice and the steadiness with which she spoke.

But she had not counted on the appealing look in his dark eyes. "Please, Lin, I know I have no right to be heard, but we must speak. It is urgent."

She began to shake her head and close the door, but he put out one hand.

"Listen, Lin. This is vital. If you care for Jessica, if you think she would be happier wed to Cedric, then you *must* listen to me!"

Taken aback by the pleading in his voice and caught by his words, she paused. She had been unable to come to any resolution concerning Jessica and Lord Cairngrove, and still did not know what to do. She had finally convinced Jessica to see a doctor, and he had confirmed that she was indeed with child, but beyond admonishing her to rest and to try not to worry, he had said nothing about her illness. She was troubled and she must try not to be, for the good of the baby, he told them. Other than that, her nausea was a normal part of the first few months of carrying a child.

So much for medical help.

Linnet gazed uncertainly at Barton. Over the past week she had come to realize that he had crept into her heart when she wasn't looking. And it would never do. She must excise him as so much diseased tissue; she must cut him out as though he were a canker.

She was still terribly confused over the two sides of him, the tender wooer who kissed her with such gentle fervor, and the snobbish, rude boor who could think such a thing about Jessica, that she would be unfaithful to the earl. He knew her, had talked to her, spent time with her. How could he imagine that she would take another lover, Jessica the most faithful of women? Surely she could not be so dim a female as to become infatuated with a man she could not even respect!

He still stood, patiently awaiting her word. His dark eyes had never left her face.

It would do no good to send him away until he had his say, she thought, and so she held the door open wider and motioned him in. If he served any purpose at all, perhaps she could vent some more of her anger at his hideous imbecility. Wordlessly, she led him to the parlor.

She looked haggard with worry, Barton thought, watching her pace around the room, her slim hands moving knickknacks and straightening pictures. Her movements were jerky and nervous, unlike her usual calm grace, and though she was tidily dressed, as always, stray dusky ringlets escaped her tight bun.

"I was right, wasn't I?"

"I beg your pardon?" she said, turning toward him.

"Jessica is with child."

"Yes, with *Cairngrove's* child." There was an edge of hardness to her tone.

Barton flinched, as if cut by the touch of a whip. "I . . . Lin, I apologize for my beastly behavior. You know, even as I made that horrible comment I knew it was ludicrous. My miserable mouth ran away with itself. I was stunned by my own idiocy. Please, *please* accept my abject apology."

Linnet looked up, startled into making direct eye contact by the sincere tone to his apology.

There was a question in her eyes, and Barton found he did not need it verbalized. He read there anger, doubt, and yet a yearning to believe him. "Yes, I mean that most sincerely. I was a bastard and deserve to be whipped in the streets for such a suggestion."

She sat down opposite him and gazed steadily into his

eyes, reading him. He watched her intelligent eyes, feeling as though she were reaching out to his soul and touching his heart, pressing insistent fingers deep inside, searching for the truth. A sweet blossom of joy and acceptance lit her brilliant eyes as she seemed to accept his sincerity. She nodded once, with a faint smile. "I do believe you mean it. I accept your apology on Jessica's behalf. I . . . I never told her what you said, or . . . or implied."

"Thank you," he said humbly. "I appreciate your forbearance even as I admit I do not deserve it. But I would not want my relationship with my new sister to start on such rocky ground."

"No fear of that," Linnet said dryly, folding her hands together. "Jess has decided she cannot face a society wedding, nor can she tell Cairngrove she is carrying his child, and so she is going to turn tail and run. She wants me to find a cottage by the seaside for us both to live in. She says that is her final decision."

"Yes, I know the outcome of her worries," Barton said. "Though I did not know of her plans to leave the city. Old Cedric is beside himself because Jessica will not see him. He is frantic."

"She loves him so much," Linnet said, a sob catching at her voice. Barton felt a pang as he saw her anguish. "But she cannot bring herself to tell him the truth!" she continued. "She believes that he will not want their child. He has said he is glad they will have no family, as he wants to devote himself to her and her only. But she *does* want it. She is completely in love with both him and the child she is carrying."

Barton had been often with his brother over the past week. He had seen how crushed he was at Jessica's behavior. He searched his knowledge of the earl and said slowly, "He is only saying that, I think—the part about being happy they will have no children—because he does not want Jessica to feel badly about not conceiving. They have been together for two years. He likely thinks she is barren. The moment he knows they are to have a child together, you will hear a different tune. I never saw a man so besotted with his own children when they were infants. Never understood it myself, until now," Barton added, his heart in his eyes as he gazed at Linnet. He knew for the first time what Cedric had felt, gazing at the woman he loved, wanting to be with her, wanting to make her and their children his life. It was a revelation that rocked him, and yet he could not afford to think about the implications at that moment. He must maintain his focus on his brother and Jessica and leave the soul-searching for another day.

She missed the look, gazing down at her hands. "What are we to do about it? Tell them both the truth?"

"I have a better plan," Barton said hesitantly, "to bring them together and give them both their heart's desire. But it will require subterfuge and your connivance, I am afraid. Are you willing to help?"

Linnet gazed again into his eyes and saw only honest determination. Yet again, Mr. Dominic Barton had amazed her. Just when she thought she understood him, he revealed a new layer, a new part of himself. She thought she could get to enjoy peeling back the layers of his soul, mining the depths of such a complicated man. She shook her head, unwilling to let herself fall under his spell again. He was not for her and well she knew it. "I dislike dishonesty and despise deceit," she said. "But I am desperate. If subterfuge will win the day, then I will lie until I turn blue. Whatever you have planned, Mr. Barton, I will go along with."

"Nic. Call me Nic, again. We may both be ostracized before this little scheme is accomplished, and it will be more comfortable if we are on first-name terms."

One eyebrow raised, she decided that as partners in

this enterprise, this web of deceit he was apparently planning, ironically enough he really should know the whole truth about his accomplice. "If your plan succeeds, we most certainly will be using first names regardless, Mr. B—Nic." She took a deep breath. "In the spirit of honesty and openness between us, I think there is something I should tell you about myself."

Ten

"Darling, you really should get up and walk about, you know. I cannot think lying abed is making you feel any better. You know the doctor said moderate exercise would do you well."

Jessica, fretfully plucking at the woolen coverlet of her bed, eyed her sister. "Do you . . . do you really think so?"

Linnet nodded. "I think that if you could get up, bathe, put on something pretty, you would feel much better."

Jessica turned her head away. "I am too tired. Maybe tomorrow."

Linnet felt her stomach clench. If everything was to work out as planned, she must accomplish this, the one tiny part of the plan that was hers and hers alone. Nic was depending on her. She glanced at the ormolu clock on the mantel. It was early afternoon; there was still time, but her sister was slow-moving and there was much to be done. "But, Jess, I truly feel," she continued, "that you must make some effort. You are letting yourself weaken, and having a baby will require all of your strength."

With a deep sigh, Jessica said, "I suppose you are right. I must not be self-indulgent now, when I have another life to think of." She touched her stomach and continued. "I still cannot fathom this, you know. That I am to be blessed with a baby. It is . . . it is almost too much. I wonder what Mama will say when she learns?"

Linnet said a silent prayer that by the time their mother learned about her new grandchild on the way, there would be no cause for any shame attached to the knowledge. "She will be happy for you, I hope. Do you most wish for a boy or a girl?" she asked, as she helped Jessica out of bed, keeping her mind occupied as two heavy-set laundry women tugged a copper bath into the room.

"I don't care, really. A boy might look like Cairngrove."

Linnet wasn't sure whether her sister meant that as a good thing, until Jessica continued.

"I should like a little boy who looked like Cedric. So handsome and h-healthy—" Her voice caught on a sob and she sat on the edge of the bed weeping into her hands.

Linnet felt a swell of impatience at the tears, but she had been speaking to a midwife in preparation for her role in her sister's new condition, and the woman had said that wild changes of mood were normal. Understanding was vital and patience a boon in such a situation. It had been enlightning, to say the least, since Linnet had not at all understood this new Jessica. Their mother had not had the same symptoms, but as the midwife had said, every woman was different, and bearing a first baby was an arduous ordeal.

And so she let Jessica weep for a minute, but then gently urged her into the bath. She washed her sister's back herself, and, aided by Jessica's maid, helped her out and wheedled her into having her hair done up. With the systematic use of bullying, cajoling, and commanding, in turn, she eventually even got her into a pretty dress, an ivory satin with blond lace frothing at the wrist and neckline. Jessica had lost weight and it fit rather loosely, but it just made her look more adorably fragile and waif-like.

And all the time Linnet kept up a steady stream of conversation. She could hear the commotion downstairs and feverishly hoped Jessica did not ask about it. Doors slammed, the low hum of voices drifted up the stairs, and on one occasion she could hear the screech of a heavy piece of furniture being moved. There was an unusual amount of traffic on the square.

But Jessica, deep in her own thoughts, remained oblivious. Finally, Linnet clasped a string of glowing pearls around Jessica's neck and gazed at her sister in the mirror. "You look beautiful."

"I look tired," Jessica said, examining her reflection. "I am so pale. And there are dark rings under my eyes I know what you are trying to do, you know," she continued, gazing at the reflection of her sister's face in the mirror.

Linnet felt a jolt to her stomach. "Y-you do?"

"Yes, of course. I am your sister. Do you think I cannot read you?"

"And yet you have gone along with it all," Linnet said, hope in her heart. "Does that mean that you have changed your mind?"

Jessica frowned. "Changed my mind? I have only gone along to humor you, little sister. But now I am exhausted and I am going to bed."

"But you have to come downstairs now," Linnet said.

"No, I don't. I have gone along with this knowing your whole purpose was just to take my mind off Cedric, but now I am weary. I . . . I know he has not called at the house for days, and I suppose that means he has given up finally. I am glad. Truly. He deserves . . . d-deserves someone to make him really happy." "Happy" was said on a sob.

Linnet felt that swell of impatience again. How could

her sister not know that the only thing that would make the earl happy was her as his bride? How blind could one woman be? "You must come downstairs, Jess."

Jessica frowned and sniffed back her tears. "Why?"

"I want to have dinner with you properly. We have not done so since the first night I arrived."

"I am too tired, dear. Please, all I want is to sit with a book. I'm not hungry."

Linnet was stymied. What to do? If she pushed too hard, Jess might get suspicious. And yet she must get her downstairs somehow.

There was one last hope. Jessica would sometimes do things she did not want to if it was for someone she cared about. Linnet had hoped to come through the day without telling too many lies to her favorite sister, but this must be done for Jessica's sake. She was going to tell an enormous bouncer, and she must hope she had some modicum of her sister's dramatic talent.

She sat down on the side of the bed. "Please, Jessica, do this for me."

Stubbornly, Jess crossed the room and reclined on her sofa, picking up a novel she had left lying on the table the day before. "I am going to rest. I am exhausted and I do not want to go downstairs."

"All right, I will have to tell you the whole truth." Linnet looked away, waiting for Jess's inevitable question.

Of course, it came. "What truth?"

"You . . . you know that Mr. B-Barton and I . . . Nic . . . have been . . . He has been very kind to me." Ah, that tremble in her voice was perfect. It might work.

Jessica, interested now, slung her feet over the edge of the sofa and let them touch the ground. "Yes. I thought there was tension between you at first, but then you seemed to get along so well, and he took you to see the sights. But the last week or so you have not been seeing him. He has not called here."

Happy that her sister was filling in so much herself, Linnet tried to word things in such a way that she would not be absolutely lying. "He . . . he has asked his leave to call on me tonight. I decided it was best not to see him anymore because I was becoming too fond of him." That much was true.

"Oh, Lin, I had no idea!" Jessica crossed the space between them and sat on the bed beside her. "Do you . . . do you love him?"

"I d-don't know." True, too.

"But he has asked to see you alone?"

Not quite the truth. Linnet stayed silent.

"What could he want?" Jessica said, frowning and fingering her pearls. "Did he give you any indication what he wanted to speak to you about?"

"Jess, I just do not feel able to see him alone. He is . . . he is very attractive, is he not?" All true, Linnet thought feverishly, knowing her face was flushing an unbecoming red. Jessica was watching her face.

"He is. He has not made any forward advances, has he?"

Linnet shrugged. "He . . . kissed me. On one of the darkened paths in Vauxhall."

Jessica gasped. "And now he wishes to see you alone? I do not think that wise at all. I will go down with you, dear. There is no telling what a man may say alone with a woman. I like Nic very much, but he is a rake."

Linnet's eyes widened. Was he really? She had not known that, though she supposed she should have by his demeanor. If ever there was a man who had a way with women, Dominic Barton was that man. She almost giggled when she remembered the look on his face when she had revealed that she was Jessica's sister, and a *schoolteacher*. He had been shocked by her close relationship to Jess, but positively horrified that she was a teacher, though, with an ironic twist to his elegant eyebrows, he had said that it "explained much." It was the first time, he told her, he had ever kissed a teacher.

"Let us go down, then," Jess said calmly.

At the last moment Linnet realized that she needed to give the signal. She rang for the maid and told the girl to have tea ready in the parlor, the agreed-upon sign that they were ready to come down now. The maid smirked and curtsied, and said she would make sure all was ready.

Jessica took Linnet's arm and, leaning heavily on her sister, walked out of the room and to the head of the stairs. As they descended, the sound of piano music drifted up, and Jessica said, "Nic must already be here and be playing the piano. I did not know he was that proficient."

Linnet stayed silent. When they reached the bottom, Linnet could feel the jolt of surprise that shook Jessica at the sight of her staff lined up before the parlor doors. Two liveried footmen, dressed in the Cairngrove colors of green and gold, opened the doors and ushered the ladies in.

There, at the end of the parlor by the fireplace, was a soberly garbed vicar. The mantel was covered with pale flowers, ivory and blush. Candles glowed in the evening gloom.

And there, near the vicar, dressed in his immaculate evening best, stood Cairngrove, his bluff, handsome face glowing ruddy in the candlelight. Beside him stood Barton with a grin of delight lighting his handsome face.

"Welcome, my sister-to-be," he said, "to your wedding."

Eleven

Jessica trembled and her eyes widened. "What is going on?" she demanded. She sounded frightened.

Cairngrove came forward, and Linnet dropped her sister's arm and moved away from her. This was between them now. She had done her part and Barton had done his; it was up to Cairngrove to do the rest.

The earl dropped to one knee.

Barton came to Linnet's side and stood with her. She took in the whole room with one glance, from the creamy orchids and lilies to the blush-pink roses and flickering candles. "You have done a magnificent job," she whispered.

"Thank you," he said. "Let's hope it was all for a purpose." He fell silent once again.

"My darling," Cairngrove said, "I know everything and I want to . . ." He took a deep breath, and then continued. "First, I want to offer you my deepest apologies for pushing you into a society wedding. All I have ever wanted is you, my dearest, and if that means retiring to our country estate for the rest of our lives together, then I will gladly acquiesce, just so long as I have you. Will you marry me, tonight, here, this minute?"

"But . . ." Tears welled up in Jessica's eyes. Her mouth formed a word, but neither Linnet nor Barton could hear.

But Cairngrove evidently heard. He stood and gathered Jessica into his arms. "I know about the baby," he whispered, "and I am overwhelmed with joy, and yet so very sad that you thought I would not want something so . . . so precious as our own dear baby. It makes this day doubly blessed. I am only saddened that I did not do this two years ago. Marry me now and let us make up for it. Help me make everything right again."

Linnet felt tears well up in her eyes as she saw her sister melt into the earl's arms. All of the doubts, all of the uncertainty had been swept away by his words; so simple a solution after all of the fuss and unhappiness. How much easier it would have been if Jess had just been honest with the earl. Cairngrove kissed her gently and then guided her to stand with him in front of the waiting vicar, who smiled and started the words to the ceremony.

Linnet felt her arm gripped by Barton and gazed over at him.

"Am I forgiven?" he whispered.

"For what?" she asked, smiling up at him.

His dark eyes gleamed, and he reached out to touch her lips gently with his fingertips. "For everything. For being a boor and an ass. For judging your sister when I knew nothing about her. For interfering and for doubting. You, the schoolteacher, have taught me how little I understood about life and love, when I thought I was the one who could give love lessons."

Linnet felt all of her anger and coldness melt. He had done so much and proved himself capable of growing and changing, and of accepting change. He had made this beautiful moment possible. "I forgive you," she said, looking up at him with glowing eyes. "And judging from the look on Jessica's face, there is nothing to forgive." They both looked toward the happy couple, who were now sealing their vows with a kiss.

"There is something else," Barton said. His voice was tight with tension.

"What is it?" Linnet asked, looking again into Barton's dark, expressive eyes. There was tenderness there, an expression she had never before seen in a man's eyes, except in Cairngrove's when he gazed at Jessica. Could it be? . . . No. Surely she was reading the wrong things.

"Lin, I love you. I love you so very much. Do you think? . . . Can you ever find it in your heart? . . ." He could not finish.

"You love me? Are you? . . ." She was overwhelmed with hope. And yet afraid to hope. She turned to face him and put her hands on his shoulders. "Oh, Nic, are you sure?"

Laughing out loud, Nic said, "Yes, I am quite sure. I have never been so sure of anything in my whole life! When you have never felt it before and it floods into your heart . . . and then old Cedric has shown me the way, you know. My brother has taught me that love is so precious, one must capture it and gently hold it and nurture it." He touched her hair, her cheek, ran his fingertip down her jawline to her chin, and said, "Lin, I love you. Will you marry me? Please say yes. Marry me."

"M-marry you?" Linnet felt her heart pound. Marry him. Marry Nic—Nic who made her skin flush with heat, Nic who made her tremble and sigh and toss and turn in her bed at night. Nic, who had had the courage to realize his mistakes and correct them in so magnificent a fashion. "Yes . . . yes, I will!"

"Now?"

"N-now?" Panicked, Linnet turned and saw an expectant look on Cairngrove's face. Jessica was smiling up at him, beaming with love and joy. And the elderly vicar was waiting with a smile on his seamed face. She turned back to Nic, who had pulled out an official-looking form, and with it, a small velvet box.

"Now. This night. Marry me and come home with me. I have the license, I have the ring. . . ." He popped open the box to display a lovely opal surrounded by fiery diamonds that winked and sparkled in the candlelight.

Linnet, stunned and disbelieving, looked to her sister, who leaned on her new husband's arm. "Jess?"

Jessica gently said, "Only your heart can tell you, Lin. If you are the slightest bit unsure . . ."

"Oh, but I'm not," Lin cried, realizing in that moment that she had never been so sure of anything in her life. Nic had proven himself to be everything she had never thought to find in a man, and more. And he loved her! She saw it glowing in his eyes, for mingled amid the passion and longing and desire was that tenderness and joy. "I am sure," she whispered. "I cannot quite believe it, but I am sure!"

And so they were married.

The next hours passed as a dream with a second wedding ceremony and then a late dinner, just the two newly married couples. But after the laughter and chatter ended, when Jessica and Cairngrove started casting longing looks at each other and at the stairs they would ascend in a short while, Lin realized with a start that she did not know where she and her new husband—husband, what a strange new word in her vocabulary—would spend the night. It had all happened so quickly that her head was whirling.

She turned to him with consternation. "Nic, you only have bachelor rooms in London. Where—?"

He threw back his head and laughed. "My dearest schoolteacher, my little instructress, do you not think that if I went to the trouble to get a ring and a license that I would not think of our first night together as man and wife?"

"I . . . I d-don't know," she said shyly. Her whole body flushed with heat and then went icy cold at even that oblique reference to their joining as man and wife.

"Then believe me," he whispered. "I have thought of little else. I am ready if you are, and we do have a place to lay our heads tonight."

They said their good nights. Jessica's was long and tender.

"Are you happy, dearest?" she said, her hands on Linnet's shoulders.

"I think so. But I am too stunned to know how much. But Jess, oh, Jess, what about you? I have not given a thought to your well-being. Will you be all right here alone? . . . Of course, you will not be alone. . . ."

"No, I won't be alone. I think much of my sickness was worry. I still feel weak, but Cedric says we will have a full-time nurse now, and he will coddle me. You *know* he will. Go and be happy and do not worry about me. Everything will be fine now. So go . . . go to your husband."

"Are you sure?"

Jessica nodded, tears in her eyes. "I am sure of so many things now. Cedric wrote to his eldest son telling him he was to be married. Telling him *everything*. And William wrote back, saying that he and his sister and brother were all agreed; they only wanted his happiness. He told me he has the letter for me to read. They said they trust him and love him, and will love any wife he marries. It soothes the last of my worries. I can face anyone or anything now. Cedric wants Mama and the children to come live with us, if she wants to. He is so kind!"

The sisters—new brides, and both on the same night—bade each other a fond farewell.

Nic escorted Linnet to an elegant coach. While they had supped, Nic had ordered Meg to pack all of Linnet's things, and the trunks were loaded on the carriage already. They rode through the dark, gaslit streets, and Lin felt Nic's arms steal around her. His lips touched her cheek gently, reverently. He cleared his throat in the darkness, and said, "My dear, I understand that you have not had long to get used to the idea of marrying me. It is all new to you. If you need time before we . . . well, before we make love for the first time, I will understand."

Lin felt a deep thrill of love and tenderness. "Oh, Nic, I don't want to wait!" She heard her own voice, heard the eagerness, and stopped, abashed. Would he think her fast, would he—

"Lin, my love . . . ," he whispered, and enveloped her in his arms. His kisses were full of promise and passion, and Linnet found herself responding, learning and teaching, giving and taking.

Soon, too soon, the carriage stopped, and Nic helped his new bride out. They stood in front of an elegant town home ablaze with light. He escorted her in, helped her off with her wrap, and swung her up in his arms, carrying her up the long, winding staircase.

"We do have a serving staff," he whispered in her ear. "But I wanted no one around at this moment. You will meet them tomorrow. Tonight, my little schoolmistress, we have more important things to concern us."

He carried her into a chamber, and she gasped as she took in the sight. It was alight with a hundred candles, and over the gold silk bedcover and the linen sheets where the bedcover was pulled back, was a covering of rose petals, their delicate scent filling the air. He let her slide down until she was standing, and held her close, his body trembling against hers.

"My enchanting Linnet, let me show you my love, let me give you my love tonight and every night for the rest of our lives."

They melted together as his lips covered hers in a long and lingering kiss. His body hardened as hers softened, and they sank down to lay among the rose petals. Together, exchanging kiss after kiss and caresses that became more sensual through the long night, Nic and Lin gave and took lessons in love.

THE QUIZZING-GLASS BRIDE

Hayley Ann Solomon

One

"*Mistress* Fern, I am usually as mild mannered as spring time, but if you wear them . . . them . . . *spectacles* to meet the marquis, it's handin' in me notice I am, and that be fact!"

Mimsy Garett glared defiantly at the little mistress. It was her grand title to be referred to as "dresser," now, just as if she were living in London, and she took the title most seriously.

"How am I to arrange your hair, such a beautiful color, the color of spun gold even if it *don't* curl the way it ought to? Bless me, we must order in some more curling papers. I must speak to Mrs. Fidget at once about that. . . . But I daresay I am runnin' off me subject. . . ."

Fern, sitting docilely in front of the glass, was relieved. If only Mimsy would keep off the wretched subject of her spectacles, she could rest easy. But no! It was too much, of course, to hope. The dresser was rattling on again, playing with Fern's short, cropped strands in front of the glass, just as if she were in short skirts rather than a lady grown. Her tone was heartily indignant.

"*How,* Mistress Fern, am I to arrange your . . . your *glorious* hair if you persist in wearing them spectacles? It is not possible, and don't you say otherwise! Oh, I *do* wish we had not called Jenkins in to cut it! Still, no one can quibble about its condition. . . . Now where was I?"

Fern muttered something inaudible and rather unlady-like, but fortunately Mimsy was too distracted to hear.

"Oh! The spectacles. Remember the Addingtons' ball. . . ."

Fern groaned. She *did* remember. It was a hideous occasion, chaperoned by Lady Winterton, for Mama had the fever, and it had been an unqualified disaster.

Somehow, Fern had landed behind a great potted plant all evening, squashed between the dowagers' chairs and a large trestle of lemonade. She was certain it was the spectacles, for several unkind young ladies actually tittered behind their handkerchiefs and pointed them out to the gentlemen. Those who had subsequently scribbled their names in her dance card had been constrained, almost as if they were doing her some kind of huge kindness. Naturally, in the face of such condescension she had been defiant, though not actually rude, as Lady Winterton would have her mama believe.

Nevertheless, the whole sad matter was best forgotten. Fern had endured most of her first season in this excruciating manner, then returned shortly thereafter to the country, there to be buried in her beloved books and garden, with only the occasional scold to remind her of her folly.

Now, however, there seemed to be no way to forget the past as Mimsy hovered over her with a brush, easing out the classically cropped tangles with vigorous strokes that made her eyes sting but added incredible luster to the soft, shoulder-length lashings of spun gold. Unfortunately, of course, it was dead straight, sadly unmodish despite the new cropped style.

"I shall enhance this mass with a hairpiece and pile it high in a coiffure, just like Lady Winterton and Lady Ashleigh wear theirs in town. Now don't you pout! You are too *old* to wear nothing but the odd ribbon; you don't want Lord Warwick thinking you be naught but a country miss, or worse, a *dowd!*"

The dresser clapped her hands to her mouth in horror. Fern merely sat obediently, offering no comment of her own. So Mimsy continued. "I might be old, like, but I am up to the rig, don't you fear! I have studied all of them London fashion plates, I have, and I know *exactly* what is required! You shall borrow Lady Reynolds's amethyst combs, along with the tiara, and I shall pile your hair up in coils, with just a few ringlets dripping down. . . ."

"Mimsy, your head is in the clouds! I don't *have* ringlets to drip down, remember? And if you think curling papers in my cropped hair will help, they shan't! Remember how we tried last summer. . . ."

"Now, now, Miss Fern, don't despair! We shall prevail! Try and try again is what Mimsy always says! And there is no saying wot we can't find a hairpiece wot have curls, there isn't! But *not* with the spectacles! Don't want the marquis to run off in fright before he has ever even met you!"

"He has *already* met me! Five years ago, when I was a scrubby little brat with a toothless grin and nothing to recommend me but my barley sugar, which I gave to his horses."

"Mistress Fern! Was he very angry? Gennelmen don't like nobody fiddlin' with their cattles' feed! Most particular they are that way!"

"He threatened to spank me, I believe, then gave me a tweak upon my chin and confided that Rascal—that was the horse's name, though I believe it applied equally to the owner—had an infernally sweet tooth and that was why his pockets were always sticky—from sugar lumps."

"A whopper if ever I heard one, for Lord Warwick is the greatest *nonpareil* of our time! Fancy him saying such a thing, when all of London knows him to be fastidious in his dress! Which is why, Mistress Fern, you are to look like a fairy princess. Nothing short of that will hold his eye."

Fern thought it would take more than the absence of spectacles to hold the famous marquis's eye. And why anyone should think *she* could, a little mouse from the country who was more bookish than bold, just because her mama and his were bosom buddies ever so long ago—not to mention the fact that his land marched upon their own, Evensides—she could not fathom.

But the whole household seemed to expect it of her, and everyone was murmuring and muttering here and there about bridals and trousseaus, just because Warwick had written a very polite missive to her father.

The contents she had not been fully apprised of, but anyone would think the man had offered for her, the way the household was topsy-turvy! And he could not have, surely, without at least conversing with her first, or paying his addresses, or even offering to stand up with her at any number of the country balls where he surely must have attended, though she had never actually *seen* him very well.

Five years was a long time for a scrubby little child, and all she could really remember of him was whiskers, which he had apparently shaved off when entering the Sixth Hussars. This she knew from Mimsy, who made it her business to know all of London's *on dits* and pass them on—sometimes with shocking candor—to the little mistress.

"Cook is making a grand feast, she is, with cockles and lobster, and of course a partridge pie, though Mrs. Fidget is inclined to think that rather plain, so she has added a perigord to the menu, and the gamekeeper is bringing in pheasant and such . . ."

"I shall not be able to eat a thing; indeed, my stomach

is turning already at the thought," Fern muttered. "Can I not say I have the headache and be done with it?"

"Mistress Fern! You must surely be funning, or else the most tiresomely ungrateful chit wot ever needed a great good dustin' of the rear end . . . Now don't look at me so. I've known you since you were in leadin' strings. . . ."

"Mimsy! This is only dinner! What in the world do I have to be grateful *for?*"

"Well! When a gennelman such as the rank of marquis, mind, offers for a country chit like you—not that you aren't passing pleasing, mind, with a beautiful heart when you are not scowlin' 'orribly, and a rare seat on a 'orse . . ."

"Mimsy!" But Mimsy was on a roll.

"Not wot, without those spectacles you have the finest, clearest green eyes I have ever seen, and the purest skin, though you refuse my lanolin and lime decoctions. However, me not ever bein' one wot takes offense, like . . ."

"Mimsy!" But Fern was, sadly, ignored by a greater force.

"I reckon you are rare beautiful, like, with those tanglin' black lashes wot Lady Winterton would die for, and make no mistake. No need for them newfangled corsetry wot makes you breathe like a stuck pig . . ."

"Mimsy!" Fern practically bellowed now. Most unladylike, but she had little other option and just cause.

Mimsy blinked. "You ought not to yell like that, mistress. Be bringin' the house down you will, and your mama with the headache . . ."

"*I* have the headache! What do you mean, Lord Warwick has offered?"

"Don't you *know?*" The dresser, for once, looked speechless.

"I know nothing except that the Marquis of Warwick is dining with us tonight and I am to wear this horrible flounced creation from Madame Audesley of Bond Street. Also, that I am to behave myself, to speak only when I am spoken to—though *that,* as you know, Mimsy, is practically impossible—and I am to be gracious, but civil, if you have the foggiest notion what *that* implies! I did ask Mama, but that was before the headache set in, and she was obliged to seek her chambers with sal volatile and laudanum, I suspect. Oh, Mimsy! What does this mean?"

"It means, luv, that 'is lordship has asked for your hand. Comin' to look you over like, before the matter is signed and sealed."

"How do you know?"

"Well, Nancy, the under maid, had it from Stevens wot works 'cross the boundary, like. On 'is lordship's estate. I don't 'old with gossip from the lower orders, but Edgemont whispered it to me this morning, and he, I reckon, had it off the master, 'oo was frettin' over 'is port and expectin' Mr. Potters up from London, like."

"Mr. Potters the lawyer?"

"Yes, and you can be sure it is about your portion, and such. Not that Lord Warwick needs anybody's dowry, mind, but there it is. Now don't get in a pother over it, love. Doubtless if Lord and Lady Reynolds have not told you, they 'ave their reasons. Maybe thought you'd be afeared."

"Run *away,* more like! This is outrageous!"

"It is better than a season, luv, where you stand around bein' nothin' but a wallflower! And as the Marchioness of Warwick, think of the *respect* you will receive! And you will 'ave your own carriage, and Lady Willis and Lady Stonecroft and yes, even Lady Winterton, with 'er ghastly pug face, will 'ave to make their curtsies to you, and cede you precedence at table. Oh, Mistress Fern, a rare treat it will be!"

Mimsy, caught up in the excitement, almost made Fern

laugh. She was too shocked to do so, however, so she chose a seat by the window and sat down, more to steel her nerves than to take a rest.

"Mimsy, you are sure?"

"Oh, as certain as anything, luv! Now do be a dear and stand still for me while I check those pins. The gown—see how it shimmers—needs some adjustment."

"It needs to be burned, more like! It feels heavy with all these hoops—I can't see why I need them; they are usually only required at court—and flounces. I look like a large green pudding. And I will *not* marry Lord Warwick!"

"*Mistress* Fern!" Mimsy did not know whether she was more shocked by this outrageous statement or by Fern's callous dismissal of the gown, which had taken hundreds of hours in the sewing.

"You are funning; ah yes, I see it now. But you really must stand still, luv, this material is thick, and the beading is difficult to pin. . . ."

Fern's head swam. It was useless scolding Mimsy. She loved and adored Fern, as Fern was sure her parents did not, or at least, not in the ordinary way. They were civil, but not doting. Mimsy was strict, but Fern could twist her around her little finger and very often did.

No, she would save her wrath for her papa, or even for arrogant Lord Warwick, who had not even bothered to ask her opinion on the matter. It would serve them both right, she thought defiantly, if she flouted them at the aisle. But that was silliness talking. Fern, very well bred, would not *think* of making such a scandal. She would just have to see to it that Lord Warwick changed his mind, after all.

Lord Warwick, the object of this attention, did not seem to be aware of the disaster awaiting him. He threw the reins of a magnificent new stallion at Peters, the groom, and grinned. "She will be a rare goer, that one! Feed her some oats tonight, and we will test out her strength in the morning."

"Aye, me lord. Anything else?"

"No. Just have the carriage sent 'round in an hour, when I am out of all this stable grime."

It took Warwick and his valet precisely fifty-nine minutes to announce themselves satisfied. After a steaming bath, brought up hot from the kitchens, wherein Warwick had scanned the *Gazette* with moderate interest, the ritual of shaving had occurred without incident. Then had come the donning of the doeskin breeches in the lightest shade of buff, and the corresponding matter of the shirt and coat, into which he had been eased with both care and consummate skill. In truth, Warwick preferred the form-fitting accoutrements thus described to the more lax attire donned in the country. This might well be because such garments, unpadded as they were, were highly complementary to the marquis's lithe and muscular person, but was probably more out of force of habit, as he spent the better part of his time in London.

Be that as it may, he looked, as always, a veritable marvel of understated masculinity in his wine-colored dress coat and his white shirt. This was complemented by a starched cravat that was whiter yet, if such a thing could be possible, and tied with Warwick's usual visionary grace.

At his throat was a single, defining pin, an oval-shaped diamond that was almost legendary among the Upper Five Thousand, and a source of great envy to many of his friends and enemies. Yes, enemies Warwick had, since his rapier wit was matched only by his skill with the rapier itself. It was many a man who had felt the edge of his foil, and several who had been wounded for want of tact, or for libeling someone of the fairer sex.

Now he seemed unconcerned with his dilatory past, checking his fob with a languid air that showed none of his inner qualms. Yes: Warwick, though God-like in stature, was human, too, it seemed. It would be positively insane to suggest that hovering on the brink of marriage he should not feel a trifle curious as to the nature of his bride or what she had become. He remembered only too well the scruffy little brat feeding sugar lumps—or were they barley cubes?—to his prize cattle. Truth to tell, it was this fact that clinched the deal, for the chit must harbor some softer feelings to be so kind, and some courage to be so bold.

But mostly, of course, it was his mama, the Duchess of Hargreaves, to whom he was the only son and heir. The duke, of course, had indicated several times that it was time for him to settle down, but his mama—oh, his mama of the beseeching eyes, of the wheedling, meddling, muddling ways, oh, it was his dear mama who had led him to such a stand. Not that he minded, terribly—he was raised to believe that duty came before inclination—but he was curious. What had become of that untidy little chit, with her tangle of hair and her bonnet in a riot of feathers—most, he suspected, from the henhouse, rather than from any modish milliner. His lips curved a little at the memory, causing Rivers, his valet, to flutter about him, adjuring him not to spoil the line of his neckerchief.

Warwick stared at him coldly. "And when, Rivers, have I ever performed such sacrilege?"

To which Rivers, of course, had no response. Warwick, at all times, was perfect. Simply, unutterably, splendidly, perfect.

* * *

When the carriage rolled off at only two minutes past its appointed hour, a great murmuring arose from within the stately residence. A procession of the butler, the housekeeper, and several of the upper-house staff unbent a little to permit the uncorking of two bottles of Warwick's finest Madeira. For the lower staff, a dram of fruit punch had been ready stilled, ever since news of the nuptials mysteriously wafted through the servants' quarters. A fitting occasion, they felt, for such deviation from the customary abstinence. Warwick, doubtless to be in his cups upon his return, would surely neither notice nor begrudge them.

Thus it was, that quite unbeknown to him—or his unwilling bride—Warwick was toasted with due reverence at precisely five minutes before he reached Evensides.

Two

Fern set down her spectacles with determination. She sniffed. The hall clock had chimed the hour and Mimsy had already hastened her a dozen times, begging her not to keep Warwick, who had been announced a half hour since, waiting. Even her mama had sent up a message and a little nosegay with some illegible words scrawled upon the note.

Fern knew she ought to hurry, but somehow, she could not. The swathes of heavy green brocade weighed her down, and the beading, though perfectly stitched, seemed gaudy in the candlelight of darkening dusk.

Perhaps if she had been permitted a coronet of flowers, she would have felt lighthearted, but the heavy tiara with its thick golden peaks, and the matching set of heirloom sapphires about her neck seemed to do nothing more than add to her gloom.

As for her spectacles—the abigail had frowned, her mama had frowned, and Mimsy—dear Mimsy had flatly refused to allow them.

"For once," she had said firmly, "Miss Fern will look like a lady born and bred. If I have to arrange her hairpiece about them spectacles she will look like a regular quiz and I shall sink, positively sink, from mortification!"

Such impertinence would ordinarily have earned her a sharp reprimand from Lady Reynolds, with her die-away airs, but tonight it received no more than a nod of approval.

"Quite right, Garett. Never thought to hear such good sense from you. Gracious, Daughter, you are almost beautiful without them!"

Fern took no real comfort in this announcement, for it was useless, she supposed, to point out that she was as blind as a bat without the round, metal frames to which she had slowly become accustomed.

Now, she checked herself one last time in the glass, but of course could see nothing more than a fuzzy blur and a great deal of the loathsome green. She sighed, her statuesque figure tucked behind flounces and the hoops she detested. She was dressed to Lady Reynolds's precise satisfaction—she being an avid fashion plate reader—but nonetheless felt something rather like an unripened pumpkin. It was all rather appalling.

The only comfort, she supposed, was that Warwick would turn tail and flee at the sight. She bit her lip, refusing to allow the image of her first meeting with him to shadow her immediate resolve. He had shown to advantage, then, but *then* she had been a green girl, probably dazzled by his éclat and social graces. These he was now sadly lacking, else he might have had the courtesy to seek her out himself, rather than high-handedly assuming her compliance! Grimly trailing her skirts across the lighted corridor, Miss Reynolds thanked heavens she had no need of any candle taper, for she was trembling so much she would have been burned.

Warwick was too well bred to show his impatience, but after a quarter of an hour of desultory conversation first with Sir Peter Reynolds and then with his lady wife, his eyes wandered to the hall clock. Surely it had chimed the hour this fifteen minutes and more? It had. He sighed. Doubtless the chit was fussing over her gown or dithering over her jewels, in the manner, he supposed, of all females. His thoughts took an indulgent turn. She was probably nervous, breathless with her conquest and anticipation.

He must remember to be extra charming, to draw her out with romantic witticisms. Maybe not romantic precisely—how *could* they be, when he vividly remembered the smudge of grime on her upturned cheeks and the merry way in which she handled his prize Arabians, just as if they were common cart horses rather than powerful beasts worth a king's ransom or more? No, he did not think he would be romantic. Merely charming.

His eyes turned from the clock to the great hall stair, with its alabaster banisters and faded velvet carpets. Blue, he thought, but his attention was diverted by footsteps. Not the butler, this time, but Miss Reynolds herself, he supposed, as he gazed up in amusement at the grim tiara upon her head. Poor dear! That was Lady Reynolds's doing, he supposed. The tangle of hair he remembered was slightly darker now, and piled high upon her head in a modish coiffure quite outrageous for the country and more suitable to . . . No, his thoughts would not stray to ladies of impure virtue. Not tonight, at any rate, when he was face-to-face with his intended.

Was that a spot on her face? No, merely a patch. Lady Reynolds, it seemed, had gone to town. Pity about the garish gown . . . but such defects could always be rectified. Warwick watched the lady's progress down the stairs. She neither smiled nor flirted nor so much as acknowledged his presence. Puzzling. Warwick—accustomed to an enormous range of such expressions, some of them quite blatant—was miffed. He was used to being fawned over, gushed over, and lavished with unimaginable eyelash batting—enough to whip up a small breeze. Miss Reynolds performed none of these usual feminine wiles. Instead, she stood as stiff as a board upon the stairs, almost as if she was immobilized. Warwick's features relaxed. She was a bundle of nerves! She had to be.

There was no other conceivable explanation for such a reception.

His good heart—for beneath his flippancy there was an excellent heart—bade him fly to the rescue, like a veritable knight of old. He therefore did not permit her to take the last steps of the lonely procession alone, but ascended two or three himself, bowed courteously, and extended his hand. Lady Reynolds, behind him, could be heard gushing with pleasure, emitting such words as "thrilling" and "masterful."

Sadly, however, her daughter did not seem to concur, for she stared at him directly in the face, scrunched up her features in the most horrible manner, and ignored his outstretched hand.

My God! She had snubbed him! Worse was to come, for from there Miss Reynolds, sensing something was amiss, lost her footing and tumbled helter-skelter down the stairs, her skirts billowing about in hopeless disarray. Warwick, still stunned, had just time to notice two very intriguing ankles beneath the balloon of a ball gown, before servants appeared to help the lady from her predicament.

Lady Reynolds—a person he could *not* like, despite his mother's long-standing friendship with her—then chose this inauspicious moment to swoon, so instead of following his intended into the dining hall, he was forced to catch the mother in his arms. He balked at administering smelling salts, and was thankful that she appeared to have a whole contingent of servants perfectly accustomed to such histrionics. Sir Peter, twirling his whiskers, then had the brilliant notion of pouring glasses of port from a crystal decanter, unconcerned that his daughter was at dinner and his wife lying prone upon a decorative Egyptian chaise longue at the foot of the stairs.

Warwick, of a sudden, wanted to laugh. The situation was so farcical as to actually be funny. He regretted not following his impulses, now, and seeking Fern out. But his mama had been adamant. The correct form was to approach the father. Warwick, who almost never visited this part of the country, or this particular country seat of his, had agreed for the sake of convenience.

The House of Lords had been convening over several crucial land- and tax-reform issues, and it was naturally his place to be in attendance. Besides, there had been Lotta the ballet dancer and Nikita the opera singer . . . too many expensive diversions, he supposed. He gulped down his port and suggested they adjourn to dinner, since neither of his hosts seemed to have the presence of mind to suggest such a logical course.

Sir Peter, pouring himself an even stiffer drink than the first, agreed, mildly remarking to his wife that Warwick would not be impressed by such antics. Whereupon Lady Reynolds sat bolt upright on her seat and demanded to know how she could ever have come by such an unfeeling husband, and what Lord Warwick could be thinking, she shuddered to think.

She *would* have shuddered, had she known, but fortunately, since Lord Warwick was a consummate gentleman and perfectly used to winding females around his elegant gloved thumb—she never did.

Instead, he lent her his arm most cordially, and they adjourned to the dinner table, where Fern was seated, scowling horribly and rubbing her eyes.

Warwick, glancing at her sharply, suspected tears, but was too arrested by her headpiece to do anything other than cough, for surely, *surely,* that was a wig the chit was wearing? It was too dark for the magnificent shade of blond he detected beneath. He chortled, then miraculously transformed the chortle into a genteel cough.

Lady Reynolds, now restored, rang her little silver bell at once. "Water, Jenkins. His lordship is coughing. Oh, I *do* hope you are not succumbing to the chill—so inclement this time of year . . ."

But his lordship, his gaze still arrested upon Fern, was too busy choking back his laughter to make any civil comment. Instead, he accepted the water and gulped at it until his customary sangfroid was restored. But why to goodness was the lady behaving in so peculiar a manner?

He knew for certain there was no madness in the family, and the one time he had conversed with Fern, she had seemed completely charming, if a trifle young for his tastes. And yes, despite Miss Reynolds's stated belief that he had not noticed her at country balls, he had, at one. It was just before he had left for the Peninsular, when he was still whiskered and half green himself.

He had not stood up with her, of course, for that would have exposed her to the worst type of gossip and speculation. Warwick knew that his every move was watched and reported on ad nauseam in anonymous little columns like the *Tattler*, and the more conservative but nonetheless interested *Gazette*. For some reason, he did not want Fern to become the latest *on dit* of London. He had therefore bowed rather formally—she had described it as coldly—and taken her hand in the prescribed manner.

But he had moved on, leaving Fern with no small qualms and some disappointed little feeling at the pit of her stomach. Perhaps it was because of the intimacy of their first meeting, with nothing but Rascal the Arabian stallion to interfere with their brief, but somehow memorable, conversation.

Fern told herself she did not care, and had come rapidly to the conclusion that Warwick was too high in the instep, too proud for his own good, and uncivil to a fault, all allegations that were spectacularly unfounded, but which he had never disproved to Miss Reynolds's satisfaction.

Then, of course, Fern had had her one terrible season, and had returned to Evensides without seeing either him or indeed *any* of his illustrious peers again. Naturally, being a sensible and proud little person, she had told herself that it did not signify in the least. She had her stable of horses, her garden, and her still, wherein she produced honey wine, pots and pots of lavender, and all kinds of interesting potions. She was too young to concern herself with the business of marriage, and indeed, why should she? There was always Squire Winlock if all else failed, but she rather thought she would prefer to be an old maid.

"Fern, dear, I am certain after the meal Lord Warwick will wish to hear you play."

"Upon the *harp?*" The incredulity in her tone could not go unobserved. Warwick refrained from raising his eyebrows, as he might have to anyone other than his betrothed, and Lady Reynolds glared meaningfully at her incomprehensible daughter. She had quite forgotten, of course, the crucial matter of the spectacles.

"Well, naturally, for you excel in the instrument, and I am certain his lordship would be pleased to hear."

"Mama . . ." Fern cast beseeching eyes at Lady Reynolds, but it was perfectly useless. She wondered frantically whether to mention the spectacles, but thought she might be sunk in deeper disgrace if she did—deeper than she was in already. Perhaps it was her imagination, but she was certain even Edgemont the butler was frowning his disapproval.

Trapped, she agreed, thinking, rather sadly, that perhaps it was all for the best. Warwick would be so revolted by her performance that he would feel perfectly in his rights to withdraw his offer. After all, nothing was formalized, there had been no announcement, and she frantically hoped no banns. It would be a small thing for him to elegantly withdraw.

Indeed, she hoped he did. But something inside her was miserable, hopelessly miserable, and she was forced to scrub at her eyes again, so that Warwick eyed her keenly and her mama actually kicked her under the table. And how her slippered feet *hurt!*

"Ouch!" Fern glared at her mother, then remembered herself. Warwick, more acute than some might think, almost *precisely* inferred what had occurred. His sympathies, strangely, were aroused. Whatever the chit was up to, he was certain she would be in disgrace for a sennight at least if he did not intervene.

"Actually, it is such a fine night I think I might prefer to promenade a little, if you don't mind. The air shall clear my head, and the stars at Evensides seem particularly bright."

Lady Reynolds seemed clearly put out by this announcement.

"Oh, but Lord Warwick, I did so *particularly* wish you to hear Fern play! She might be tiresomely modest, but even I, who have no ear at all—though Lord Derby once said I could sing like an angel—knows that my daughter has a talent!"

Talent for trouble, more like, Warwick thought grimly, raising an inquiring brow in Fern's direction.

"It is naturally up to you, then, Miss Reynolds. I shall be delighted to listen to a recital, but equally delighted, if you prefer, to take a stroll with you upon the balcony."

He was being reasonable, and moderate, but Fern felt unconscionably cross. Caught between the frying pan and the fire! If she played, she would make a fool of herself; if she strolled, she would very likely trip over her skirts and fall headlong to her death. She did not, even to herself, think of the more likely danger—that she would fall headlong, not to her death, but in love.

For Lord Warwick, despite his arrogant assumptions, was everything she remembered. Not that she could actually *see* him, of course, but she could almost *feel* him across the table from her, and every nerve, somehow, was strained. She was certain that if she took the offered turn on the balcony, she would do something perfectly reprehensible, like offering up her lips to be kissed. Then, of course, there would be no crying off. For a second the prospect was tempting, but Fern did not want Warwick to triumph thus. She was positive it would be bad for his psyche. Besides, he was rude and arrogant and grossly overbearing.

She must never allow herself to forget that he had not so much as dignified her with a proposal. Not even a decent conversation, let alone a proposal! Her bodice swelled a little with indignation. She churned her anger up, for else, she knew, she would disgrace herself by responding to his charm. Oh, he was charming, undoubtedly—the whole of London seemed to speak of little else. And a rake, too, she suspected, though naturally a well-brought-up lady like herself could have little knowledge of such matters.

Warwick, eyeing her across the table, wondered what she was thinking. Her thoughts were obviously tumultuous, for her breathing was slightly shallower, and her cheeks, flushed before, were now almost crimson. His dark eyes lighted with sudden amusement. He would wager a pony her thoughts were less discreet than her modish gown, which revealed nothing at all of her form.

"Well?" Sir Peter's tone was sharp as he took a sip of flame-colored liquid. "No good dithering, miss! Which is it to be? Lord Warwick, I trust you do not need a chaperon for this stroll of yours?"

"Oh, no, for I see the balcony is alight with candles,

and I assure you I shall take Miss Reynolds no farther than that window seat over there." Warwick lifted his gloved fingers toward the balcony door. It was made of glass, so Miss Reynolds, peering out sharply, could see what *he* saw.

An empty bench and a tall, wrought-iron candelabra flaming with tapers of various lengths. In all, there must have been fifty lit. Fern was astonished at the amount, for her parents, though fashionable, were generally frugal. Then she realized that they must have been expecting such a request, and she felt the strangest combination of confusion, yearning, and outright fury at being manipulated so.

"I believe I shall play, after all." She blurted out the words before she had time to reconsider. Sir Peter and Warwick looked astonished—Sir Peter because he was longing for his port and had thought he could retire to the library, Lord Warwick because he had formed the distinct impression that the lady did not wish to play. Only Lady Reynolds looked satisfied, clapping her hands genteelly and murmuring that although she was not a *doting* mama, Lord Warwick would see that she had done her duty by her daughter.

The daughter, stricken and appalled by what she had just suggested, rose stiffly from the table, hoping that the white blur in front of her was, in fact, the hallway, and not the antechamber that led off from the dining room. Luck, for once, was with her, so that no one noticed anything amiss, save perhaps the footman, who thought she was behaving uncommonly odd for someone who had been sliding down the banisters for years.

For Fern, sad to say, was walking as stiff as a ramrod, concentrating on keeping her tiara aloft, her headpiece in place—she could feel the pins loosen as she walked—and her eyes strictly ahead of her, from where she could marginally see the large, blurry objects that threatened to obstruct her path.

Finally, though, she was seated by the instrument and it was no more than a second before Lord Warwick was at her elbow, muttering in low, velvety words that only she could hear.

Three

"Miss Reynolds, are you perfectly well?"

"Perfectly, I thank you." The answer came out cooler than she intended, for in truth Lord Warwick's presence flustered her quite unaccountably and she would not for the world have him know it. She fixed a quizzing glass to her eye, which increased the effect of cold hauteur. A quizzing glass!

The Marquis of Warwick, heir to the dukedom of Hargreaves, had never had a quizzing glass fixed on his person in all of his life. If anyone quizzed, it was he. He did so with a practiced air guaranteed to depress the pretensions of any young jackanapes fool enough to be impertinent. But to be quizzed by his betrothed! From the tips of his soft slippers to the . . . Well, she had not yet reached his fine countenance yet; she seemed arrested at his breeches.

Lord Warwick, eyeing the brilliant gold peeking out from the darker coils of the headpiece, wondered if it was he, not she, who was going mad. The girl was as cold as ice toward him, yet he felt fire in his veins and the most overwhelming urge to throw her up on his horse and carry her off into the night.

Instead, he gently removed the glass from her hands, commenting firmly that it was not his pleasure to be quizzed. At which the lady, who had been frantically trying to catch at least a glimpse of him, colored up wildly, for she had focused altogether on the wrong part, due entirely to her own folly. She wondered if he knew, and suspected he did, which made her scowl fearsomely.

Warwick compounded his sin by ignoring her displeasure and offering to turn her pages, to which she responded with an impertinent shrug. It was so pointedly rude that it would have earned her a horrified gasp from her mama if only she had seen it.

Lady Reynolds, fortunately, had not, for she was firmly occupied with securing her wrap. Sir Peter was ordering the first footman to stoke the embers, so he, too, did not notice Fern's rancor.

Warwick did, though, and he wondered at it. It was almost as if the girl had set her back up against him, but for the life of him he could not fathom why. He decided, grimly, that he would certainly find out, if he had to carry her kicking to the altar.

"I do not require the pages turned, thank you. I shall play a little air I know by heart."

Warwick shrugged and took a seat, feeling foolish hovering over her when she evidently did not require it. The sensation was novel to him, for most young ladies positively *threw* their music sheets at him, batting their eyelashes wildly and thinking of every excuse under the sun—from lemonade to the burning desire to be fanned—to keep him at their sides. But Fern, evidently, was not like those ladies. He wondered in surprise why he sighed faintly at this discovery. He must be becoming a coxcomb, to be miffed at so minor a rejection!

Lost in thought, he did not notice Sir Peter eyeing him keenly, or Lady Reynolds casting shrewd eyes upon his person. Nor did he notice Fern's fingers move to the strings, until the first discordant notes. He tried not to wince, and coughed genteelly instead. Then again, came a jangling that set his nerves on edge.

"Gracious, Fern, you are funning us!" Lady Reynolds gasped.

But Fern was not funning; she simply could not see to save her life. She had thought she might get away with something simple, but of course, without her spectacles or even the quizzing glass, she could not see to find the first string. The whole matter, quite simply, was perfectly hopeless.

Tears of mortification stung her eyes, for although she wanted to be rid of Lord Warwick, and she was certain this display would accomplish the matter, she felt a great depression of spirits. This, in addition to the natural feelings of anger at her predicament. Oh, if only she had not allowed Mimsy and her mama to bully her so! Surely her iron spectacles, with their charming blue satin ribbon, would have been preferable to this? But there was no going back, no wishing she had worn a simple muslin with her hair unfettered by clips and pins! No wishing that the damnable tiara, heavy upon her head, could be consigned to the devil, or indeed that the whole company be so consigned! Everyone—even Waters, the third footman, was staring at her agog.

She rose from her seat a little unsteadily and held up her head a trifle higher than she might normally have done. Lord Warwick, rather than being annoyed, began admiring her for her backbone. She glared, with quite enormous, glorious, sparkling green eyes, at her audience.

"You will forgive me if I retire. I am tired, and I have the headache. Lord Warwick, pray do not feel obliged to tender your addresses. I understand perfectly if you have undergone a change of heart. As a matter of fact, I release you utterly from any arrangements you may already have made. Naturally I do not have the details, since I was never consulted, but I surmise there must have been some settlements."

At which both her parents gasped in shock and annoyance, and Lord Warwick very nearly clapped his hands. So, she had spunk, the little one. And at last he thought he understood what ailed her.

The little termagant had wished to be courted, by God! Well, if he could just uncover a trifle more of the evening's mysteries, he might oblige. On the other hand, he should probably make a very hasty exit and thank his lucky stars. For the present, however, he satisfied himself with bowing and extending his hand. It was ignored, again, but he was not so easily set aside this time.

Lady Reynolds, in the process of swooning yet again, missed the most disturbing occurrence of all. Warwick swept forward and placed his arms about Fern's waist in a grip that was light yet nevertheless hinted of steel. Fern gasped, for she had not seen the extended hand, but she certainly felt the consequences of ignoring it!

Sir Peter signaled for another brandy and sank back into his chair. He was perfectly unused to such goings-on in his own home, but if it would save the settlements, he would be a sorry sort of papa not to turn a blind eye to this outrageous behavior.

Fern struggled, but Warwick murmured firmly that it was wiser that she did not. In a louder tone, he very civilly invited her onto the balcony again, "for," he said, "you undoubtedly require a restorative, Miss Reynolds, and the air is really most clement for headaches and such."

At which the third footman nimbly moved to open the balcony door, which could be accessed from the music room, just as easily as from the more formal dining area. Sir Peter retired, at last, with his paper, and Lady Reynolds, still not yet recovered from her shocks, lay moaning upon the sofa, both the housekeeper and the upper housemaid now busily in attendance.

Fern was trapped. Short of screaming—and even *her*

volatile nature did not permit this—there was nothing to do but to acquiesce, and to try to ignore, quite utterly, the masculine arm encompassing the only part of her gown not resembling a pumpkin.

A task easier said than done, for the gloved hand was like velvet, warm and heady against her skin. Their arms seemed to touch, and though she had been wearing gloves in the approved manner, these had been discarded before the debacle of her performance. She wriggled a little, but it was hard to do so and still maintain a shred of her dignity.

Besides, the more she wriggled, the heavier seemed to be his arm upon her waist, until she thought she was trapped in some kind of heavenly vise. For heavenly it was, though she was loath to admit it, and loath, too, to question why her body trembled so, or why her breathing became so shallow just because she could feel his own breath upon her neck.

The candles outside were still glowing, flickering merrily in the enormous candelabra lit with such painstaking care by Mrs. Fidget, the housekeeper. Fern could just make out the flicker, though not the wrought-iron castings of the elaborate structure. She did not need to though, for Lord Warwick was leading her, as if in a dance.

Not a quadrille, she thought, *but a waltz.* She had only to turn just slightly to be encased in those arms of steel. Contrarily, she turned away, but was pulled back faster than she expected, so now her mouth was within inches of his own. She had never been so close to a gentleman in her life, and now she really did feel faint!

Her knees felt like they were going to cave beneath her, but amazingly, they were resilient. Warwick, completely lost to all sense of decorum, drew her closer yet, so that her lips almost touched his shirt, and she smelled the wild excesses of rosewater and musk that he splashed liberally upon his person.

"You are really a very tiresome creature, Miss Reynolds."

The words were drawled, but Warwick was anything but composed as he looked down upon those dreamy, soft emerald eyes. He had never really expected to want to kiss his intended, a fact that now surprised him slightly. Now, he very much wanted to, especially as she was licking those lips in a most intriguing manner, but he suspected it was agitation rather than affection that prompted her.

"You don't understand!" Fern pulled away, at last. The air was freezing after the intimacy of his arms.

"Then pray, do enlighten me!"

"You think you can . . . can . . . maul me like this just because of some contracts you have signed with Papa! Well, I assure you that is not the case! I am sorry if I have wasted your time, Lord Warwick, but since I was never apprised of your intentions, I do not think I can be so very much to blame!"

"Which is a backhanded apology if ever I heard one! And how are you so knowledgeable of my intentions *now,* Miss Reynolds?"

"Oh, half the house staff is! It is a pity, I assure you, I am not a common housemaid! Then I would have known of the marriage plans an eon ago, I am sure! But since no one cared to apprise me of my illustrious good fortune, I am afraid I now stand in ignorance."

"And on your high ropes!"

"Yes, well I said you could call it off."

"Is that what you want?"

Fern bit her teeth and lied. She was too ashamed of the strange sensations that he aroused in her to do anything else. "It is, Warwick. And now, if you will excuse me . . ."

"I shan't. Not before I have kissed you, that is."

"You are abominable!"

"And *you* are behaving like a mannerless brat! I should have spanked you when I had the opportunity."

"Oh!"

"Yes, oh! And now, if you please, you shall permit me to kiss you. Ordinarily I would have waited for the banns, but I find the matter is most urgent."

Fern thought he meant it was urgent to convince her, but Lord Warwick was fascinated to find he meant urgent in the quite literal sense.

He wanted Fern; he wanted to stop her quarrelsome objections with a thorough kissing. He wanted her to smile with blinding happiness and proclaim herself the most satisfied lady alive. Quite why he should want such an absurdity, when a convenient, trouble-free nuptial was all he really aspired to, he did not know. But with all his heart he wanted it, and he wanted it not next month, nor next quarter, but now, this very moment.

He pulled the coroneted head closer, and Fern, for once, was bereft of all speech. Dimly the candles flickered in her consciousness; then all she could think of was Lord Riccardo Warwick and his consuming masculine presence. She could feel, rather than see, his smooth, clean-shaven skin and his starched cravat with its lustrous pin bedded deep in the folds.

She could feel his hands upon her, then his mouth, gentle, but oh, so demanding. It was a sweeter kiss than she could have dreamed possible, yet it promised of more sweetness still. When Warwick felt her rigid body relax, he laughed a little in some secret triumph and kissed her again, and her tangled lashes, too.

Fern moaned a little and extended her long, very lovely neck. He touched it lightly with his thumb, but was shocked moments later to feel a very heavy object land on his feet. Since he had changed out of his riding clothes, he was wearing shoes, rather than the more traditional boots. They were highly polished and as soft as doeskin.

"Hell and damnation! What the devil was that?"

The moment was broken. Fern, horrified, broke from his arms. She did not have to see to know what had happened. The wretched tiara had slipped its clips and tumbled to the ground. Or, more specifically, to his feet. She realized, with mortification, that it was solid gold. The sapphires were as large as wren's eggs. Her head ached—quite truly, it did—and so, evidently, did his feet. In a few seconds, she was sure, Mimsy's splendid coiffure would be in pieces about her head. Her humiliation would be complete.

Ignoring his arms—which were stretched out with the offending jewels—she gathered her skirts and ran. Sheer good luck stopped her from either tripping or walking into a windowpane. The candelabra, thankfully, was well out of her shortsighted path. Warwick thought to follow her, then stopped dead in his tracks. His heart was beating most erratically for a rake, but worse, he was laughing. He thought perhaps it would be best if he departed. Fern—dear, lovely, wonderfully wild Fern—might not understand his sudden mirth.

In truth, neither did he, only he knew for sure that he wanted Fern, and more, that the feeling was reciprocated in kind. Despite her strange behavior, her indifferent manners, and her obvious prejudice against him, she felt as compelled as he did to abandon good sense and kiss and surrender to inner passion. Fern had always had an inner passion. He had known it on that day, five years ago, when she had stolen past his under groom and fed poor Rascal barley sugar.

He had glimpsed it again when her eyes sparked fury and chagrin, but most of all, her mouth had given away a hundred sweet secrets. Now all he had to do was to get to the bottom of the peculiar mystery of her aversion to him, and he would be home and dry. Oh! He had also to post the banns and send a notice in to the *Gazette*. He did not, he thought, wish to wait long.

With a little whistle, he let himself out a side door. Edgemont, erect at his post at the grand entrance, was horrified. When he found Miss Fern's tiara lying about as if it were of no more moment than a pair of nankeen breeches, his horror was complete. Word spread through the lower order like wildfire. Miss Fern was no longer to be a grand marchioness. No, nor a duchess either, not even when the Duke of Hargreaves popped his cork. It was no wonder, then, that when Miss Reynolds was finally served her morning chocolate, the face of her maid was quite as miserable as her own.

Four

The gentleman, poised on the point of knocking, dropped his gloved hand silently to his side, tossed his top hat on a hall table, and regarded the single occupant of Sir Peter's extensive library with ill-concealed interest. He was unaware how arresting he looked, with his curly, shoulder-length hair and his dark, smoldering eyes. His locks were not guinea gold like the lady's, but sandy, revealing faint lights as he moved. When he smiled, his chin dimpled. He was not smiling now, only staring curiously within.

There was no sign of Sir Peter, of course, for everyone knew him to be far from bookish, preferring the hunting fields to the rosewood confines of the Evensides library. So it was a lady he watched with unconcealed interest.

She was dressed in a simple gown of rose sarcenet, with a tantalizing underslip of the purest white—silk, he thought, but he could not be sure. She was turned from him, a book open upon her lap. She had not read a word for ages. He could see, for the fifth page of *Ivanhoe* was stained with tears.

He made a small movement, then startled in surprise. It was not the bright, abundant gold locks that arrested him, for he had glimpsed them the night before, beneath the appalling headpiece. What captured his attention was the revealing satin ribbon dangling down the nape of her neck.

What a clodpoll he was! The lady wore *spectacles!* It would explain much, he thought, especially her cutting of him at the outset, when she had rudely brushed past his extended hand. Oh, there had been myriad clues. . . . Now that he thought on them he was only astonished he had not perceived it before.

What a pother over nothing!

He peered at her closely. The spectacles were charming and distinctive. Common iron, with loops at the end of each temple for a securing ribbon. A bit dark, perhaps, for her piquant face, but that could be rectified. Good Lord, he could have gold ones wrought if she so wished! It was not that uncommon—Lady Asterley had famous silver spectacles; there was the new tortoiseshell. . . . But he ran ahead of himself. He was not home and hosed yet, he was certain.

Ivanhoe was growing wetter. The lady was now weeping quite freely. He wondered whether it would be diplomatic to depart unseen, or have himself announced.

The decision was wrested from him by the lady herself, who looked up at the precise moment he was pondering this conundrum. The book slid from her lap with a large crash, and she jumped up guiltily, affording the gentleman an utterly guileless smile.

"I am sorry, sir. You have caught me trespassing on Sir Peter's library! I am not usually such a watering pot, only . . ."

"Only?"

"Oh, I should not burden a stranger with my troubles! Step inside, and I shall call a servant. Sir Peter is hunting, I believe, but if it is urgent a footman can be sent. . . ."

Warwick did not hear where the footman could be sent. He was too astonished to vouchsafe anything but the mildest reply as he regarded her with suddenly acute eyes. Good Lord, she behaved as though she did not recognize him! And her charming demeanor was at such odds with her behavior the previous night, it could hardly be credited!

"Miss Reynolds, do you not know who I am?"

Fern looked startled. "Should I? Your countenance is certainly familiar, but I cannot perfectly recall ever being introduced. But I am such a shatterbrain, you must forgive me! If we have met, it was probably in London, and my first season, you know, was an unmitigated disaster!"

"That I cannot believe!" Warwick was gallant more by habit than by choice. His mind was far too active wondering how the devil the girl did not recognize him. Either she was playing a very deep game, or he must tread carefully. Perhaps, if she did not recognize him, it would give him a fresh start, time to talk to her without her prejudices or angers or fears. Fern might slap Lord Warwick in the face the next time they met, but she would surely treat a stranger with more courtesy! Warwick decided rather whimsically that he would rather be the stranger.

He smiled meltingly at Fern, so that she blinked, her honest, direct gaze a staggering contrast from their last encounter. He inferred it was both the spectacles and the happy circumstance that she'd not just had a bridegroom summarily foisted upon her. Or, at least, that *he* was not that groom! Bother Mama! He should never have taken her advice and approached Sir Peter first. He should have realized from the outset that Fern would have a mind of her own. Now was his chance to get to know that mind, and he was damned if he was going to own to being Warwick!

He took her hand. "We had the pleasure of a dance a while back. I cannot exactly remember whose ball it was, but it was a great crush."

"Oh, then it must have been Lady Addington's. She

is famous for her squeezes, and the others, I believe, were all rather moderate."

"Yes, Lady Addington's, then. It must have been. You look delightful."

"With my spectacles?" Fern made a face.

"Especially with your spectacles. They distinguish you."

Fern's eyes lit up. Warwick thought that they shone brighter than flames on the finest wax candles.

"Do you think so? Mama thinks they are perfectly abhorrent, and my dresser despises them. I would myself, probably, only it is so good to actually *see,* and not to have to stumble over everything, or . . . or . . ." The smile faded from those luminous eyes. Warwick thought he knew why. The memories from yesterday must have been painful indeed. He felt a stab of remorse for not realizing sooner what the problem had been.

Fern spoke again. "I am very much afraid, sir, that I am in disgrace. *And* in a dreadfully morbid frame of mind, so it would be best if I excuse myself from your company right now. I shall arrange to have a tea tray sent 'round. . . ."

"No!" The words were loud and rather too adamant for a stranger.

Fern raised her brows a little. "No to the tea tray, or no to my departure?"

"No to your departure. I forbid it. I am perfectly at ease with morbid people, for I am morbid myself. I will rattle around in this library like a caged animal if I don't have something young and pretty to look at! If Sir Peter is at hunt, he will be an age, and you cannot deny it!"

"No, but neither is it proper to remain."

"Oh, bother proper! Haven't you ever wanted to rebel, Miss Reynolds, and do something just because it *isn't* permitted?"

"Frequently, sir, but I try to quell the impulse."

"Do you always succeed?"

Fern looked abashed, then smiled again. "Almost never, I am afraid."

"Then stay with me. No one will know. This wing of the house is seldom used, I believe."

"Gracious, how can you know that?"

A slip of the tongue, but all of London knew Sir Peter never went near his library. Warwick lied glibly. "Oh, an educated guess! The wing smells of Holland covers."

Fern relaxed. "You are right, of course. It is all store-rooms up here. All except this marvelous library, which houses the most splendid works imaginable. I come here for solitude, though Mama disapproves of my always having my nose in a book."

"I suppose she must. It is such a very *pretty* nose."

Fern grinned. "You seem determined to cheer me from the doldrums, sir."

"I am. In fact, it is my mission. Here, I shall pick up your Scott and restore it to its shelf. Then you shall tell Uncle Rick everything."

"Rick?"

Blow it, he had better be careful. He had nearly slipped up again. Lord Riccardo Warwick then lied as smoothly as if he was born to it. "Yes, short for Eric, Viscount Sandford, but we shall not stand on ceremony, you or I."

Fern nodded, and Warwick congratulated himself on his quick thinking. It was not such a terrible lie, after all, since Sandford was one of his lesser titles.

"Come on, then. Why was the beautiful princess crying?"

"I was not crying—I detest tears. I was merely sniffing."

"So why were you sniffing, then?"

"It would be improper to tell."

"Ah." Warwick's eyes gleamed, but he pressed his

point no further. Yes, she was blushing quite deliciously, and it was perfectly impossible to simply stand there and not take her in his arms. But he was good. He had to be, if he did not want this delightful creature to turn into a glaring virago again.

"May I take a seat?"

"But of course! Where are my manners?"

Lord Warwick had wondered that several times in the last twenty-four hours, but he declined to point this out.

"I really should go," Fern said.

"No, stay. You interest me."

"How so?"

"Oh, you have a story to tell that is sadder than mine. I see it in those sparkling eyes. Tell as much as you can—it will help pass the time."

"My life is no entertainment, sir!"

"No, but nor is it tragedy. Sometimes it helps to talk, and I, quite providentially, happen to be here. Better than a pillow."

"A pillow?" Fern looked bewildered.

"Every lady of my acquaintance whispers her agonies of first love into a pillow. I am surprised you do not know of such a practice."

Fern laughed. "Oh, but I do! I have done so several times!"

"You have been in love so often?" Warwick looked whimsically shocked.

Fern held out her ungloved fingers. They were smooth and pale, healthy half-moons at the tip of each nail. He noticed this fleetingly as she began counting mischievously.

"Indeed! With my dance master, with a great brute of a man who threatened me when I merely fed one of his horses, with . . . Oh, this is a silly game. I shall not continue."

"Now why am I so interested in that third person?"

He asked this softly, almost to himself, but his eyes met Fern's directly. "Tell me of the dance master."

"He was tall and gangly, but oh, his steps were heavenly and he taught me to waltz."

"Good God! What did Lady Reynolds have to say about this?"

"Nothing, for she never knew. We kept it a complete secret. I was devastated when he left to become secretary to Lord Garadeen."

"But you came 'round, I collect? You are heart-whole once more?"

"Oh, indeed! Until, that is, I met—oh! We shall talk of something else. This is not at all diverting."

"Au contraire. I am diverted. Does this mean you fell in love, again, with the brute?"

"Yes, though I don't know why! He threatened me quite abominably and he wore whiskers."

"What is wrong with whiskers? They are a mark of distinction!"

"They are prickly." Fern made a face. "But he had the most magnificent Arabian imaginable, so I forgave him this small defect."

"And the third?"

Fern blushed. "He is not actually the third, for he is just another, more arrogant version of the second. Only older. I daresay his whiskers are uglier."

"You did not see them, then?"

"No, for I am as blind as a bat without my spectacles, and Mama refused to permit them when we met for dinner. It was an unmitigated disaster."

"Poor Fern! I shall call you that, for I feel we shall be firm friends."

Fern sniffed suspiciously, and her eyes filled with tears. Warwick could see the blur behind her hated spectacles.

"How do you know you love him, then, if you have not seen him?"

"I do not, for he is arrogant and unfeeling and did not even have the decency to propose, only talking of settlements and such, just as if I were a common chattel, not a person at all!" Fern's tone was indignant.

"He should undoubtedly be whipped." Warwick's tone was perfectly serious, but his eyes danced. He had been right! She was miffed! But why in the world did she persist in believing him whiskered? Surely, when they had kissed, she had been disabused of such a strange notion? He wondered how to tactfully probe this mystery, but paused, as Fern continued.

"Yes, he should be whipped, but I daresay he was punished enough when my tiara fell on his foot. It is solid gold and as heavy as lead, I can assure you! I shall never wear it again—it gave me a frightful headache and caused me to walk like a . . . like a . . ."

"Like a dowager with an attitude?"

"Precisely, though I can't see how you should picture it all so clearly!"

"Believe me, I can picture it." Warwick thought he would choke on his laughter. His eyes twinkled bright with hilarity. Fortunately, the library was dark, with little natural light and several heavy velvet drapes, so Fern remained wholly unsuspicious.

"You are very comforting. I feel you understand, which is a marvel, for my parents cannot, and I assure you if I were any younger it would be bread and water for a week!"

"Then they must be unfeeling monsters. How came you to love this paragon?"

"I told you, I do not love him at all! Well, only a little, and only because he seemed to understand when I said I did not want to play. He tried to cover for me. It was really very kind."

"Did you thank him?"

"No, I was abominably rude."

"Surely not? You seem such a gentle creature!"

"I am, in the general way, but he stirred up the most nonsensical feelings and caught me . . . staring at him with a quizzing glass. I was mortified beyond belief!"

"Ah, those whiskers. Were they terribly bristly?"

Fern groaned. "It was not the whiskers that arrested my attention!"

"No?"

"No! And don't you *dare* ask me what it *was* that captured my notice, for I swear I shall throw that pitcher of lemonade at you!"

"Ah. I perceive, at last, your dilemma. You were caught in unmaidenly pursuit."

Fern blushed fiercely at the very memory. "It was not pursuit, precisely, but interest. He is a remarkably handsome man. That is, I think he is."

"You don't know?"

"No, for all I could see of him was a blur, fuzzy at the edges. But he used to be passing handsome, and he has not, to my certain knowledge, grown fat."

"That must be a relief! How came you by such knowledge?"

"If you must know, he kissed me on the balcony. Shocking behavior, but I don't see what else he could have done, for my parents practically forced him into it, much to my extreme mortification!"

"And delight?"

"You ask too much for a stranger!"

"We are not strangers; we are friends. Would you not confide so in a sister?"

"Yes, but I have none!"

"Voilà, then! I am of some use! You may unburden your feelings."

"You are not my sister, but I shall not quibble. I have

done enough reprehensible things this past quarter to know that one more cannot matter. You help me clear the muddle from my head, Lord Sandford."

"Then it is well. So tell. Did the kiss delight you?"

"Yes, but I have no notion why, after his abominable behavior toward me!"

"Well, he has been punished for it, as you say. Why don't you just explain to him the matter of the spectacles?"

"He would think I was having second thoughts."

"You are."

"I am not! I have always loved him! Well, for five years at any rate. Clandestine and odd, maybe, but real, nonetheless! I used to look for him at so many balls, but it was only once that he ever acknowledged me, and then in such a hideously toplofty manner I was crushed."

"So tell him. If he wants to wed you . . ."

"That is the point! After last night, he would be a bedlamite if he did! I released him from any obligation, and if I go to him now, it will simply look as though I regret it."

"You do." The logic was unarguable.

Fern sighed. "Yes, but for the *right* reasons. He will suspect the *wrong* ones."

"That you are an unconscionable little fortune hunter with nothing but rank in your heart?"

"You put it severely, but I must thank you. Yes, that is how he would see it. He would think I was merely regretting my fit of bad temper."

"You will not give him the benefit of deciding for himself?"

"No, for I will be mortified either way. He does not love me, you see. He cannot, if he chooses to ignore me all these years, then haggle with Mr. Potters over bits of land!"

Warwick, who knew perfectly well that he had not

haggled, had not had the remotest interest, even, in settlements, bit his tongue. He could not defend himself for fear of giving away the game. And somehow, he did not feel that this particular game had played itself to its conclusion.

"What shall you do, then? Closet yourself away with your potions?"

"No, for Mama will wear me down to the bone. If I do not marry him, I shall never live down the disgrace."

"Then you should remove immediately to London! Have you no relatives?"

"None at all. Or none who would bear the cost of an extra mouth to feed when I have been so undeserving! No, I shall have to do something more drastic, I fear. I shall disguise myself as a boy—for I am not so green as to think London a safe place for a lady on her own—and I shall seek work of some kind. Perhaps as a scrivener, for my handwriting is as neat as ninepence even if I say so myself."

"Your parents shall die of mortification!"

"They might, but more likely they will wash their hands of me. It is better than spending the rest of my life in their black books, I think, being a pensioner in my own home."

Warwick thought not, but he did not wish to quibble at so interesting a point. So he asked the obvious. "Why not just simply a marchioness?"

Fern looked up sharply. "So! You guessed the identity of my suitor?"

"But naturally. It is the talk of the neighborhood and I am judged, in some circles, to be quite astute, Miss Reynolds."

"Well, you are. No, I can't be a marchioness. The poor man is probably thanking his lucky stars for his narrow escape. You have not heard the worst."

"Good Lord, there is more?"

"Indeed. I attempted Bach's air on G. A trifling little piece, I assure you, though pleasant—Bach is always pleasant."

"How unexceptional. I fail to perceive the problem!"

"The problem is that I was seated farther from the harp than I thought, so started on the incorrect note! I tried frantically to make the correction, but succeeded only in a series of excruciating twangs that must have sent his lordship into whoops! Or spasms of despair, since he was honor bound to marry me!"

"So you cried off?"

"Of course! There was no other option!"

"You could have explained—"

"And sounded like a whining little ninnyhammer? I think not. No, I shall leave on the next chaise for London. If I simply disappear, he need feel no qualms about terminating the arrangement. If I stay, Papa will doubtless threaten to sue for breach. I would sink with mortification, then!"

"Yes, I see that. But all the same, Miss Reynolds, I cannot permit you to take the stage by yourself, disguise or no."

"Well, I agree it is not . . . *convenable,* as my French governess would say, but there is no other option."

"There is. You shall disguise yourself as a page in my household and travel under my protection. I assure you, the path of a viscount is smoother than that of the common stage. And the carriage, I might mention, is a great deal better sprung."

Fern jerked up her eyes. They were so expressive, it was like watching a mirror, framed, of course, in iron, like the ubiquitous spectacles. Doubt warred with hope. Excitement warred with flat despair. He waited in stillness, for much hung on her answer, and he feared she might waver or doubt his pure intentions. Which *were,* by the way, pure, unlike his desires. These he steadfastly ignored, despite their obtrusive nature.

It seemed he would like nothing better than an illicit day of pleasure with his bride-to-be. His "quizzing-glass bride," he liked to think of her, though she would have gasped in horror. The patience paid off.

After several moments of painful deliberation, Miss Fern made the hardest and bravest decision of her life. She would alienate her family, disgrace her name, but surely, *surely,* save the man she loved from annoyance. He would not be forced to marry her. Neither would he be dragged through the courts for breach. Fern smiled brilliantly at Viscount Sandford. Her lips curved delightfully, but in the translucent green of her eyes, there was no answering laughter.

Five

Fern struggled through a note to her parents, then sealed it quickly before she had a chance to change her mind. They would never understand her reasoning—*she* hardly did, only she knew for certain it would be a shabby thing to do to foist herself upon Warwick. Of course, she told herself crossly, if he had only taken the time to get to know her, he might have saved her a lot of bother. He would never, most likely, have proposed, and therefore never exposed himself to issues of breach.

She had little doubt that Sir Peter, stuck with a daughter whose first season had been an unmitigated disaster, would stop at nothing to get her firmly established. He would undoubtedly therefore threaten breach, knowing full well the famous Hargreaves dislike of scandal. All very well, but the direct consequences of all this conniving would be that she was foisted upon a man who despised her! And if he didn't now, he soon would, when he was leg-shackled forever in such distasteful circumstances.

A small voice told Fern that she was foolish, that she should seize her chances and marry the man of her dreams. Unfortunately, it was not just *she* who dreamed of him, but also half the unwed ladies of London. The wed ones, too, if rumor was correct. The Marquis of Warwick, she suspected, was a rake. Which brought her full circle again. Rakes do not take kindly to having their hands forced. He would hate her, hate her spectacles, and hate her pet parrot, Kate. She simply could not bear that, for she and Kate went way back to the fourth county fair, where she was purchased for threepence from a sailor.

Her language had never been expurgated, of course, but oh, she was the most intelligent creature alive! Fern could not imagine life without her. Even Mimsy indulged her, which was saying a lot, for she did not normally hold with birds and had been severely disapproving from the first. Now she and Kate had called a truce.

Kate no longer squawked "Washerwoman washerwoman!" when Miss Garret entered Fern's chamber, and Miss Garett, upon occasion, poked seeds in through the bars.

The parrot, blue tailed and bright, eyed Fern suspiciously. "Squawk! Squawk!" she said.

"Yes, of course you shall come! I cannot think that one extra piece of luggage will burden the viscount a great deal. He seemed a very pleasant gentleman!"

The parrot, satisfied, stopped squawking and cocked her head against the bars.

"Yes, you are wondering what is to be done. So am I. But if we keep wondering, we shall lose our nerve. I shall take all of my pin money for the next quarter and pray that something comes up. Why, we might even apprentice ourselves to an apothecary! I have always been interested in potions. Or I could seek work as a clerk. There is always a need, I am perfectly certain, for educated gentlemen who can read and write. It might be fascinating, Kate! What say you?"

But the words that Kate squawked were not suitable for a young lady's ears. Fern ignored her, therefore, and finished her final note—addressed to Mimsy, this time—painstakingly dotting each *i* and blotting her work so that it would not smudge from either ink or tears.

* * *

It was not until her baggage was safely stowed—Kate conveniently covered on the floor between them—that the coach had made its first jolting start. The shudder was due, Fern realized, more to a rut in the road than to any defect with the carriage itself. This was very tastefully outfitted, in dark royal blue velvet with squabs that were functional rather than flowery. A man's chaise, for though it paid painstaking attention to detail, it was not extravagantly embellished like Lady Reynolds's was. It was paneled in oak with copper trim and made the other occupant seem larger and more intimidating than he had seemed before. Also, rather more immaculate, for he was dressed for driving, in a coat that sported four capes and fitted his form rather too perfectly for strict maidenly comfort.

Fern tried not to stare, then revised her strategy to trying not to be caught staring—there was no doubt about it, she had underestimated Viscount Sandford. He was a magnificent specimen of a man.

"Satisfied?"

"Beg pardon?"

"I only wondered if I passed muster. You have been staring at me through those spectacles of yours these five minutes past!"

"Oh! How impertinent of me! I must beg your pardon, of course."

"Not at all. I find the situation quite novel. It is usually I, you see, who does the scrutinizing."

Fern did see. She could quite see, and she colored up quite horribly. Actually, Warwick, eyeing her with amusement, did not think her delicate flush horrible at all, but poor Fern, distracted, was not to know—or be comforted—by this fact.

"Squawk, squawk!"

"What the blazes?"

"Fine as ninepence! Fine as ninepence! Squawk!"

"Miss Reynolds, am I going crazy or is there a . . ."

"Parrot! It is a parrot, Lord Sandford! I do trust you do not mind? She has a wicked tongue at times, but I simply could not leave her, and since there is all this carriage space . . ."

"Oh, yes. Quite. I quite see the need to bring . . . eh . . . Polly?"

"No! Polly is for pirates! My parrot is Kate. Do you wish to see her, or shall I keep her covered?"

"Oh, by all means uncover her, if her modesty is not offended!"

Fern grinned. "It would take a lot to offend Kate's modesty, I am afraid. She is a wicked bird!" She removed the dark cover from Kate's golden cage. Kate glared at the viscount.

"Squawk!"

"Now, Kate! Don't be rude! Allow me to introduce Viscount Sandford."

The parrot regarded Warwick with stubborn, unblinking eyes.

"Fine pair of legs. Fine pair of legs!" she squawked.

Fern could have sunk through the carriage floor, so exactly did the parrot mirror her wayward thoughts. "Be respectable, or I shall cover you up."

"Spare my blushes. Spare my blushes!"

"You shameless old biddy! You could not blush if you tried! Now hush, will you? We are trying to talk."

"Talk, talk talk talk, talk *talk,* talk talk talk!"

"Good God, cover her up for the love of Jacob!"

"I shall, for she is being impertinent."

"Squawk!"

"And please put her on your side. My nerves won't stand for her coming between us."

"Jabberwit! Jabberwit!' '"

"You must think me a complete hoyden."

"It does not mater what *I* think. It is Warwick's judgment that matters, is it not?"

"If he saw me now he would think me a hoyden. This shirt scratches."

Personally, Warwick did not think Fern should concern herself with the scratchiness of her borrowed plumes, but rather with the tightness. Her abundant curves were clearly visible beneath the tight cambric, causing him to change his plans with swift decision.

He rapped smartly on the carriage door, using his silver-topped cane for emphasis. The horses slowed almost at once.

"Lester, a change of plan. We shall not dine at Trentham, but rather press on to London. You may fetch yourself a tankard of ale at the change, and procure for me a packed lunch. A cold collation will suit perfectly."

He did not refer to his occupant, and the coachman, his eyes respectfully upon Warwick, did not peer any farther inside. Instead, he doffed his cap in acknowledgement and returned to his box.

"There! I hope you do not find me high-handed, but your attire will cause comment."

"Oh! I quite thought I looked perfect! I've had these clothes for an age. We used—my brother and I—to go on all sorts of wild pranks in them. That is where I got Kate."

Warwick ignored the last part of her statement and began calmly with the first.

"Your brother is . . ."

"Peter Reynolds, like my father. He is at Oxford, worse luck for me."

"You are lonely!" The tone held discovery and a smidgen of sympathy that Fern found herself drawn to.

"Only a little. But Peter and I always had such fun, always crept away to the fairs—which Mama disapproved of, you know, on account of the boxing and the cant language."

"Yes, I see. But Peter?"

"Oh, he was a great good gun! Found me these clothes and we had a quizzing good time! We were never caught, but it came close at times!"

"You have grown, I infer, since then."

"Yes, for I find myself surprisingly uncomfortable, when normally I just bless the freedom of . . . of . . ."

Fern blushed. She had been just about to make a most serious mistake. It was not *comme il faut,* even in the worst of circles, for a lady to allude to a gentleman's unmentionables.

Warwick's eyes danced, but he came to her assistance, offering the more mild term "shirtsleeves," though of course these, too, were rather risqué for a lady to mention. Fern snatched at the offering gratefully, muttering "shirtsleeves" under her breath several times as if to erase suspicion of the other, more damning comment. Warwick nodded sagely, hard-pressed indeed not to laugh outright. Well, Fern was not a prude at least. He did not think he could stand a prudish wife.

He looked forward to getting to know her better and blessed strange circumstance for this chance. It was not every day a gentleman got to inspect his bride so minutely! Before the wedding, that is. After, of course, it was always too late. Fern looked prettier than ever in her boyish clothes, with her hair unfettered, even by a ribbon. It looked just marvelous, a golden stream of sunshine in the darkened chaise.

He wanted to run his fingers through it, for it looked softer than the finest china silk. He restrained himself, however, permitting himself the reward of just one glimpse at that white shirt, far too revealing for its purposes! He would have to, of course, gently broach the topic again.

"As my page, you will naturally wear my livery. It is rather smart, I think you will find. Crimson velvet with gold trim. I shall spare your blushes by not requiring the usual clocked stockings, but Martha, my housekeeper, shall sew up some garments suitable for a young boy in service. In the meanwhile, I suggest you keep to your chamber away from the other servants. You are not yet, you know, quite believable in your part."

Fern gazed at him in rapt amazement. "My lord! I am only traveling to London with you! This ruse was simply meant to confound innkeepers and tollgates and such. You can't, surely, mean to actually take me into your household?"

"Why ever not?"

"Because it is scandalous, that is why! I cannot keep up such a charade indefinitely, and I shall have to earn my keep! I am not going to bludge on a total stranger!"

"You are not bludging. You are going to be my page. You shall earn an honest day's work and receive wages."

Fern felt herself in far deeper than she had imagined. Warwick's jaw had a familiar strength about it that she found alarming. Perhaps he and the marquis were not so dissimilar after all! Certainly, she had felt that odd twinge of . . . awareness upon this trip, a complicating factor even she could not fathom, though why she suddenly wished to be kissed so often, the Lord only knew. Perhaps she was ill, or sickening for something.

Be that as it may, Sanford was looking quite obstinate, and she hardly knew how to respond. Her stupid heart was beating faster, too, which made serious thought an utter impossibility—absurd and childish, but the truth, nonetheless.

"That would be most improper, my lord." Now she was being trite and prissy, but how else could she respond?

He countered at once. "More improper than running

off in a closed chaise, unchaperoned, with an accredited rake?"

"Are you an accredited rake?"

"Indeed, though I do not boast of it."

"You might have told me before I agreed to this trip!"

"You were desperate. I could think of no other way to help, and you have to agree, my behavior has been impeccable."

Too impeccable! Though their knees were practically touching, he had taken care never to make the smallest contact, despite the ruts in the road. Though her lips were behaving utterly traitorously, he never so much as tried to kiss her! It was actually more mortifying because he was a rake!

Fern's voice was small as she answered. "You have been all that is gentlemanly."

"Good. Then why quibble at honest employment?"

"I would rather hire myself out as a clerk."

"They are not hiring clerks at the moment. It is too late in the year."

"An apothecary's apprentice, then!"

"You have no references. You need references, skill, and influence."

"A scullery maid?"

"Don't be ridiculous. I may allow you to cavort about London because your parents are hen-witted, but I shall certainly not permit you to be a scullery maid!"

"How does being a scullery maid differ from being a page?"

There was a moment's silence as Fern suddenly recollected that pages were no longer the mode. In fact, she realized, they had disappeared almost entirely from society, though several more elderly noblemen still retained their services.

"Pages are not in vogue anymore!"

"I do not follow fashions. I set them."

"You are going to make me a fashion?"

"Very possibly. It might be amusing. But first I shall teach you how to be a page. You will black my boots, choose out my garments, stitch anything that needs to be repaired, help me with my ablutions. . . ."

"You can't be serious!"

"Never more, though naturally I shall spare a thought for your maidenly modesty. But the rest of my staff cannot be allowed to suspect you are not what you seem. Therefore, of course, you shall sleep on a pallet on the floor beside me. Otherwise, it will be the servants' quarters and certain discovery."

"How long do you propose this . . . preposterous scheme?"

"Not long. Only long enough for Warwick to cry off and for your parents to have no wherewithal to cry breach. I shouldn't imagine the matter will take long. Warwick will hardly kick his heels at Evensides while the Reynolds scour the country for you."

Fern looked thoughtful. "They won't be able to make the search public, either, for fear of my reputation being damaged. Without a reputation, Warwick cannot be expected to uphold his pledge."

"Precisely. So your sojourn as a page should not be long. It might prove edifying. Think of it as an adventure. You thirst for adventure, don't you, Fern?"

Fern startled, for he read her mind acutely. What is more, he was gazing at her so closely that her heart stopped for a second, and it was nearly *she* who disgraced herself by reaching for *him*. Instead, she saved her dignity by regarding her boots—adorable Hessians, two sizes too small for her brother—and nodding.

"I do, though I am not sure that this adventure is going to have a happy conclusion. My father and mother will likely disown me."

"Let us not grow gloomy. Besides, if that happens, I

have a closet full of boots to shine!" With a private smile, Riccardo, Marquis of Warwick, tilted her chin in his hands. It surprised him, still, how her very touch made him shiver. He had not responded to a woman like this since he had been a green lad, years ago. And Fern felt it too. He knew it, by the manner in which her mouth opened, oh, so invitingly, and the way her fingers trembled fleetingly. At her throat, a little pulse danced backward and forward, barely detectable beneath her boyishly tied neckerchief.

"Trust me."

"I want to, but I don't see . . ."

"Just trust me. I would not for one minute permit this charade if I did not think a positive outcome possible. It is possible, in more ways than you know, but at the risk of sounding mysterious, I must ask you not to inquire further. Trust your instincts, Fern."

"My instincts are to run!"

"Are they? Then they are at fault, for I mean you no harm."

Miss Reynolds looked suddenly contrite. "I was funning. I feel safe with you, and though I cannot fathom what you may mean, I do trust you. I shall stay and be your page, though the notion is archaic, and I am certain your staff shall think it a very strange thing!"

"They might, but they are also devoted to me and perfectly used to my queer starts. You are just one of a string, you know!"

Fern wondered how many other young ladies had served as his page. Somehow, she felt a vicious stab of jealousy that caught her totally off guard. She was staggered by its intensity. And it was not Eric, Lord Sandford whom she loved, but the arrogant Lord Riccardo Warwick! She had never thought of herself as fickle—worse, wanton, for both men seemed to stir up unmaidenly desires—but she had to admit it must be possible. The thought was not encouraging, but it sent a flicker of triumph across Warwick's countenance. It was a singular thing, he found, to read a lady's thoughts.

His baser self suggested that now was the time to take her in his arms and reveal all. Surely, now that she was reaching these interesting conclusions, he should reap the benefits? They could return at once to Evensides and confirm their betrothal. Doubtless Sir Peter and Lady Reynolds would be too relieved to scold or place any bar to the ceremony.

But what of Fern? Her feelings were still new and tender. If she thought she'd been tricked or betrayed, she might set herself further against him. This time, the damage might be perfectly irrevocable. He had been highhanded in assuming her acceptance. He must pay the price. The charade must last its course. When the time was right, he would know it. Or he hoped he would!

He fought to maintain his composure, for Fern, her oval face framed prettily by her spectacles, presented the most frustrating, delightful, teasing, adorable, and perfectly annoying sight. He could not think, he could not curl out his paper, he could not read his estate reports, he could do nothing, in fact, except smell her sweet scent. It wafted through the carriage, canceling out the more masculine smells of tobacco and Spanish Madeira. His legs, encased in doeskin breeches that immaculately fitted his form, almost—almost—touched the scrubby fawn breeches of his companion. If he shifted but an inch . . . the warmth from Fern was devastating. He wondered if she felt the attraction, too, or if it was simply he who was going mad by small degrees.

"Here!" he said roughly, throwing her a carriage blanket." Put this about your knees. It will keep out the draft."

And my desires, he thought but did not say.

Obediently, Fern covered herself modestly, from top

to toe, so that only her Hessians peeked out from under the warm, soft kersymere. She was grateful for the blanket, though far too warm for its use. Warwick's legs, nearly touching her own, were the purest torture. She had not expected that. She sank down even farther into the blanket, so that only her spectacles and cheekbones were visible. He noticed, with some small satisfaction, that they were flushed.

Six

Lady Reynolds felt a trifle better after a day laid up with a bilious attack. It occurred to her, after taking her constitutionals, that she really ought to inquire after her tiresome daughter. Doubtless she was buried in some dreary chronicle or other, but she supposed it was her parental duty to intervene.

A quiet talk where she was brought to conceive the folly of her ways and the great generosity of Lord Warwick must be undertaken. Lady Reynolds sniffed at her smelling salts dramatically. Oh, to be beset with such children! Peter almost sent down from Oxford, and Fern behaving so peculiarly as to send away even the most ardent suitor! And it was no good blaming it all on the spectacles; everyone knew Fern could play the harp like an angel, yet she had chosen to make an abysmal mull of things.

Honestly! Anyone would think she *wanted* to be an old maid, rather than the Marchioness of Warwick. It was most provoking. Buoyed up with annoyance, Lady Reynolds rose effortlessly from the sofa to which she had now removed and marched down the long corridor to Sir Peter's lesser-used wing. If the tiresome child was anywhere, it would be in the library.

The door was closed. Lady Reynolds pushed it open with a great thump of her cane. She was not old enough to use one, but everyone knew she had a poor constitution and failing nerves. The stick was a useful confirmation of this, and also a swift means of entering through stiff doors. Sometimes, she found, it took far too long to await the arrival of a footman.

Now she looked about her in irritation. The room was empty save for a sparrow that seemed to have made its way through one of the half-open windows. She shooed it away, then shut the window in displeasure. She disapproved of air; it was calamitous to the constitution. But where was Fern? Surely she could not have ridden off without a groom? Not with Lord Warwick still riding about the neighborhood?

What if they were to meet? What if she were wearing her awful, shabby, red velvet riding habit rather than the smart new blue one Lady Reynolds had specifically ordered up? What if Fern had discarded a bonnet and worn just a simple ribbon instead? She groaned.

After all her hard work! It had been a nightmare choosing just the correct evening gown for Fern. The stubborn girl had hated it, too. There was really no accounting for tastes. Now where was she? Lady Reynolds left the library smartly, her previous weakness no longer in evidence at all.

"Timothy!"

"Ma'am?" A footman glided up behind her.

"Where is Miss Fern?"

"Begging your pardon, ma'am, I don't know. She has not been in to breakfast, nor lunch either."

"Did she leave a note?"

"I believe so. It is on the mantel in your chamber. Mrs. Fidget bade me place it there as soon as she noticed it."

"Which was?"

"This morning, ma'am, just after the milk was delivered in. I remember, because Cook was baking buns in the kitchen and the smell . . ."

"Thank you, Timothy. You may go."

"Yes, ma'am."

Contrite, the footman turned on his heel. He never could remember not to engage his betters in talk. The butler would give him a regular earwigging if he'd heard. Fortunately, Timothy rather thought he was otherwise engaged. The silver plate, laid out in splendid rows on the scullery table, all required polishing. Edgemont would be supervising for weeks!

Fern never got to hear Lady Reynolds's screams, not her swoons, nor her absolute hysterics on reading the carefully penned note. She never got to see the household set on its ears, the maids in tears, or Sir Peter cursing in a preposterously ungentlemanly fashion. It was just as well, for she would have felt more guilty than she already did, her splendid resolve wavering at the magnificence of Lord Sandford's London address, bordered everywhere with topiary gardens and a great, wide turning circle for the horses.

She was peculiarly silent as his lordship bade her alight from the chaise and hold the door open for him in the prescribed manner. It was comical, really, doing things the wrong way, alighting first, rather than last, helping rather than being helped. Fern would have enjoyed it, were she not certain of curious gazes cast her way both from the coachman and from the waiting servants lining the entrance to the illustrious residence.

Warwick marched up the stairs scowling. His staff bowed and curtsied as if on cue, which made him scowl all the more.

"Good afternoon. Have I not told you all a dozen times or more not to stand on ceremony with me?"

"But my lord! It is only fitting that we welcome you home. You have been away this age!"

"Nonsense! A week is not an age. Now disperse, all of you, or I shall be most displeased."

At which Fern was amazed to see the household vanish almost completely into thin air. Warwick chuckled.

"A motley lot, but as loyal as blazes. They can't bear seeing me angry. It is most dishonorable, I suppose, but the knowledge can be useful."

"Like when you are trying to smuggle in a charlatan page?"

"Precisely. But after you are garbed, you shall be presented. And I doubt if anyone shall suspect an iota!"

"I wish I could share in your confidence."

"You worry too much. Enjoy your adventure, Mistress Fern!"

"While my heart is sinking?"

"I shall fix it for you. But come, I shall take you through the vinery. It is a short and private way to my personal wing."

He extended a hand. Fern hesitated a moment, but she was trembling so much, she felt in need of the support. His palm was warm, even through the glove, and strong. Fern felt that strange surge of headiness again. And suddenly, quite remarkably, she threw herself into her adventure, not caring anymore what the outcome might be.

"If we are seen it will look passing strange to your servants!"

"Oh, it would only be Anders the head gardener, and he is as blind as you are!"

"Well, that is a relief! Poor man! I wonder if he has ever been fitted for spectacles?"

"Miss Reynolds, can you please stop worrying about my household staff? I need to get you inside before we are noticed, and if you carry on like a regular jaw-me-dead we shall not make it to the first door!"

"The first? Are there many?"

"Yes, for this house was built as a fortress. It is very old, as you can tell, and the first Lord War—that is, the first . . . viscount . . . seemed to have a particular penchant for Gothic-style doors. There is one on each floor, then another slightly after to limit drafts. I don't know if they do, but they are the bane of my servants' lives! Each time they bring up a pitcher of hot water, they have to open and shut about seven doors. I think it is seven—it may be more. . . ."

"It is a wonder that they do not complain!"

"Oh, they do, most volubly." Warwick grinned. "I take no notice, for it ensures my privacy! People think twice about knocking when there are seven oak doors to negotiate!"

"Crafty and cunning. I admire your spirit."

"And I admire you." There, it was said at last. Warwick, finding himself at the first door, opened it quickly and pushed Fern through, safe from prying eyes.

"Beg pardon?"

"I said I admire you, Fern. You cannot cut up at me for that!"

"No." Fern was smiling. She had no idea why she was so curiously happy, or why she followed meekly while he snatched her hand and positively raced through a labyrinth of doors and bells—they all seemed to chime on opening, an interesting mechanism, but Fern was too breathless to explore, somehow.

Finally they were in his private suite. More elaborate than she had expected of a mere viscount, but tasteful and uncluttered. The centerpiece of the room was a huge tester bed, surrounded with drapes of soft vellum, quite different from the usual heavy brocades or velvet. Chocolate brown and silvers dominated the chamber, from the sterling silver finishes on the locks and door handles, to the silver candelabras, to the sparkling eighteenth century vases filled with peonies and roses.

The paneled walls were all brown, severe against the silver, but lightened by the chocolate chaise longue with floss squabs, the rosewood chests, the single Chippendale

chair, and a host of books, all leather-bound, scattered
invitingly on two beautifully wrought tables, the bases
of both finished in silver.

"Oh!"

"You are pleased."

"Yes, for my brother's room sports nothing but guns,
and Papa's—on the odd occasion I have glimpsed it—is
very spartan, save for a stuffed hog's head."

"Good God! I have not much to compete with, then!"

Fern laughed, though she was suddenly feeling tre-
mendously shy in her scandalous circumstances. "I suppose not, though I still think I should like this room,
even if I had seen the chamber of the regent himself."

"Which I pray God you never will, for he is a likeable
fellow, but definitely not to be trusted in the presence
of a beautiful woman."

"I am not beautiful."

"You mistake the matter. Where can you have con-
ceived such an addle-witted notion?"

"My spectacles . . ."

"Are adorable. They lend you distinction."

Fern dropped her eyes. "You are quite the kindest man
I have ever met."

"I am not being kind, Fern. I am being selfish."

"Selfish?"

"Yes, now black my boots for God's sake, before I
lose my admirable control."

Bewildered, Fern did not understand the sudden
change of tone or the darkening of his eyes. She did
know, however, that it had been hours since she had
thought longingly of Warwick. It had been hours, indeed,
that she had watched the smooth line of *this* lord's lips
and hungered to be kissed, or to wrap her arms about
his broad shoulders and trace out the dimple that appeared from time to time in his masculine chin—*When
he laughs*, she thought. She wanted to make him laugh.

It was half *his* fault she had all these wanton notions—if he did not wear such close-fitting clothes, or was considerate enough to harbor a potbelly like the squire or a dozen other gentlemen of her acquaintance, she would not now be so . . . obsessed. He was watching her, she knew, from those dark, quizzical eyes of his. She must say something; she must not stand rooted to the floor like a silly clutter head!

"How do you black boots? I have never seen it done." The dimple definitely reappeared.

"I shall show you. In the Peninsular, I grew into the habit of doing it myself. There is a secret to it."

"There is?"

He nodded solemnly. "Swear you will not tell another living soul, or my valet will have my head!"

"I swear."

"It is champagne. You mix champagne with the boot black, and the shine is incomparable."

"What a sinful waste!"

"Which is only to show what an ignorant young wisp of a thing you are, for my boots are the envy of all of London!"

"Now *that* is a patent falsehood, my lord! I have it on the best authority that the Marquis of Warwick's are."

"Bother the marquis. I shall ring for my housekeeper. She shall have you outfitted in no time; then you may commence with your duties."

"Shining boots?"

"On second thought, no. Your ignorance is disturbing. You may interfere with many things, but not, I think, my neckerchief or my boots! My valet would have serious convulsions, and he is a decent sort of fellow. I would not wish such a tragic end for him."

Fern giggled. Warwick regarded her sternly, but she was not deceived. She had grown used to the telltale dimple and the twinkle that illuminated those deep brown eyes.

"You shall read to me. A novel use for a page, but one that I would find pleasant. By the by, you *do* actually play the harp, do you not?"

"It is considered my greatest accomplishment!"

For some reason, Warwick started coughing most alarmingly. Fern stepped forward, but the moment passed quite quickly.

"Then the evening with the marquis was an aberration?"

Fern groaned. "Oh, do not remind me of it! I quite wished to sink! It was hideous! It was a wonder he did not flee there and then, rather than stay to kiss me on the balcony!"

"I am sure he found the latter more to his tastes."

"Don't let us talk of Warwick. It is an excruciating chapter for me, but I believe it has ended."

Warwick, who had been on the point of summoning a footman, stopped in his tracks and regarded Fern with a curious, indefinable expression in those aristocratic eyes. "Ended?"

Fern nodded firmly. "I have been very foolish. I see, now, that Warwick must be consigned with the dance master and the beast."

"You mean . . ."

"Calf love. I have had a lucky escape, for I am certain, if you had not rescued me, I would have landed up wedding him. My inclinations were exactly to *do* so, you see. I may not have had the resolve to resist, with Mama and Papa and his lordship himself all so implacable. . . ."

"But it would have been a mistake?"

"Assuredly. It *always* would have been. But I thought I had one advantage. I thought I loved him."

"And now?"

"Now I know I don't."

"How can you be so certain?"

Fern shook her head, but her color was high again.

A glimmer of a smile crept onto Warwick's lips. He thought—he hoped—he knew the answer to this riddle. Fern did not love Warwick, for she had transferred her affections to him. And a very good thing, too, he thought, for it was becoming harder and harder to play out the charade. Perhaps, if her feelings had undergone such a transformation, she would not long have to be his page. Fern, in the first bloom of womanhood, had felt the undeniable attraction between them but had not understood it. Now she was feeling that same attraction compounded by something deeper, something more intimate—friendship and trust. It was a powerful combination. He knew, for he felt it every bit as much as Fern, only it was revealed to him, whereas Fern was working from instincts alone. He wondered who was suffering the most and decided, ruefully, it was probably him.

How easy it would be to seize her in his arms and carry her off to the great tester bed! But he would be a cad if he did so, so he mildly proceeded to ring his bell, call for the housekeeper, describe the livery he required, and keep Fern in stitches with little anecdotes from his wild youth.

At dinner—which was a quiet affair, on account of Fern miraculously having all her livery bar a crucial topcoat, which needed stitching but meant she could not yet be presented to the servants—Warwick made himself as amiable as he possibly could. This put Fern at her ease, for with nightfall, and the necessity to light candles, she was feeling increasingly more uncomfortable. When her pallet on the floor was carried in, she found it hard to meet his eye, or to thank the two footmen who had carried it up the stairs and past all seven doors.

They stared at her curiously, bowed low to his lordship, then disappeared, causing no further disturbance bar the arrival of the tea tray, carried in by no less than the housekeeper, the butler, the under butler, and an upper housemaid. At which Warwick raised his brows loftily but offered no comment.

In the kitchens there was a frenzy of activity and speculation, for Anders, it seemed, had noted the pages hands—"as white and as soft as bleedin' silk," he'd described it. The housekeeper had noticed the lad's becoming pallor, the maids had noticed the high color and the soft voice, "which" as they said, "was more like a friggin' lady's than a blamin' page's" and so on. Be that as it may, Fern lived in happy ignorance of the fact that her secret had been discovered, and Warwick in the sublime knowledge that his servants, reprehensibly curious, were loyal to a fault. Miss Reynolds's secret was still perfectly safe.

The housekeeper sent up the topcoat in record time, having stitched her hands off to preserve the young lady's modesty. She had also sent up, to Warwick's secret amusement, a hot posset—so that "the page could get a good night's sleep and none of them shenanigans" at which she stared severely at Warwick—and a plate of cookies. The negus she recommended to him, "better than the port, what could addle your brains," and she frowned blightingly over the pallet, commenting over and over that it was "not fitting."

Warwick's eyes twinkled. "The sheets fit perfectly, my good woman."

At which he received a baleful glare from the second most senior person on his household staff. She had also been his nurse when he had been in swaddling clothes, which might account for the fact that she was not cowed by his aristocratic bearing or by his suddenly haughty manner. "I hope you know what you is doing, my lord. Innocent pages an' all . . ."

"The page shall remain innocent, Annie. Trust me on this."

At which comment the housekeeper transformed immediately into a wreath of smiles, curtsied most obediently, cast Fern a shrewd glance of appraisal and a melting half curtsy, then left.

"You must think I employ the most impertinent servants in England!"

"They love you."

"Come, your wits must be addling. My housekeeper glares, has the impertinence to suggest *negus . . .*"

"Negus is very palatable, I believe."

"Then *you* have it!"

"You are being churlish, but I am not deceived."

"No?"

"No! For your dimple gives you away, my lord. You are nicer than you would have people suspect. Now wipe that frown from your face, or I shall not read to you."

Bother the reading, Warwick thought, eyeing Fern's slim legs and neat ankles, masterfully outlined in the page's clothes. Really, it was worse than the tight cambric shirt of before! But naturally he did not speak his thoughts. If he had, Fern might not have been so willing to oblige him.

Seven

Miss Reynolds, her heart set on making herself useful, thumbed through the leather-bound pages with genuine interest. Warwick, watching her choose from his collection, delighted at the way her eyes lit up at his choices.

"You are interested in hot-air balloons!"

"Yes, I am having some silks stitched at this very moment. I should like to try my hand at an ascension."

"How splendid!" Fern clapped her hands.

"I shall take you up, if you like."

"Oh, above all things! When will you be ready?"

"In the summer, when it is crisp but not cold. We need winds, but no rain, and a perfectly clear sky."

Fern tried to hide her disappointment. "I shall not be with you in the summer, my lord. . . ."

"Rick. Can't you call me Rick? I always call you Fern."

"It is not proper for a page to address you so!"

"A lot of things are not proper, Fern. That is the great adventure!"

Fern hesitated. Oh, how she longed for this man! It was not calf's love, she knew, though the physical attraction was now as strong as ever it had been for Warwick.

"Very well, I shall call you Rick. In private."

"Good. If you want to be with me in the summer, you may."

"I won't be here that long. As soon as Lord Warwick has left Evensides, I must go back. We always knew it would be so."

"With no wedding to please your family?"

"No. That is what we wanted, is it not?"

"Not precisely. *I* always wanted a wedding."

"Then why did you help me sneak away, engage in this ridiculous charade, browbeat me . . ."

"I never browbeat you!"

"No, but you are so . . . terribly convincing you might just as well have!"

"Are we quarreling? It is pleasant to have a first quarrel."

"I do not find it pleasant!" Fern set her book down with a crash and glared. It was well that the servants did not see her, for she did not look at all like a page, with her eyebrows arched and her magnificent green eyes flashing like waves across the ocean tides.

"Come here and let me kiss you."

"What?"

"Young ladies do not say 'what.' They say 'pardon.' "

"Gentlemen do not usually make such outrageous suggestions!"

Now that Fern's secret desires were about to become an actuality, her upbringing warred with her inclination. She was not frightened, precisely, but her heart beat erratically, and there was just a tiny part of her that was alarmed.

Had he lured her here for just this? It was unspeakable if he had—*worse* that she found the notion so tempting—but somehow, she could not believe his motives had been dishonorable.

Warwick watched her with a faint smile. "Is it outrageous? I might be a coxcomb, but I had quite thought you might oblige me in this!"

"I had quite thought you were above reproach!"

"I am. Fern, will you do me the great honor of being, not my page—which I find quite antiquated, frankly—but my wife?"

"Your . . . You do not know what you say!"

"I do. Fern, if you were not in this fix, if there was no Lord Warwick . . . would your inclinations lead you to me?"

The room was suddenly shadowed as the sun sank gracefully for the night. The candles, already lit, flickered gently, but yielded no real light. It was not fully dark enough. Fern could almost hear the silence, could hear his impatient breathing, could feel the light touch upon her gloved hand. A page's smart white glove. It could be traded for a lady's if she said the word.

"My inclinations are not relevant, Lord Sandford."

"They will always be relevant to me. Fern, dearest, say you will marry me."

"You hardly know me!"

"I know enough to know I shall not find happiness with anyone else. Do you think your mama could settle for a mere viscount?"

"She will doubtless swoon."

"With happiness?"

"No, with annoyance."

"Then I cannot hope?"

"Of course you can! Mama swoons at anything! And if I am in her black books for the day, well, so be it. It shall be no different from most days, I assure you!"

"Then you will kiss me?"

"Be quiet, Lord Sandford, and just do it."

So, with great aplomb, Lord Sandford—or Lord Warwick, to be more strictly accurate—did.

Then he removed her spectacles and did it again. It took a few moments for the memories of a certain candlelit balcony to stir. They were a few wild, heady, blurry, intoxicating moments. How was it possible for Lord Eric

Sandford and Lord Riccardo Warwick to feel so identical? To rouse the self-same tremors, to be the same height, the same masterful blur? Even their names—Eric, Rick, Riccardo, Rick . . . Fern gasped. She groped for her spectacles. She stared very hard at Lord—bother it, at Rick. The dimple was very much in evidence, but so too the charming beast of five years ago. How could she not have seen it before? It was perfectly clear, despite the fading light. The glow in Warwick's eyes was tender but just faintly amused at her slow realization.

Fern did not stop to think. She fiercely slapped the smile off Lord Warwick's debonair countenance—for she owed him that, surely? Then, perfectly sensibly, she kissed him again.

Postscript

The wedding of Miss Fern Reynolds and his lordship, the Marquis of Warwick took place in summer amid a great deal of fanfare and pomp. Lady Fern was still the despair of her mama, for she refused to pay due regard to her trousseau or to her newly acquired rank.

It was quite *comme il faut* for a betrothed to be treated with the elevated status due her new position—this Fern found to be true, with a tedious stream of morning callers, toadies, petitioners. Oh, the list was endless! So, to her mama's annoyance, she escaped—to the orchards that bounded the Evensides property from Warwick's. What in the Lord she did there all day, her mama could never conceive, but since she always dutifully brought home a basket of oranges, eyes suspiciously bright, she never did complain.

On the day of the wedding, Fern was not beset by nerves but by a wild excitement that her mama found unmaidenly and her papa found unedifying. But Fern, stubborn as always, did not seem to care. She wore a gown of the utmost simplicity, styled in rosewater silks. Her hair, unbound, hung loose from her head. Her locks were straight, cropped, classical, and as bright as the morning sun.

Upon her head was no coronet, no tiara—Lady Reynolds wept daily at this piece of stubbornness—but a single rose. On her nose, the most glorious pair of

spectacles ever witnessed—even by the most fashion
conscious of critics. They were wrought from purest
gold, gossamer thin, and *light*. Fern thought them as light
as the air that she breathed: Lord Warwick's best wedding
gift by far!

The pomp of the church was awe-inspiring. Fern
nearly faltered, for up until that moment she had not
really thought of herself as the Marchioness of Warwick,
or of Riccardo as a true marquis. Well, she had, of
course, until she'd been his page, until his staff had re-
galed her with numerous anecdotes . . . she smiled.

He was waiting for her, immaculate, as always, in full
court dress, with the ubiquitous diamond pin at his throat
and a tricorn tucked smartly under one arm. Fern could
hardly breathe, for his eyes were dark, and though she
looked, there was no dimple in that famous chin. He had
never been more serious in his life.

He was waiting for her, and she cared nothing at all
that Lady Willis and Lady Stonecroft, and yes, even Lady
Winterton, were curtsying as she made her way up the
aisle. But Mimsy did—dear Miss Garret—who had loved
Fern since she was only so high—*she* noticed, and it was
she who wept for the purest joy.

The vows were simple, but Fern had to remove her
spectacles twice, for they were blurred with tears. Warwick, fortunately, had an excellent handkerchief, and he
murmured a great deal of nonsense that brought the gurgle back to her laugh and the flush back to her modest
cheeks.

The dinner was huge, the grandeur all that the Duchess of Hargreaves—fussing about with table arrangements and place cards, to the complete distraction of the
housekeeper—desired. Warwick had brought Fern to his
mother that same memorable night, for sleeping on the
pallet bed had become out of the question and far too
great a temptation for them both. Fortunately, the duchess

lived in Cavendish Square, very close to Warwick's London quarters.

They had taken instantly to each other, though the duchess moaned over Fern's bright hair and impeccable skin.

"See, I am a crusty old crab," she had said, wrapped up heavily in a fur coat to her throat and a turban that almost entirely covered her head. It sparkled bright with jewels. Fern had laughed and liked her, despite the fact that she prodded prodigiously hard with her ivory fan, and that her eyes were shrewd and probing.

"Squawk!" had commented Kate.

"Talk?" said the duchess. And she had, endlessly, with the parrot interrupting at short intervals. True to her elevated status, she dined now upon platefuls of seeds and pine nuts. Every so often the duke, a quiet man but fond of pets, snuck her some unidentifiable but sticky treat. Fern could hardly contain her mirth.

Two days before the wedding, the duchess, pleased with her new daughter, announced in a booming voice that it was *she* who could take all the credit for the bridals. Her handsome son refrained with difficulty from mentioning how close her bad advice—to approach Sir Peter and not his daughter—had come to ruining everything. But they were very fond of the old dear and consequently endured the endless thunder of carriages, the rolling out of carpets, the fanfare, the footmen, the outriders, all that was necessary to the grandeur of the occasion. For the duchess doted on pomp and in Lady Reynolds, who up until now had only *aspired* to such heights, she had found a kindred spirit.

Unfortunately, now, at the height of the bridal festivities, when plain Miss Fern Reynolds was transformed into her very regal ladyship the Marchioness of Warwick, the future Duchess Hargreaves, the bride and groom had vanished completely. It was really extremely vexatious, especially as the orchestra was striking up for a waltz and no one in the entire spectrum of guests was more elegantly attired or more nimble of foot than the wedding couple.

Lady Reynolds, Their Graces the Duke and Duchess of Hargreaves, Sir Peter, Peter Reynolds Jr., and almost all of the noble guests, tut-tutted in disapproval.

But Fern and Riccardo did not care a whit. If anyone had cared to look, they would have found them floating high above the topiary gardens in a crimson balloon made of the finest Chinese silk. If they had looked any farther, they might also have seen a sharp yellow beak and a bright feathered blue tail aloft in the basket.

"Kiss kiss kiss . . . *kiss* kiss kiss," came the impertinent squawk. Warwick, following this advice precisely, threw a dark cloth over the gilded cage. It was really, Kate thought, *most* unfair.

From Best-selling Author
Fern Michaels

__Wish List	0-8217-7363-1	$7.50US/$9.50CAN
__Yesterday	0-8217-6785-2	$7.50US/$9.50CAN
__The Guest List	0-8217-6657-0	$7.50US/$9.50CAN
__Finders Keepers	0-8217-7364-X	$7.50US/$9.50CAN
__Annie's Rainbow	0-8217-7366-6	$7.50US/$9.50CAN
__Dear Emily	0-8217-7365-8	$7.50US/$9.50CAN
__Sara's Song	0-8217-5856-X	$6.99US/$8.50CAN
__Celebration	0-8217-6452-7	$6.99US/$8.99CAN
__Vegas Heat	0-8217-7207-4	$7.50US/$9.50CAN
__Vegas Rich	0-8217-7206-6	$7.50US/$9.50CAN
__Vegas Sunrise	0-8217-7208-2	$7.50US/$9.50CAN
__What Your Wish For	0-8217-6828-X	$7.99US/$9.99CAN
__Charming Lily	0-8217-7019-5	$7.99US/$9.99CAN

Call toll free **1-888-345-BOOK** to order by phone or use this coupon to order by mail.

Name_____

Address _____

City_____ State _____ Zip _____

Please send me the books I have checked above.

I am enclosing $_____

Plus postage and handling* $_____

Sales tax (in New York and Tennessee) $_____

Total amount enclosed $_____

*Add $2.50 for the first book and $.50 for each additional book.

Send check or money order (no cash or CODs) to: **Kensington Publishing Corp., 850 Third Avenue, New York, NY 10022**

Prices and numbers subject to change without notice. All orders subject to availability.

Come visit our website at **www.kensingtonbooks.com**.